SUSAN HUGHES grew up near
Northumberland. For as long as she
a part of her life. When she didn't l
climbing trees, catching water boat
carting in country lanes with the kic

After University she worked in ... .. .y .. ..g ...
frenetic 'Big Bang' boom of financial de-regulation, before marriage
and family life led to a desire for a change of gear. A move to the
rural West Country enabled her to raise her sons near the coast,
encouraged her to indulge her penchant for visiting country piles,
while also keeping up her reading habit by patronising the local
bookstore.

She became a writer almost by accident, after she found a handful
of WWI silk postcards in a box of her grandmother's possessions.
The romantic greeting on one of these inspired her to weave a story
around its imagined sender and recipient. It became her first novel,
A Kiss from France. She is now working on her second book.

To find out more about the author:
www.susanhughes.net
Twitter: www.twitter.com/su_sanhughes
Pinterest: www.pinterest.com/hughes7584

Earning high wages?
Yus, five quid a week.
A woman too, mind you,
I calls it dim sweet.

Madeleine Ida Beauford (1917)

First World War Timeline

1914

28 June	Archduke Franz Ferdinand, heir to Austrian-Hungarian throne, assassinated in Sarajevo, Bosnia.
28 July	Austria-Hungary declares war on Serbia.
1 August	Germany declares war on Russia. Outbreak of war.
3 August	Germany declares war on France.
4 August	Germany invades neutral Belgium and Great Britain declares war on Germany. United States declares policy of neutrality.
8 August	Defence of the Realm Act (DORA) gives British Government wide-ranging powers, including censorship, commandeering of public services and industry for armaments production and reduction in pub licensing hours, for the war's duration.
5 September	Stalemate and trench warfare follows first Battle of the Marne.
19 October	First Battle of Ypres begins.

1915

19 January	First German Zeppelin attack on England.

4 February	German U-boat attacks on Allied and neutral shipping.
22 April	Second Battle of Ypres begins (Germans use poison gas for the first time).
7 May	U-boat sinks British liner Lusitania with loss of US lives, creating a German-US crisis and anti-German rioting in English cities.
9 June	Ministry of Munitions established to address shell shortage issue, on which the British failure at the Battle of Neuve Chapelle was blamed.
17 July	Women's Right to Serve March in London as women demonstrate for the right to work in munitions factories in support of the war effort.
16 October	Derby Scheme introduced in Great Britain. Men to register their voluntary commitment to serve if called up.
19 December	Sir Douglas Haig replaces Sir John French as Commander of the British Expeditionary Force.
28 December	Dardanelles campaign failure leads to withdrawal of Allied troops from Gallipoli.

1916

24 January	The First Military Service Bill passed in Great Britain, leading to conscription of single men aged 18–45, followed in May by the call up of married men.
1 July	Battle of The Somme begins. It ends with enormous casualties and no winner.
28 November	First German Gotha aeroplane raid on Great Britain.
7 December	David Lloyd George replaces Herbert Asquith as GB Prime Minister.

1917

31 January	Germany announces unrestricted submarine warfare, leading to food shortages in Great Britain.
6 April	United States declares war on Germany.
13 June	First of the London daylight air raids when twenty German Gotha Planes dropped 100 bombs on the English capital and killed 162 civilians, including eighteen children at Upper North Street School, Poplar, E14.
31 July	Third Battle of Ypres (Passchendaele) begins.

1918

February	Great Britain introduces rationing in London. Rest of United Kingdom rationed in the summer.
3 March	Russia and Germany sign the Treaty of Brest-Litovsk.
21 March	Germany launches its Spring Offensive on the Western Front.
11 April	Field Marshall Sir Douglas Haig, Commander-in-Chief of the British Armies in France, sends his 'Backs to the Wall' communiqué, urging the Allies to 'fight on to the end'.
18 July	The Allies seize the initiative.
8 August	The German army is forced back to The Hindenburg Line.
27 September	First Allied breakthrough of The Hindenburg Line; more follow.
4 October	Germany and Austria send a peace note to US President, Woodrow Wilson, requesting an armistice.
9 November	The German Kaiser abdicates.
11 November	Armistice Day. Fighting ceases at 11am after 4 years, 3 months and 14 days.

Pre-Decimal British Monetary System

One guinea (gn.) = £1 1s 0d (twenty-one shillings)
One pound = £1 0s 0d (twenty shillings)
A crown = 5s or 5/- (five shillings)
A half a crown = 2s 6d or 2/6 (two shillings and sixpence)
A florin = 2s or 2/- (two shillings)
Twelve pence = 12d (one shilling)
A sixpence = 6d
A penny = 1d
A halfpenny = 1/2d
A farthing = 1/4d

British Money Slang

A quid = £1 (one pound)
A two bob bit = 2/- (two shillings or a florin)
A bob = 1/- (a shilling)
A tanner = 6d (sixpence)
Three penny bit = 3d (three pence)

1917

Chapter One

Taking advantage of a few rare moments of privacy, Lizzie Fenwick pulled down the wooden lavatory seat lid and sat on it. In the dim yellow glow given off by the gaslight, her eyes greedily searched the pencilled handwriting for the words that had set her heart a flutter yesterday.

I am promised some leave.

A delicious shiver ran along her spine. Finally, she might meet Harry Slater – the soldier with whom she had been sharing secret, intimate thoughts and sentiments.

"You cock tease."

Damn that other Tommy at the dance last night! Her cheeks suddenly flashed crimson as the vulgar words uttered against her detonated in her head and threatened to spoil her happy daydreaming. She pressed her precious letter from France against her chest. Yesterday evening, that other soldier had kept pestering her, playing on her conscience – seeing as how he was prepared to die for his country – to try to persuade her to do what he considered to be her patriotic duty by letting him have his way with her before he went back to the Front.

"What're you waiting for?" her friend, Peggy, had called over her shoulder as she disappeared into the blackout with yet another soldier's arm around her waist. "You might be dead tomorrow!"

Unlike Peggy, who had succumbed to the widespread khaki

fever which manifested itself wherever a group of men in uniform congregated, Lizzie considered herself spoken for. Of course, she had rebuffed the over-amorous Tommy. He hadn't taken it well. Now she gave a little huff of irritation because he had become an unwelcome blot on her ideal of the handsome, brave, honourable and patriotic soldier with whom she could fall in love. She batted away the unwanted thoughts and scanned the rest of the letter as she looked for confirmation of the romantic image she held in her mind of her distant correspondent.

Somewhere in France
2 April 1917

Dear Elizabeth
I noticed it is six months to the day that I picked your little note out of the box of ammunition shells. Since then I have looked forward to each letter from you. They brighten up my life here in this miserable trench, with the din of artillery all around and the threat of death never very far away, and help keep me sane. I look at your glorious photograph and pray that the next sniper's bullet or German shell doesn't have my name on it so I might stay alive long enough to be able to meet you.

She recalled how she had sent Harry Slater that small portrait photograph of herself – one that showed her comely features off to best effect – and how their letters had gradually started to carry meanings beyond the mere words on the page, inviting beguiling, tempting fantasies into her head. Now, however, after her disconcerting experience last night, the possibility of actually meeting her correspondent insinuated a little worm of doubt into her mind.

What if, in the flesh, he proved to be a disappointment? Not as she had imagined him? At the back of her mind there lurked the taxing issue of whether he would also expect her to do her 'patriotic duty', just as that pushy Tommy had. She sucked in her breath at the thought.

The lavatory door handle rattled and made Lizzie start. "Hey, hurry up, you in there. I'm plaitin' me legs out here."

She realised the other lodging house occupants were up, ready for the early morning shift at the munitions and now belligerently demanding their turn, so she pulled the lavatory chain to deflect any suspicion and opened the door.

Back in her room, her breath made a cloud in the air. She bent over the wash stand to crack the ice on the water jug with her toothbrush handle before splashing the freezing water onto her face. Her sharp intake of breath caused the other two occupants to stir.

"Gawdsake, I'm trying to sleep." The muffled complaint came from the bed nearest the wash stand.

"And the Lord knows you need your beauty sleep," jibed an Irish voice from the other bed.

Two fingers forming a V emerged from the bedcovers opposite in reply.

Lizzie put some paste onto her toothbrush to give her teeth a quick clean, and before the other two women got up she squeezed between the beds and got dressed, her back to them so she could transfer her precious letter to her skirt pocket. She would read it again later, if she got the chance. She pulled the covers up over the bed, even though she knew another body would soon occupy it while she worked her next shift.

"Why doesn't that miserly bitch let us have a fire?" Peggy Wood railed against their landlady as she pulled the covers up tighter around her neck.

"And which eejit's going to carry a scuttle full of coals up three flights of stairs and then get up at the crack of dawn every day to light it?" grumbled Mary Maguire. "I had enough of that in service."

And me, thought Lizzie, although a nice warm fire would be welcome, and might help cure the damp patch spreading over the stained and blistered distemper on the wall near her bed.

Peggy threw off her covers, pulled a face and dragged herself out of bed. As soon as the cold registered, she began to hop up and down in front of the tarnished brass rail which was crammed with clothes.

"When you've finished doing St Vitus's dance," said Lizzie, "I'll be waiting downstairs."

"I need something especially nice to wear." Peggy began to rifle through the clothes, despite knowing her choice was limited and her munitions overalls would put paid to any high fashion. "George and the Dragon are gracing us with their presence today."

"No royals are coming today, as far as I know," said Lizzie.

"Keep your hands off my things," warned Mary.

"Pity they don't send their handsome son instead. Now that Prince of Wales could boost my morale any day."

"Come on, Peg, move yourself or we'll miss the bus," Lizzie, who was proud of her unblemished attendance record and didn't intend to be late, called over her shoulder as she left the room.

"It's all right for you!" she heard Peggy shout after her. "You'd look good in a sack."

Lizzie liked the relative stillness of the lower half of the house just before dawn; before the noise and bustle of those on the first shift edged out the silence. She walked down the elegant staircase of this once wealthy merchant's house, the top floor of which was now divided into mean little rooms let to female munitions workers. Apart from their rooms, only the kitchen wasn't off limits.

As was her custom, she stopped for a moment in front of the

only large mirror in the house and swept her long Titian hair up into a wooden comb at the back of her head. Finished, she inspected her hands before leaning more closely towards her reflection and scrutinising her face and neck for any signs of the yellow which would mark out her occupation. She was satisfied to see only her creamy, pale complexion, and was pleased that the Ven-yusa cream she had been using seemed to be living up to its advertised claims.

What would Harry Slater think of me if I turned up looking like a canary?

The thought made her smile, but reminded her of her earlier dilemma.

Of course, it would be so much more daring to find out what he was really like in person, wouldn't it? And it would be such a pity to waste all those exciting and captivating emotions and feelings his letters stirred in her. Anyway, wasn't she just a little bit intrigued? Out loud, she said, "Mrs Harry Slater" just to see how it sounded, before going down to the basement to make some tea and scrape her meagre portion of butter and jam onto her allocation of half a slice of bread for her breakfast.

The bus disgorged its horde of passengers opposite the fire station in industrial Silvertown, next to the old caustic soda works which had been commandeered as a munitions factory by the Government. The familiar overpowering stench of rotten eggs from the chemical works and other nearby factories, mixed with the pungent sour-sweetness of the Tate & Lyle sugar refinery, assailed Lizzie's nostrils as she stepped down onto the road. Somewhere behind her a door banged shut and a window rattled, making her glance at the dilapidated tenements and rundown houses opposite the munitions. It certainly wasn't the wealthy and more fashionable West End, where she used to live and work.

Immediately she was engulfed in a wave of colour and noise as the throng of women, many arm-in-arm, their laughter and chatter peppered with ribald comments, surged along the narrow street. The few men on the bus peeled away from the female crowd as soon as they alighted. Out of the corner of her eye, Lizzie spotted Peggy.

"I'm not going to ask." When she had left, her friend had still been undecided on what to wear.

"Cadged a ride on the front of Fred Waller's bicycle." She rubbed her bottom.

Poor Fred Waller, thought Lizzie. *It'll take him all day to recover.*

The crowd slowed as they stopped to clock in. Lizzie stamped her feet on the frosty ground and clapped her gloved hands together.

"Eeh, I'm perished."

"Be grateful you're not at the Front," chided an anonymous male voice.

The two women raised their eyebrows and pretended to look chastened. When they reached the rack of numbered cards on the wall, Lizzie jostled Peggy playfully to one side to get her card in the slot underneath the wall clock ahead of her friend. She cranked the handle to make sure the time of twenty-five past six had printed on the card – irrefutable proof she had turned up for her shift on time.

"Beat you!" she laughed.

Peggy gave her a gentle shove in return as they walked off towards the cloakroom. Lizzie often thought that this area – barely big enough to hold the 500 women and girls employed here – was as explosive as the munitions factory itself, when petty gripes and female jealousies mixed dangerously with feelings of exhaustion and the stress of being at war. As a result, she usually tried to get changed into her munitions overalls as quickly as possible to avoid any altercation.

Lizzie took a certain pride in her khaki-coloured cotton twill work garb. She knew it was drab and purely functional, and allowed for no personal accessories for fear a spark might combust, but it made her feel patriotic and that she was doing her duty – just as much as the lads fighting – to help win the war.

She squeezed past the crush of bodies as she dodged arms and elbows, and left Peggy somewhere behind her in the mass of womanhood. As soon as she pushed open the heavy doors into the Danger Building, the fumes combined with the ceaseless roar of the machinery and the heat hit her. She still hadn't got used to it. She walked down the concrete floor, crammed with row after row of benches and machinery. As usual, she ignored the blackboard which proclaimed, 'When the boys come back, we are not going to keep you any longer, girls' to find her station for another shift filling shells with trinitrotoluene.

Just as she turned to get to her position, she felt a tug at her back. Peggy feebly called out her name before she fell against her and collapsed onto the floor in a dead faint.

Lizzie bent down to help her. "C'mon, lass, buck up or you'll get in trouble again."

Other workers crowded in for their shift as they carelessly skirted round them. Peggy opened her eyes. Suddenly above the din of the machinery, a barrage of offensive remarks was hurled in their direction.

"No need to guess what's 'up' with her!" a shrill female voice called. "Been granting favours to our war heroes again, has she?"

A florid-faced man minced around his machine table, leaned backwards on it and pretended to lift an imaginary skirt while opening his legs wide.

"Ooh! Soldier, you're so brave." He mimicked a high-pitched feminine voice. "I'll do *anything* to help the war effort."

A continual roar of suggestive noise rose above the machinery. Lizzie felt her face colour. A slender, neat woman stepped out of the crowd.

"You should be thankful us women are rallying round," she cried, "doing all this hard work to keep this country going while our men are away fighting, risking life and limb." Her eyes swept over the onlookers.

"*We* are risking life and limb every second here, you stupid bitch." The voice was aggressive and harsh, its owner hidden by machinery. "What do you think this is – a tea dance?"

The woman muttered, "Well at least they've got the guts to go and fight…"

Her expression told Lizzie that as soon as the words left her mouth, she wished them unsaid.

"And your 'brave' husband went willingly, did he?" A large, disagreeable looking man stepped out in front of her and blocked her path. "Jack Wilson had to have a bayonet in his back just to get him on the train at Victoria, I heard."

Savage laughter echoed around the gathered crowd.

"You leave her alone, Evans." A male worker with a limp and half his face ravaged by an angry red battle scar confronted the disagreeable man. "We all know you had some help to avoid the call up."

The two men squared up to each other, their differences in height and physique making for an uneven fight. Other workers egged them on until someone hissed, "Fawcett!" and the crowd parted to disclose the factory manager standing in the gap. Everything about him, from his highly polished shoes, well-cut black suit and turned down collar to his tidy moustache, small round glasses and bowler hat, distinguished him immediately from the dull, practical uniforms of the workers. He looked totally at odds with the machinery and din in the background, but pulled up to his full height, with his back ram-rod straight and his hands on his hips, there was no doubt he was in charge.

"What are you lot waiting for?" he scolded the crowd. "You're well aware there's a big push on." He walked towards the trio of women and nodded at Lizzie. "Miss Fenwick. Go on, get her out of here. She can have ten minutes to come round. If she needs any longer, send her to Miss Henderson." He glanced down at Peggy. "And I'm sure you are aware you are wearing incorrect footwear for this area. Make sure you rectify that before you come back in here."

Lizzie and the other woman helped Peggy up, and as they led her away Lizzie sensed the manager watching them.

"And not a minute more or it comes off your wages!" she heard Fawcett shout, although she had the impression it was said more for the benefit of the other workers than for themselves.

The few stragglers left in the cloakroom glanced sideways at the three women before they walked off, their voices reduced to a whisper. Peggy slumped down onto a chair.

"Put your head down between your knees."

"Yes, Eunice." Peggy rested her arms on her thighs and let her hands dangle over the edges of her knees. She noticed the yellow tinge on the ends of her fingers, but quickly shifted her gaze to the bright red laces which enlivened her dull brown boots.

"I expect you stayed up all night at the dance again, did you?" Eunice's tone was, as usual, that of a disapproving and disappointed parent talking to a disobedient child.

"No point sitting in your lodgings feeling sorry for yourself just 'cos we're at war. Life's for living." Peggy craned her head upwards, looking for support from Lizzie. "Ain't that right?"

Lizzie, who had had cause to come to Peggy's aid twice recently in the factory, was disappointingly non-committal, but suggested she should see the welfare officer if she felt unwell again.

"That meow? She's not one of us, so you needn't bother mentioning her, or any other swank pot." Peggy attempted to stand up, but crumpled back down onto her chair.

"Do we need another little chat?" She felt the slight pressure of Eunice's hand on her shoulder.

"It's all right. Honest. It's just the heat." Peggy feebly wafted her hand in front of her face like a fan, but she felt the room closing in on her.

"Have you taken something to get rid?"

She heard in the tone a competing mix of concern and exasperation, and supposed that was how a mother might scold a daughter.

"Didn't I tell you before?" Eunice chastised her before she could reply. "This larking about with soldiers is all very well, but taken too far, well…it's always the woman who pays the price."

At her workstation, Lizzie discovered her machine monkey, used to compress the TNT into shells, wasn't working. She had to tell the tool setter.

"Up to their usual tricks?" He shook his head. "Anyone'd think they wanted Germany to win."

As Lizzie pulled down her protective cap veil and put on her gloves, she thought what a kick this occupation gave her and how much she enjoyed the mixed camaraderie of working next to men in the factory. It was just a pity some men refused to accept women doing this sort of work and revelled in sabotaging their efforts. However, she knew it wasn't worth making a fuss – she'd seen too many confrontations flare up over nothing in this environment, and now the Government was threatening to comb out another half a million men from protected industries for the army, any animosity between the sexes was only likely to get worse.

At the end of her shift, Lizzie pushed her knuckles into the small of her back and stretched her body to alleviate the aches in her joints and the stiffness in her knees.

"No better than being a slavey," the female workmate on her left complained. "I'm done in."

Lizzie shoved to the back of her mind the inconvenient truth that, like domestic service, munitions work was thankless toil – and a damned sight more dangerous.

"At least the wages are better," she volunteered. "And I can spend them on whatever I like. I've also got a life of my own. Never had that in service."

"I suppose." The girl didn't sound convinced. "Doesn't it play on your conscience just a bit? This work. I mean, I know they're the enemy, but these shells are going to kill some mother's son, some woman's husband."

Lizzie kept to herself her qualms about helping to fill ammunition shells whose end result would be maiming and death. After all, hadn't she gone on the Right to Serve March back in July 1915 to demand women be allowed to work in munitions? Seven months ago she had done her first shift.

"Well, at least no one can say we haven't proved ourselves and done our bit for the war. It might be the making of us yet."

"Be careful what you wish for."

Chapter Two

Eunice Wilson heard the expected knock and took her coat from the wall peg. She opened the front door to Peggy, whom she saw drag her eyes away from the sign in the window proclaiming 'A man from this house is fighting for King and Country' to give her a brief smile of acknowledgement. *Probably thinks that's a bit rich*, Eunice mused, before slotting her arm through the younger girl's ready to walk off.

"I won't be long, Alfie," Eunice called to a skinny, dark-haired boy in short pants with his shirt tail hanging out, who was playing a game of marbles surrounded by similarly unkempt children. "Mind you behave yourself till I get back."

He gave her a quick backwards glance to show he had heard her.

"And tuck your shirt tail in!"

Further along the street the two women passed a gaggle of men talking in indignant tones as they pored over a newspaper. She recognised them as local men who, for one reason or another, had been spared conscription.

"More than three an' a half years since the war started, and now the Yanks have finally got off the bleedin' fence," one said with undisguised bitterness.

They saw Eunice and Peggy and nodded acknowledgement.

"It should end then, now America's in," said Peggy, trying to muster some interest.

"Please, God. And soon," replied Eunice as she took a halfpenny piece from her purse to give to the newspaper hawker loitering at the end of the street, easily selling his newspapers on the back of the war headlines. As usual she was desperate to read the latest news, but she decided she ought to give Peggy her full attention. In the event, they sat in silence on the bus, each wrapped up in their own thoughts, until they alighted at the usual stop for the munitions. Instead of heading towards the factory, they crossed the road and turned into a side street. Peggy stopped suddenly, and Eunice, who had walked on a few more paces, turned around to see what the matter was. She saw the girl's hand resting on her stomach, an odd look in her eyes.

Eunice's dark brows creased. "You haven't felt it move, have you?"

Peggy shook her head.

"Because if you have…"

"I'm not that far on yet."

Eunice walked back towards Peggy, rubbed her hands up and down the girl's coat sleeves, and said, "Be brave."

Peggy gave her a twisted smile, nodded, and they walked on down the dingy street to a terraced house near the end.

Inside, Eunice's nose wrinkled at the fatty smell of an earlier cooked meal which lingered in the dimly-lit, narrow hallway before Dora Catchpole, a bulky potato-faced woman with a Scotch accent, took Peggy by the arm and led her down to the kitchen.

"Don't ye worry," she called over her shoulder. "I'll put her on her way."

"Take your drawers off, hoick your skirts up and lay here," Dora Catchpole instructed Peggy. "We'll soon have ye right."

Peggy leaned back on the kitchen table, which had been covered in newspapers, her legs splayed and bent towards her chest so the woman could go about her business.

"It won't hurt, will it?" Peggy asked in a faint voice.

"Just relax, lassie. I cannae get started if you're all tense."

Peggy stared, unblinking, at the cracked and yellowed ceiling. She began to hum quietly to herself until she felt the woman touch her and she flinched. Dora Catchpole cursed under her breath.

"Sorry," Peggy whispered.

When she had the sensation of something being inserted, she gripped the edges of the table and squeezed her eyes shut.

"Just get it over with, please," she whimpered.

"If ye can keep still and stop your wee legs from shaking, I'll be finished the sooner."

Peggy glanced down once or twice and, beyond the rapid rise and fall of her own chest, saw only the top of the woman's head. She focused on the jagged line of chalk white skin exposed by Dora Catchpole's untidy hair parting and tried not to think about what was happening.

I'm doing the right thing.

She didn't want to bring such a carelessly conceived child into the world; one she would only have to abandon to its fate if it was born. A child deserved a mother's love. A momentary vision of a man in khaki uniform flashed in front of her eyes. Melbourne, he'd said he came from. Australia. The other side of the world. She liked his funny accent and his determination to have a good time while on leave in London, and found his eagerness to sample all its many pleasures before he went back to the trenches mirrored her own. She'd been rather enamoured of his mischievous hazel eyes and the crinkles that appeared either side of them when he laughed.

Without warning, a pain – like a knife had been twisted in her insides – ripped through her. She cried out. Her fingers gripped the edge of the table harder. A trickle of warm liquid dribbled down the inside of her thighs and she couldn't hold in the tears.

*

Eunice paced up and down a little way from the house, side-stepping discarded cigarette packets, greasy fish and chip papers and other detritus which littered the road. She watched an emaciated dachshund foul the road before being kicked hard by a passing stranger: the action had, she knew, nothing to do with the dog's toilet habits. She didn't meet the man's gaze, and was careful not to meet the eyes of any other passers-by, lest they might guess what her purpose there was.

She accepted Dora Catchpole provided a necessary service. Who was she to judge? Her own useless womb hadn't needed any help from the likes of Crochet Hook Dora to expel all of her dead babies, until she'd kept hold of Alfie, her precious boy. She supposed she could rail at the unfairness of the world, but what was the use? It didn't change anything. She prayed Peggy would be all right and that she'd learn her lesson.

"Well, that was three guineas well spent," said Peggy, her voice strained and her face drained of all colour as she focused on buttoning her coat against the bitter cold, not meeting Eunice's gaze. "She told me nature'd do the rest in a few hours, and to take some aspirin for the cramps."

Eunice thought it'd take more than a few aspirins as she wrestled with the prurient need to ask whether the stories about the crochet hook, rubber tube or syringe full of liquid were true, but she fought the impulse off.

"I've to go to hospital if the…bleeding doesn't stop." Peggy swallowed hard. "And she warned me not to mention her name if… anything goes wrong." She looked past Eunice, a frightened wildness in her eyes like a cornered animal.

The older woman put her arms around Peggy and said, "There, there," as if she was comforting a small child. "Come and stop with me for a while. Until it's all done."

*

Eunice always felt a little sick when she anticipated reading the war headlines, but they exerted a horrible fascination and she was addicted to them. As she fully took in the news, she began a solitary waltz around the kitchen with the newspaper held in front of her like a dance partner. *An army of two million!* Surely America's entrance into the war augured an end to her life of suspended animation. Nearly ten months her husband, Jack, had been gone. *Felt like ten years some days*, she thought. Since then she had answered the call for women to join the war effort and taken work in munitions, pleased to be doing her bit and glad of the extra money – anything to help her to forget the bouts of stomach churning anxiety about her husband's safety over in Flanders and her fear of the Zeppelins' bombs at home.

She glanced at the letter rack on the mantelpiece as she went into the front parlour and picked up Jack's latest letter, checking the postmark and date. The time between his letters seemed to be getting longer. Or was she imagining it? On her fingers she counted aloud the days that had elapsed since its arrival. It distressed her to think how many opportunities there had been in the interval for him to be killed or maimed.

She looked at the hastily scribbled letter, which was really no more than a note, thanking her for the home baked cake and newly knitted socks, but even so it had the censor's black marks on it. She had to rely on the newspapers and gossip to tell her what was going on over there, although more and more she was starting to doubt the veracity of what she learned. Other women's husbands wrote them letters to keep up their morale; not Jack. She always felt there was an edge to his comments, but she knew they reflected their differences about the war. Perhaps she deserved it, she told herself.

Unconsciously she tapped the edge of the envelope against the palm of her hand. Part remembered sentences floated into her mind.

"Everyone's joining up, Jack. They say it'll all be over by Christmas."

"Of course it will. And that old soak Asquith's taken the pledge."

"Ada Brown's going round telling everyone that you're allergic to serge."

"Is no one listening to Kitchener? It's going to be a long and bloody war."

"Maisie Grieve asked if we were changing our name to von Wilson. It's beyond embarrassing."

"It's a rich man's war and a poor man's fight. Don't you understand? Working men will be the cannon fodder."

And then Mrs Earnshaw, who had lost her husband at Loos and had two sons who had enlisted at the start, had spat in Jack's face because she felt she had the right since he hadn't joined the rush to the Colours. That had been the final straw.

"Ma! Ma!" The front door banged against the hall wall. "Look!" Her son burst into the room, full of life and filthy dirty, brandishing a piece of twisted metal in front of him.

"Kill the Kaiser! Kill the Kaiser!" Alfie thrust the shrapnel back and forth like a weapon.

The last time he had said that, the day war was declared, Jack had cuffed him hard round the ear.

"See, Ma! Isn't it a beauty?"

Eunice put her finger to her lips. "Shh! Peggy's upstairs, a bit under the weather." Frowning, she said, "Oh, Alfie."

She felt it wasn't right to go and scavenge bombed areas, even if it was only for bits of enemy shell. She wasn't even sure it was allowed these days; the Government seemed to have outlawed even the simplest pleasures. It was too upsetting, going to gawp at any devastation, and it seemed disrespectful to the victims. However, she acknowledged that owning a piece of German shrapnel was too tempting a souvenir for a five-year-old boy to forgo.

In the kitchen, Eunice brushed him down then washed the dirt from his knees with a damp cloth – he wasn't due a bath until the end of the week – but she saw no sign of contrition. As she fussed over him, he stopped admiring his loot.

"Am I the man of the house now?"

Eunice nodded. "Why, I suppose you are, love – till your father comes back."

She thought at once of the sealed envelope Jack had left, to be given to their son in the event he did not come back, and which she had been unable to stop herself from steaming open.

> *My dear boy, Alfie*
> *This is my farewell in case anything should happen*
> *to me. Keep at your schooling and make your mother*
> *proud, but most of all be a good son to her.*
> > *Always remember that I love you.*
> *Da xxxx*

With a sudden involuntary movement, she grabbed hold of Alfie and hugged him tight. She kissed the top of his head and breathed in the smell of his hair, redolent of the coal-tar soap she used to wash it, as she felt a rush of love for her only living child.

"What would I do without you?"

Chapter Three

At Aldgate, Lizzie waited with Peggy for the next bus to take them back to their lodging house in Bow. *You could talk the hind leg off a donkey*, she had been thinking with some amusement as her friend rattled on, fifty to the dozen, about something or other – her recent 'little problem', as Peggy had put it, of two months' ago seemingly behind her – when she became aware of a sudden lull in the general hubbub around them. She put a hand on Peggy's arm.

"What?"

Groups of people stood still and pointed upwards.

"It's not a Z...Zepp, is it?"

"They only come at night."

Lizzie shielded her eyes against the sun's glare.

"Look!" cried Peggy as she pointed at the sky.

Above her, Lizzie at first saw only a single plane, but then, out of the azure June sky, came an arc of planes flying in perfect formation. She thought they looked like large birds freely riding the air currents.

"I think they're ours..."

A barrage of anti-aircraft guns hammered into action, and their thunderous roar tore through the unusual stillness. Both women watched the enemy planes zigzag right and left as they evaded the white puffs of smoke from exploding anti-aircraft shells which were breaking all around them.

"They're sending planes now, not Zepps!"

31

"And in broad daylight!"

"Holy Mary, Mother of God!"

The two friends made a sudden dash for safety. Lizzie felt her nerves unravelling amid the unmistakeable scream of falling bombs and rumble of explosions nearby. The pair were forced to dodge shocked passengers who tumbled off a tram at a standstill in the middle of the road, and had to plough their way through shoppers who scattered in alarm from a once orderly queue outside a grocery. They just managed to sidestep a man with a briefcase, mesmerised by the spectacle.

"It's an air raid!" Lizzie screamed at him, horrified at the cascade of cigar-shaped bombs, silhouetted against the blue sky, which hurtled down towards them.

Immediately she yanked Peggy into the doorway of a boarded up German bakery shop, where they huddled together, their bodies rigid with fear, an arm placed over their heads as a flimsy shield. Lizzie sucked in her breath as the dull boom of a direct hit close by made the makeshift wooden hoardings behind reverberate violently against them, and then came an explosion which was so colossal that the ground beneath them actually shuddered. Lizzie's ears buzzed from the hellish noise. She gripped Peggy ever tighter as they cowered together, their faces pressed hard into each other's clothing. Their muffled sobs of distress pulsed out like SOS messages, while the far away anti-aircraft guns continued to pound.

"I think the world's ending," whispered Peggy.

Time seemed to stand still. They waited, afraid to move as an eerie quiet descended. Without warning, Peggy's knees gave way and her body drooped like a marionette whose strings had been cut. Lizzie attempted to prop her up.

"Here, give me your hand."

The faint wail of a fire engine in the distance cut the silence, and Lizzie felt a strange surge of exultation that they were still alive.

The pair stepped out into the bright sunshine of Aldgate High Street. Underneath their feet shards of glass crackled and broke like ice, and loose papers from blown-out offices floated about in the street and flapped in their faces, each time making them start. Other survivors, like strange amorphous creatures, blundered about covered in a fine grey residue of dust from destroyed and crumbling masonry.

A baleful hum started, and the hairs on the back of Lizzie's neck stood up as she recognised the poignant chorus of pain and suffering. Peggy tripped and almost fell. A strangled scream escaped her lips as her terrified eyes looked down on a mangled female body. Immediately she turned her head away and retched. Lizzie's hand flew to her mouth, but then she realised that it was a shop window dummy, blown through the shattered glass frontage of the Albion Clothing Store. As her gaze darted back and forth, she saw that several other mannequins were grotesquely mixed with the bodies of real people who lay dead or wounded in the road, and she swallowed down the bitterness of the raw bile that rose in her throat when she looked on gaping wounds in soft human flesh.

She walked past a pile of rubble, which minutes ago had been two shops, just as her eyes lit on a jagged crater in the middle of the road. It looked as if it had been carved out by some massive supernatural force. But it was the solitary owner-less briefcase that was teetering on its edge which made her face twist in revulsion and horror. She did not dare look down into the hole. The nightmarish sound of howling and crying which echoed all around her had started to make her temples throb, but she knew she had to shut it all out and force herself to help others.

She kneeled down beside a woman, who lay like a cadaver on the pavement. Her hands trembled as she touched the body, but the victim blinked and opened her eyes. Lizzie exhaled with relief.

"It's Eunice," Lizzie heard Peggy croak, and watched her wipe away acrid spit with the back of her gloved hand as she came abreast of them. "Eunice Wilson." She kneeled down by the woman and hugged her.

Lizzie's brow puckered, and then she recognised Eunice as the woman who had been abused about her husband in the factory a few months ago, and who had given Peggy a talking to. She left them together as she moved off to help others.

After about fifteen minutes two ambulances arrived. The ambulance women looked pale, but had a sense of urgency about them, making no apologies for being spread so thin – this was not the only place of death and destruction. Eunice said she was fine; she didn't need to go to hospital. When a handful of motor taxis showed up, willing to take less seriously injured passengers, Peggy helped her into one of them and gave the driver the street name.

"Poplar?"

Peggy nodded and got in the cab with Eunice, while Lizzie asked if anyone else wanted to go east. No one else did. She felt she could do more good by staying behind, but her friend's urgent wave held sway. As soon as they were out of sight of the carnage, Peggy pulled herself together enough to grill the taxi driver for any gossip about the raid. He told them he'd heard that the Royals had been hit, but said that it was a good job it was just the Royal Docks flanking the Thames and not the munitions, "Else the whole of the East End might've gone up with it."

"At least we're still here." This thought seemed to perk Peggy up. "We've cheated the Grim Reaper again."

It dawned on Lizzie then that her friend seemed to thrive on the fear and danger of their daily existence, an essential part of her live-in-the-moment attitude. "After all," Peggy was fond of saying, "You never know when you might cop it." Lizzie glanced over at their other passenger. Eunice Wilson had remained silent, and sat with her hands together on her lap as she stared out of the cab window.

As they got three quarters of the way along the East India Dock Road, the traffic slowed and finally came to a standstill. Lizzie watched a man approaching from the opposite direction; his gait was that of an automaton.

The cabbie addressed him. "What's the hold-up?"

"The school…"

Lizzie noticed Eunice's body stiffen before she leaned forward towards the driver.

"Ask him what school?"

"Those German bastards…"

Eunice had the cab door open now. "What school?"

The man shook his head in shocked disbelief. "Upper North Street. They've bombed it."

Eunice made a helpless noise in her throat, like a wretched wounded animal. She threw herself out of the cab. In an instant she was gone.

"Go after her. I'll settle up here. Go on." Lizzie attempted to pay the fare, but the cabbie waved her away.

"Least I could do. God bless that poor woman."

Afterwards, Lizzie would think: *Never in a month of Sundays before war was declared would a London taxi driver give you a free ride.*

As she turned the corner into Upper North Street, she saw men and women dashing to the school from neighbouring streets. Then she saw Eunice in among them, running too, but her legs buckled and she stumbled onto the pavement in front of the devastation. Lizzie saw there was little left of the school building, only a deep crater full of smashed bricks and mortar mixed up with shattered pieces of wooden school furniture. On her hands and knees, Eunice suddenly began to try to drag parts of the wreckage away. She was oblivious to the blood which smeared her hands as her own skin got razored by the sharp-edged debris. Peggy kneeled down beside her and took hold of Eunice's cut hands and encouraged her to stand up.

Despite their war injuries, Lizzie watched three Blue-Jackets help to search the avalanche of debris. Truncated conversations and comments floated around the mêlée.

"How many kids in there?"

"Not sure. Looks like the bomb hit the roof and went down through the floors to the Infants on the ground floor, and then it went off."

"Poor little mites. Didn't stand a chance."

"We should bomb the Hun's wives and nippers. See how they like it."

"It's high time we had a proper warning system – it's a scandal."

Eunice's legs suddenly gave way again, and Peggy held her up.

"Please, God," she kept whispering, "don't take my boy."

It was obvious, Lizzie thought as she watched the scene playing out in front of them, that there would be no survivors. Just as she had known four years ago when she heard the policeman's insistent knock on the door at eleven o'clock on a Friday morning – barely more than an hour after she had made up the bait tins of beef dripping sandwiches and filled the water bottles ready for her father and two brothers to take for the backshift. The policeman had told her to get down to the pit – it wasn't his job to tell her any more than that, but she had known from the look on his face what to expect. She hurried out on her way to the colliery, half a mile down the road, until she heard a fire engine's clanging bell. Then she broke into a run. The gates were shut, and a big crowd of stoic, silent women stood vigil outside the pit entrance. The underground gas explosion in the mine had left her an orphan without any close family.

The three of them stood there a long time until a woman ran up to Eunice.

"Don't give up hope, love. Mikey Smale's dad has just found him sitting on the front doorstep, large as life."

Eunice's eyes suddenly regained their spark. She broke away and dashed off headlong down the street. Automatically the two friends hurried after her. They rounded the corner into a uniform street of two storey houses, built from yellowish brick, blackened with soot and smoke from the industrial environs not far away. Eunice stood outside a house, distinguished only by the splash of colour from the well-tended window box which was filled with pink pelargonium and blue and white nemesia.

"He's not here. She said he'd be here. Why isn't he here?"

As Peggy moved towards her, Eunice suddenly lunged at the front door and, in her haste to get inside, stumbled over the gleaming white step. She staggered, but her mission kept her upright. Within seconds, dull thuds could be heard coming from the kitchen. Eunice leaned her head on one arm against the kitchen door, while with the heel of her other hand she banged out a staccato rhythm on the door jamb. Peggy steered her into the front parlour and instructed Lizzie to pour her a good slug of whisky.

Eunice sat slumped on the settee with the drink held between her hands as she stared, unblinking, into the glass.

"He was my last chance," she whispered, as if to herself.

Peggy sat down next to her and put an arm around her shoulder.

"Mikey Smale's got six brothers and sisters," Eunice cried out as she pulled herself away from Peggy. "Why couldn't it be him instead?" She closed her eyes and rocked back and forward, oblivious to the whisky sloshing over the side of the glass, until she sagged back against the antimacassar.

Lizzie shifted about from one foot to the other, an unwilling witness to this mother's all-consuming grief. She didn't know Eunice very well, and wondered how Eunice would cope with losing a loved one to a violent death. Lizzie knew the experience never left you; it became part of you, and could consume you if you let it. Peggy threw her a helpless look.

As she cast about for an excuse to leave, Lizzie's eyes were drawn to the neat row of photographs on the mantelpiece in the over-furnished yet neat and tidy room. She stepped forward to get a better look just as Eunice got up and stood in front of them. She smiled at the image of a boy, touching it gently with her fingers before she clasped it to her chest and sat back down. Lizzie watched new tears mark the well-worn tracks down her face, and saw the little smears of blood from the woman's cut hands on the edge of the photograph, but she saw that it seemed to afford Eunice some small comfort. The gesture made her think of Harry Slater: she hadn't heard from him in a while, and she had no picture of him to offer solace if the worst happened.

"You can get off, if you like." Peggy's voice cut into her thoughts. "I suppose I'd better stay here tonight."

Lizzie caught the note of reluctance in Peggy's voice, but she didn't need telling twice.

"And make sure you tell Fawcett what's happened. He'll more likely accept it from you if I don't show up tomorrow."

Peggy had been pushing her luck with her timekeeping and absences these past few months, and Lizzie knew that, though she was sometimes irked at the recent favouritism shown to Lizzie by the manager, Peggy wasn't above exploiting it for her own ends as it suited her.

Grateful to be dismissed, Lizzie walked down the street, soon moving aside to allow a gaggle of sombre women to pass her. She looked back to see them going into Eunice's. Suddenly a faint whiff of cordite, lingering in the air still, reminded her of the day she signed on for munitions work at the factory. She wasn't the only one queuing up to offer her services for the war effort; hundreds of other women thronged around the factory yard, avoiding the swarf that littered it, chattering with excitement.

"Two quid a week, just for starters!" A fresh-faced girl beside her exclaimed. "I'd better get an account at Harrods."

Lizzie grinned. She wouldn't be sorry to see the back of her meagre maid's salary of £15 0s 0d a year, but she knew the job was about more than the money. It offered an escape from the confines of her life in service, for although Doctor Keppel was a fair-minded employer and had been very good to her, she nevertheless had no life to call her own.

She continued to walk, but thoughts about the lengthening casualty lists and the appalling devastation wreaked by the enemy bombs she had witnessed today slowly eased out all other concerns.

Without warning, Peggy's voice slammed into her consciousness.

"Enjoy yourself while you can. There'll be plenty of time for regrets after the war – if you live that long."

Chapter Four

Eunice positioned herself on the stool in front of her dresser and forced herself to look at her reflection in the mirror. She stared at her flushed face and immediately regretted not having got the housework out of the way yesterday. *I look like the wreck of the Hesperus.* With one hand she pulled at a thin strand of hair that had escaped from her chignon, and with the other she fingered the faint network of red broken veins that had just started to appear on her cheeks. She leaned towards the looking glass, a line appearing between her brows as she checked her profile, and then turned to look face on into the mirror. She sighed.

She was expecting her husband home on compassionate leave today and she thought about seeing him again. Eunice knew they had parted on bad terms more than a year ago, but that was before Alfie had gone; before the incomprehensible horror of the Somme; before the personal shrines to dead husbands and sons killed in action had proliferated in neighbours' windows. Now Jack was all she had left in the world and she was desperate to make amends.

Eunice re-pinned her hair and stood up. As an afterthought she reached for the small bottle of Lily of the Valley scent and dabbed some on her wrists and neck, behind her ears and, after a second's hesitation, between her breasts. Suddenly she felt guilty. Here she was, worrying about making herself look attractive for her husband when their son was dead. Whether Jack was coming back or not, there was no getting away from that. She put on her full mourning dress of black crape and waited.

Eunice took one look at her husband as he stood on the doorstep and flung her arms around him. His wife's tears seeped unnoticed into his rough serge collar as the pair remained motionless, grief for their lost child enveloping them like a ghostly shroud.

She stepped back from him and saw at the same time the black arm band and the new stripe on his jacket sleeve. Pretending to brush some offending speck from his shoulder, she asked him what he had done to earn the promotion.

"I didn't die." He smiled, but it didn't reach his eyes. Seeing his wife's shocked reaction, he relented. "I did my duty, that's all."

Recovering herself, Eunice asked him what rank he was now.

"A one up," he said. "Lance Corporal."

They couldn't call him a shirker now.

"Well, I expect you'd like a nice cup of tea."

"I'd prefer a nice hot bath."

He dragged the battered tin bath into the kitchen from its home in the back yard and sat smoking cigarette after cigarette, while Eunice made a pot of tea anyway. They waited for the pans of hot water to boil before taking it in turns to pour them into the tub. From a kitchen chair opposite, she watched him almost shyly as he eased his pale body into the steaming water, but she didn't think she liked the newly grown moustache his new position allowed him to wear. She picked up his uniform jacket and ran her hands down the seams. Her mouth made a little moue of distaste every time she crunched another louse.

"You need to run a candle flame down the seams to kill all the eggs," he said.

She looked up from her task and saw a mocking amusement

dancing in his eyes and at the corners of his mouth. She offered a tentative smile: she accepted her task as penance.

In bed that night, torn between a crushing need to feel his caress and half afraid of rejection – she had denied him her body as punishment for not enlisting longer than she cared to remember – Eunice reached for him. He turned towards her and kissed her with a fervour reminiscent of their courtship days and early marriage.

With a catch in her voice, she whispered, "Jack, I…"

But he ignored their usual intimate preliminaries and was already pushing between her legs with a desperate, hungry urgency. Afterwards, he fell asleep instantly. She lay there in the dark and listened to his even breathing while the tears pricked her eyes.

Eunice found Jack, still clothed and on his back, laid out on the settee with one arm dangling on the carpet. Her lip curled at the sour smell of stale alcohol. Last night, she had tired of waiting for him to come home from the King's Arms and gone to bed. With a dismissive backwards glance at her husband, she stood in front of the window and wrenched open the curtains. A pale early morning light flooded the room.

"What the…?" Jack thrust himself upright, squinted at her and swung his legs down onto the floor. He rubbed his hands through his hair and shook his head to try to rouse himself.

Eunice knew very well his head was probably throbbing.

"Even watered down beer gives you a headache eventually. If you drink enough of it."

He looked up at her as she stood over him.

"Feel better now, do you?"

Here we go, his face said.

Her irritation spilled over. "Well, *I* don't. Have you any idea what it was like?" Her voice wavered. "Forcing yourself to look at your son's destroyed little body?" She swallowed down a sob. "Or

42

bits of him." Eunice started to walk backwards and forwards in front of her husband.

With an effort, he turned his head left and right with her movements, as if watching a game of tennis. Indifferent to his sensibilities or that he had his own feelings of grief to deal with, she simply hoped she was making his head spin.

"Only it wasn't really him." She could barely get the words out.

Jack hoisted himself up off the settee and swayed a little with the effort. She thought he was going to embrace her and she stepped back, but instead he lurched out of the room. She heard the back door slam and followed him. Viewed through the kitchen window, he cut a pale figure against the blackened walls of their yard. Eunice watched him strike a match and light a cigarette, the spent match thrown down onto the cobbles as he took a long, hard drag and waited until his lungs had filled with smoke before blowing it out in a plume of grey vapour, which fogged around his head in the windless air.

A bittersweet image of her husband in the days when they were just starting to get to know one another swept through Eunice's mind. Her friend had started it: the hanging around outside Repton Boxing Club with a gaggle of much younger girls as they waited for the club's rising young stars to come out after training. Eunice kept up the pretence that she didn't think much of boxing as a sport – it was, she claimed, a bit thuggish for her taste – but she was secretly flattered when Jack Wilson singled her out for his attention.

Not long afterwards, he took her to watch him at the amateur championship at Alexandra Palace, and she had been unable to take her eyes off him, mesmerised by his sheer presence in the ring and by his grace and athleticism. Nor was she immune to the attractiveness of his lithe torso above his boxing shorts. That night he was crowned lightweight champion, and she remembered the roar of the crowd in her ears and how a visceral thrill shot through her. It was also the first time he had kissed her, properly, on the lips.

She stared at the solitary figure outside. *How had it come to this?*

Jack saw her at the window, put out his cigarette and came inside.

Softened by her memories, she unfolded her crossed arms and watched him walk towards her, but as soon as she felt his touch her body stiffened, and she thrust her head down so that her chin almost rested on her chest. She could tell by the tautness of his grip on her arms that he was struggling to keep hold of his own emotions, but she knew also that he wouldn't allow himself to give way in front of her. Would she warm to him if he did? Or would she be disgusted by his show of weakness? He crooked his knees and tried to look into her eyes from below, but she refused to meet his gaze.

"Eune," he murmured, bending his forefinger and putting it under her chin to try to raise her face up to him.

She shrugged herself out of his grasp, her own resentment, frustration and grief getting the better of her, and without any warning she slapped him hard across the cheek. As she did so, something small flew from her hand and bounced across the kitchen floor and over the doorstep. Eunice pushed past Jack, and outside she threw herself down onto her knees, ignoring the hardness of the cobbles, and picked the item up. She held it to her lips and could feel the tears ready to flow, but she was determined she would not cry.

"I knew..." she struggled to get the words out "...then. When I saw this button. That it was him. My boy."

"Love..."

"He was really taken by this button, you know." Her voice was low, barely above a whisper. "He found it in my sewing box...It didn't match the others on his shirt, but he was so *definite* he wanted it, so I gave in and sewed it on for him...It was a fox – it had a picture of a fox on it." She dragged herself upright. "Where were you when they buried the bits of him?" She saw him flinch, but the need to howl

44

out her despair almost undid her. Hysterically, she cried, "Anywhere! Anywhere, rather than here. That's where you were. Do you see this?" She plucked at her black mourning weeds. "Do you? Hundreds of strangers came to the funeral. It was all over the newspapers. But not his father. More than a month it's taken you to come home."

With a note of quiet resignation, he said, "We were in the middle of a push. In France. Which is where you wanted me to be."

She ignored the first part of his comment, about doing his duty. "It was nothing to do with where *I* wanted you to be." All her pent-up recriminations came pouring out. "You always ignored *my* feelings. You just sat it out until it was inevitable. A conscript." She spat the word out. "You weren't even brave enough to be a conchie!" She stared hard at him. "I might have forgiven you for that."

The lie fell from her lips just as somewhere nearby she heard the sound of a sash window being slid open. But she was past caring if anyone heard them.

"Listen, even if I'd been told straightaway – which I wasn't – you'd prefer me to go AWOL in the middle of a battle, would you? You have no idea what it's like over there. No bloody idea." He shook his head, and she saw Jack was wrestling with his own anger now. "Would you prefer it if I'd been put in front of a firing squad for flouting orders? Would you? Christ, you couldn't even deal with me not enlisting. Imagine what the neighbours would say about your husband being shot for desertion."

Eunice heard the exasperation in his voice and she knew he was right. The pain was etched on his face, but she had gone too far to back down now.

"Oh, bugger off back to the war then," she shouted, crimson-faced.

"You'll only be satisfied when I stop one, won't you. When you read my name on a casualty list. Then you'll be proud of me."

"You're neither use nor ornament either way."

She saw the hurt in his eyes, but she turned and walked back into the house. *I'm five years older than you and halfway through my life, and what've I got to show for it?* she thought, her bitterness getting the better of her.

She had barely gone into the front parlour when she heard the front door slam. She ran out into the empty hall, where, on the floor, she saw a leaflet telling her it was 'National Baby Week, 22–28 July'. She snatched it up and wrenched open the front door.

"Why wasn't it you instead of Alfie?" she screamed at Jack's receding figure as she threw the unwanted flyer out into the street.

Chapter Five

Lizzie felt a frisson of anticipation as she looked up at the grand facade of the Corner House on Coventry Street. She had not heard from Harry Slater in over five weeks, until a telegram arrived the day before yesterday announcing his arrival back home on short leave. The way her heart leapt when she received it made her realise her correspondent might mean more to her than she had been willing to admit to herself. She remembered how it had started in jest when, like many other girls in the munitions factory, she had tucked a note into a random box of ammunition shells to wish some unknown Tommy good luck with the war and to let him know a girl back home was thinking of him. When a reply came she had given little thought to where corresponding with this stranger might lead. Its purpose was to brighten up a soldier's depressing life in the trenches – and her own too, maybe.

Lizzie went inside and stood mesmerised, transfixed by the room's huge glass chandeliers which hung from a high ceiling decorated in cream and gold. She realised at once why he had chosen this venue: he wanted to impress her. A little smile of pleasure crossed her lips. Her eyes darted back and forth across the room, but she actually had no idea what Harry Slater looked like because he hadn't sent her a photograph in exchange for hers. He had written that he was tall, dark and handsome, and it suited her to think of him like that. She could only hope that he would notice her standing there.

After a few solitary moments, Lizzie began to shift from foot to foot as her confidence ebbed. She was just beginning to think how foolish she would feel if he didn't show up, and how glad she was she had decided not to tell anyone of her planned rendezvous, when she heard an attention-drawing cough.

"Miss Fenwick?" The voice had a warm timbre to it: inviting. "Miss Elizabeth Fenwick?"

She turned to find a man in army uniform standing next to her. He clutched his cap in one hand and a photograph in the other. From the expression on his face, she wasn't sure whether he was going to continue the conversation or turn tail and leave.

Finally, he introduced himself. "Harry Slater."

Or rather she assumed that was what he said, for he spoke so quickly he could have said "Kaiser Wilhelm" for all she knew. She noticed his gaze move down her body and back up again to her face, his admiration obvious – even, she thought, a little indecent. Here was her faraway, brave soldier in person. She felt a twinge of excitement.

He looked at the photograph he held and cleared his throat behind his hand. "Ahem, your picture doesn't do you justice." He gave her a disarming lop-sided grin, which made her feel quite giddy.

When she had thought about this moment – hundreds of times since she received the telegram – all previous worries of potential disappointment were forgotten in her desire to make a good first impression. *But what shall I wear?* She didn't want her soldier to think she was frivolous and out of tune with the sombre tone of a nation at war, and so, after considerable deliberation, she settled on a fashionable mid-calf length dark green and cream check dress, which she considered flattered her well-proportioned figure and showed good taste. The hat she chose was one with an upturned brim, the better to show off her features. Finally, she pinned her small brass *On War Service* badge on her lapel, and then, almost as an afterthought, around her neck she draped her favourite pale green silk scarf – a rare extravagance, bought because she considered the colour complemented her eyes.

Now she had no time to take in his features and attire before he gestured into the middle of the room.

"This way, I have a table over here." He dragged his eyes away from her and guided her to a little table at the far side of the room, which was set for tea.

As she settled herself in her seat, she took in the crisp white linen tablecloth, the silver teapot, the delicate china cups and saucers and small plate of what passed for cakes these days. The cane back chairs were set at a slight angle to each other on the same side of the small round table, inviting intimacy. She wondered if he had contrived their placement. There was a brief moment of awkwardness, as he seemed unsure what was expected until she nodded towards the teapot.

"What? Oh. Tea. Of course," he stammered and picked up the pot.

As he poured the steaming tea, she looked at his features. No, she decided, he wasn't classically handsome, as he had implied in one of his letters, but his blue-grey eyes and dark moustache above his full lips made his face pleasing. Although his hair was short, the harsh cut hadn't quite tamed its wayward black waves, and she was amused to see the indentation where the rim of his cap had perched. Her eyes flicked to the trembling teapot in his hand. She made the assumption he was just as nervous as she. He stopped abruptly as if he felt her gaze and planted the teapot down onto the table.

"Ought I to have put the milk in first?" he asked with a slight edge of sarcasm. He placed the milk jug on the table in front of her and offered her the cup and saucer.

"No, no, that's fine. Just fine." As she reached to take them from him, she knocked over the milk jug, which spilled its contents into a small pool on the tablecloth. She let out a little cry, more at her gaucheness than at the actual mess, as both reached forward with their napkins to mop it up. She cast a glance at him from underneath her eyelashes to find him looking at her.

"No point crying over spilt milk?" He lifted his teacup, his little finger at an exaggerated and ostentatious angle, and took a sip. "Hmm. Makes a change from trench char: no hint of petrol."

She didn't get the joke, but pretended she did and countered with, "It's the same with the 'cakes'. No hint of sugar."

He laughed.

Being virtual strangers, whose knowledge of each other was limited to a handful of brief letters and postcards, they were forced to keep to banal pleasantries for a while, but the air seemed tense with unspoken words. He ate nothing and smoked incessantly, as if he needed something to do with his hands as he chatted, but he avoided any mention of the war. Lizzie felt a small knot of happiness in the pit of her stomach, and yet, without knowing why, he was not what she had expected. Nevertheless, he intrigued her. He had an indefinable attractiveness about him, but for a brief second she wondered whether he had got someone else to write the letters to her.

As she watched him and listened to his appealing baritone voice, which had just a touch of the Cockney about it, Lizzie longed for him to repeat those affectionate sentiments he had just started to confide in his letters. As if he read her thoughts, he began to reiterate his delight at finding her note in the box of ammunition shells all those months ago. Unaccountably, she found herself blushing, and to cover her reaction she babbled on about how she filled the shells and told him that they came from Silvertown Munitions. A dark cloud passed over his face. The din from the clatter of plates and cutlery and the hum of voices all around them pressed in on her and an awkward silence fell between them.

She began to convince herself that she had somehow fallen short of his expectations. *How arrogant I've been, thinking only whether I would like him. He's obviously just going through the motions until he can make his excuses and leave.* She became acutely aware of the time pressure; his leave was short, and she knew he was going back out tomorrow. She considered the possibility she would return to her lodgings with the fantasy she had woven in ruins and that she might never see him again.

"I expect you're really grateful to get some leave after all this time," she said out of desperation for him to say something encouraging.

"Leave?" He said it almost absent-mindedly. "Oh, actually it's quite comfortable in a funk hole." He warmed to his subject. "You get your own firework display every night, accompanied by the Whizz Bang Orchestra. But we have to keep it a secret," he lowered his voice, leaned closer and looked into her eyes, "or even the conchies will prefer it to hard labour."

She watched his eyes dance with mischief as he lit another cigarette.

"The best part is no one gives you a clue about what's going on or what's coming next."

She decided she had nothing to lose by aping his black humour. "Just like any other run-of-the mill job, then?"

He seemed surprised, as if he hadn't expected that reply, then his eyes crinkled and he gave a short, approving laugh.

Encouraged by his response, she continued. "Well, we've all adapted rather well to the bombs," she said, mirroring his tone. "Adds a bit of danger."

However, at the mention of the air raids his face lost all expression. Lizzie felt she had caused him to think of something painful. She silently berated herself. She watched him as he played with his teaspoon and her mind whirred with the possibility it was going to end badly after all. Suddenly, he dropped his teaspoon with a clatter.

"Look, let's get out of here," he suggested. "Find some entertainment." He pulled at his jacket collar, as if it had suddenly become too tight.

So he isn't disappointed in me after all! Buoyed by this realisation, Lizzie twisted around to get her raincoat from the back of her chair. As she did so she elbowed a passing waitress, whose pile of tin trays slid from the girl's grasp and clanged onto the hard floor. The effect on Lizzie's companion was immediate, and shocking. His face contorted in panic. He knocked over his chair as he clutched the tablecloth to get to his feet. Like a blind man, he blundered into other diners, shoving at their chairs and tables. Conversations petered out. Diners stopped to stare at the commotion. Lizzie kept her gaze downwards as she hunted in her purse for some coins to leave on the table. Not caring about the amount, she threw a handful of shillings down, grabbed her coat and handbag and walked to the door, her head held high, her eyes focused on the exit.

As she emerged into the bright sunshine, she squinted. It was hard to focus. She almost stepped into the path of one of the many motor vehicles and horse drawn carriages which surged up and down Coventry Street. When she spotted him, standing in shadow in the doorway of a boarded up shop, she hurried over.

"Harry? Are you all right?" Lizzie took in the beads of moisture on his upper lip and his grey pallor as he fought to regain his composure.

"Sorry about that," he said, not meeting her gaze as he wiped the line of sweat from his top lip with his forefinger. As if reading her thoughts, he took hold of her hand and said, "Don't go."

Chapter Six

The earlier incident with the tray walked with them like an invisible chaperone.

"Let's get a drink," he suggested eventually.

"How long have you been away?" Lizzie joked. "More than an hour yet till opening time."

"Oh yes. Another great tradition bites the dust."

She heard the note of frustration in his voice.

"What about you?" he asked, giving her that lop-sided grin again which made her knees weak. "I hope you're not" – he crooked his fingers for emphasis – "fighting the drink."

"I'd get fired if I turned up at the munitions giving off even a whiff of alcohol, and my landlady would have me out of my lodgings faster than you could say..."

"Lloyd George's beer?" he suggested.

They laughed, and each held the other's gaze for just a fraction longer than necessary. Lizzie drew her eyes away first.

"Your landlady?" he asked. "Part of the temperance movement then, is she?"

Lizzie blew air through her lips. "Oh, I don't think so. One of the girls in the lodgings saw crates of whisky and other booze in her cellar, along with tons of food tins and packets. But she puts a patriotic card in her window saying, 'This household abides by the code of voluntary rations'. Yet she's really stingy with us."

He raised one eyebrow in an exaggerated fashion and looked very stern. "Vell, I sink it iz my duty to steal all dis secret foods and drinks, gif zem to ze very hungry and thirsty Kaiser and ze German peoples and tell your authorities on zis old fraud."

Playing along, Lizzie put the back of her hand to the top of her forehead and exclaimed, like a bad actress, "You're German? A spy! Oh, no."

She made to run off, but he caught hold of her arm. At his touch, something visceral shot through her. He let go, as if worried he had overstepped the mark. Lizzie moved over to the Embankment wall and leaned on it, trying to affect nonchalance by looking out across the dirt-grey waters of the Thames. But his touch still resonated. He came and stood next to her, with his elbows on the wall, just close enough for his arm to touch her sleeve.

"She's not called DORA by any chance, is she? Your landlady?" he joked.

She flashed him an amused look.

"Don't you mind giving up so many personal freedoms because of this war?" he asked. "Having the State interfere in your private life?"

Lizzie hadn't seen the long list of civilian restrictions, imposed by the Government's Defence of the Realm Act since 1914, in that light. In many ways she felt that, as a woman, the war had brought her more, not fewer, freedoms, and she said so.

He replied, gently provocative, "Make the most of it."

"Oh?"

"I'd wager it'll only last as long as the war makes it necessary."

She turned and looked at him, her eyes challenging him.

"I'm not saying it's right. Just how it'll be."

"Some of us have more faith."

He met her gaze. "I admire your spunk, Elizabeth Fenwick."

She felt her heart flutter a little, but she didn't wish to get into any sort of serious discussion, political or otherwise, because she didn't know him that well and it might spoil things. With a slight air of desperation, she cast about for something more innocuous to talk about.

He rescued the situation by saying "Look at that," as he pointed towards the almost cloudless blue sky, "I bet there'll be a glorious sunset later."

Her eyes followed his skywards.

"I don't suppose you get much chance to think about the weather in France," Lizzie said. She thought if she mentioned that country it might draw him out a bit, since he had been silent about his experiences, other than making light of them, although she rather had the impression he was not a supporter of the war.

He tilted his head and looked sideways at her. "As a matter of fact, there's nothing I like more than a good downpour."

She gave him a sceptical look; she still felt she hadn't quite got his measure yet.

"You can get a decent bath in a shell crater."

She pretended to take him at his word, as she understood he was being sardonic again.

Behind them the hum of traffic continued to flow, punctuated by the occasional vehicle horn. She saw him tense once or twice, but there was no recurrence of the extreme reaction she had witnessed earlier. This hint of some unknown vulnerability, an echo of something painful, didn't fit in with the image she had crafted of her war hero, but she found it profoundly affecting. She thought she was a little in love with him already.

"How about we find that entertainment we promised ourselves? We passed a picture palace back there."

He offered her his arm. She felt happy, and, she thought, perhaps a little daring and very grown up. They were pleased to find a Charlie Chaplin film was showing. The main feature had started, and cast just enough light into the darkened cinema for her to notice all the furtive movement in the shadows near the back. Her escort eased down the aisle towards seats in a more central position. Although in her romantic fantasies about him he was the epitome of the perfect gentleman, Lizzie shocked herself by feeling a little disappointed at his honourable action. As the film spooled, she sensed him looking at her once or twice. She decided to be bold and offer him a little encouragement, so she placed her hand where he could reach it. She waited in a small agony of anticipation until his fingers closed gently around her gloved ones. She turned her head a fraction towards him and they exchanged a brief, intimate glance in the faint glow from the movie screen before returning their gaze to the cheerful diversion offered by the film.

When the film ended, neither moved – both seemed unwilling to leave the shared closeness their cinematic fantasy world had conjured up – until the gas lights flared back up and the moment was lost.

Outside he stopped and crooked his arm, gesturing for her to put hers through it. Approving of the offered courtesy, she obliged. They walked along, arm in arm as they threaded their way past other men in military uniform escorting girls who laughed and flirted, determined to have an evening of gaiety. As they passed an open doorway with a red canopy, adorned with faded ornate lettering, faint strains of dance music floated up towards them from the bottom of a narrow staircase. He grabbed hold of her hand.

"Come on," he laughed and led her down the stairs.

The basement room was a crush of bodies. As Lizzie followed him to the bar, prepared to go through the motions of buying her own drink thanks to the 'no treating' rule, she glanced towards the darkened corners, where cigarette smoke and dim lighting masked illicit encounters. It made her heart beat a little faster. As soon as the drinks were bought, they dashed over to an empty table before anyone else could take it, laughing at themselves for their desperate haste. However, they soon discovered the music was too loud for conversation, so when a ragtime rhythm started up, he took her arm and invited her onto the small dance space.

He held her just near enough to preserve decorum as their bodies started to move in time with the beat. They moved further apart and came together in a seamless flow of energy, abandoning themselves to the enchantment of the music. When the rhythm segued into a slow waltz, he pulled her close to him, decorum forgotten as they moved as one with the crowd of dancers. Lizzie relished the warmth of his face pressed in close to the side of her hair, despite the rough scratch of khaki against her neck, and breathed in his intoxicating musky scent. She closed her eyes to try to hold on to this feeling, which was taking her to an unknown place. They carried on swaying, as if in thrall to some hypnotic spell, even when the music picked up its rhythm again, until at last their bodies peeled away from each other.

Later, they stumbled up the steps and emerged into a blacked-out London. At the top of the stairs, he fumbled in his pockets to find his cigarettes. She heard the scratch of a match before his face was illuminated in an ethereal light as he lit first one cigarette, then another for her. At that moment she felt irresistibly drawn to him and she wondered what it would be like to be kissed by him. He passed the cigarette to her, the tiny glowing end arcing like a fairy light against the darkness. The smoothness of the action looked so practised that she knew he was used to doing this, but she found it oddly reassuring that another woman had been the recipient: it was fitting that his experience balanced out her lack of it.

Suddenly he put his arm around her waist, pulled her against him and pointed upwards into the black vastness above them. They watched the trajectory of a bright pinprick of light which moved high above them. She clutched his arm, frightened.

"It's all right. It's only a shooting star," he laughed. "Make a wish."

He didn't wait for her to respond, but took hold of her hand and walked her off into the gloom. The blackout forced them to edge slowly along The Strand as if walking a tightrope. After an awkward five minutes, he lost patience.

"Bugger this," he said and started to whistle for a motor taxi.

"Oh, oh. You can't do that. Not after ten o'clock," Lizzie informed him.

He threw the fag end of his cigarette down and crushed it with the toe of his shoe. He made to walk on, but stopped short when he was tugged back by her fully extended arm. He turned to look at her. In that moment it seemed as if some magnetic force exerted its pull on them and they were swept towards each other. He caught her up in his arms, lifting her feet off the ground, and side stepped her into a shop doorway, his urgent lips finding hers.

"God, I wish I wasn't going back out tomorrow," he whispered as he held her against him, his hot breath on her ear.

Over his shoulder, her gaze was drawn to the illuminated hotel sign on the other side of The Strand.

"There's still tonight," she said, shocked by her own blatant desire and daring recklessness.

Chapter Seven

The clerk behind the desk in the Buckingham Hotel watched them with a sly smile of collusion, and all of Lizzie's daring of five minutes ago began to ebb. In her head, two warring voices fought for supremacy. Peggy's "Life's for living. You might be dead tomorrow" vied with that of Eunice Wilson, warning that when you go larking about with soldiers, "It's always the woman who pays the price."

She hesitated in the doorway of their room. The dark, heavy Victorian style furniture and thick damask drapes made the room seem small and claustrophobic, but immediately her eyes were drawn back to her companion, who had collapsed onto the crimson sateen counterpane.

"Oh, God!" He closed his eyes as if in ecstasy. "A decent bed."

"I thought you said you were happy in your little trench." Her archness masked her building nervousness.

He opened his eyes and turned his head towards her. "Close the door and come here." He patted the bed beside him.

For all her wild imaginings, Lizzie allowed herself to be guided by him. As she lay naked beside him, she watched his gaze run over her body, his eyes blazing with admiration and desire. When he kissed her, she could still taste the faint tang of tobacco and alcohol from earlier, but when she parted her lips to accept his tongue a fizz of desire crackled along her spine. She felt his hot breath against her ear when he whispered tender words of love and encouragement, before his warm lips caressed her throat and her breasts. A delicious lick of intense pleasure flowed to her very nerve ends. When she finally let out a little moan of satisfied bliss, he continued towards his own surrender. Afterwards, as they lay together, naked limbs entwined, Lizzie was enveloped in a sweet fugue of dreamy rapture: she thought she had never felt so happy in her life.

She opened her eyes, still drowsy, and squinted over the top of the bedcovers. She made out scattered items of discarded clothing on the chair next to the bed, and beside her she could hear the steady rhythm of her lover's breathing. She reached out and touched his hair, her heart overflowing with love.

Is this what it is like to be married? To know each other so intimately, to give each other such pleasure and wake up beside each other every day? A delightful vision of a shared future life together rose up before her.

He stirred in his sleep, but didn't wake. Lizzie got up and tried not to disturb him. For all she had given herself to him, her innate modesty now prevented her from parading her nakedness like a brazen hussy before him. She pulled open the heavy curtains a fraction. It was enough to let in a thin sliver of weak dawn light so that she could see the time by the clock on the dressing table. In a little over an hour, he would be on a train going back to the danger of the Front Line, and she was afraid she might never see him again. She gazed at him. *I don't want you to go.*

She returned to the bed and slipped back in beside him. He lay on his side, his back to her, his knees pulled up towards his chest. She put her finger against the top of his spine and traced a line down the middle of his back. His limbs twitched underneath the covers before he almost jackknifed off the bed. He turned towards her, and she saw the flicker of panic on his face before his features softened into a smile as he recognised her.

"You're a sight for sore eyes," he said as he slumped back onto the bed beside her. He leaned towards her and stroked her face with the back of his hand before he pulled her close. "I only wish I could stay."

Lizzie thought of the coming days and months when she would be separated from him. She didn't know how she would bear it.

Chapter Eight

In the north facing back bedroom, Eunice stroked the coarse ear of a one-eyed scruffy teddy bear, not able to remember when or how the other eye came to be separated and lost. She pictured the delight on Alfie's face when he had pulled the bear out from under a pile of general household junk.

"Edbar."

The name had stuck, and her son and his teddy were inseparable until he started school, but it had remained part of his bedtime ritual. She let out a long sigh, put the bear down on the bed and steeled herself to complete the task she kept putting off.

First, Eunice emptied the set of drawers which contained Alfie's clothes. Just last week she had pulled out the top drawer, and the first thing she'd noticed was that the old navy jersey on the top of the pile had a hole in it. Automatically she had picked it up, intending to take it downstairs to darn before remembering her son had no further use for it. She sank her face into the softness of the jersey now, closed her eyes and inhaled the faint scent of her child. A dull ache began in her throat.

She took out the rest of the clothes. There wasn't much to sort out since he seemed to grow out of things so quickly, and many were second-hand and swapped with the neighbours' children and passed on again after that. Only the baby things were kept, folded and packed carefully away with bits of wax paper between them in an old trunk in the attic. On top of the drawers, Eunice caught sight of the tank-shaped money box. *Where's that blinking Kaiser?* said the slogan which blurred before her eyes. She wiped away the tears before she picked it up. Jack hadn't liked it. *Jack.* She had barely given her husband a second thought after Alfie had gone: her grief for her son was all-consuming.

Eunice shook the money box. The rattle of a few coins rang out into the stillness of the room. She pulled out the stopper and tipped the money into her hand. *A couple of bob and a few tanners.* She slipped the coins into her pocket, replaced the stopper on the money box and returned it to its place. Under the bed she found a jigsaw puzzle, its lid emblazoned with a Union Jack and a picture of one of the Allied generals overlaid on it. *The war's made a hero out of you, right enough,* Eunice thought grudgingly. She pulled out a few games, including Trench Football: her son's favourite. She picked up the game tray, sat down on the edge of the bed and began to manoeuvre the wooden ball from the start, at the bottom of the tray, to the finish at the opposite end, where winning required you to drop the ball into a soldier's mouth painted on the tray. She only got as far as the second leg of the maze, where she succumbed to the hazard of a hole cut in the surface and her ball was swallowed up in an instant.

"Stupid game. Stupid, stupid game."

Eunice threw it aside onto the bed and put her hands over her face. She began to rock back and forwards, keening. A voice started up in her head: *You supported the war. It's your own fault.* She nodded, unable to argue with this incontrovertible fact as her guilt pounded her like a steam hammer.

"Yes!" she screamed. "Yes, I did. I supported the *bloody war!* This godforsaken, awful, bloody war!"

A picture of Alfie, playing marbles in the street, his shirt tail hanging out as always, filled her brain until it gave way to a vision of all the children she had given birth to and lost, with Jack standing looking on. All at once she began to grieve for them all over again.

She had no idea how long she had been in here. She picked up the clothes and the games, took hold of Edbar and went across the narrow landing into her room, where she put the bear on her pillow before she walked downstairs. At the bottom, Eunice saw a pair of her son's shoes – his Sunday best – placed to the left of the door.

"Maa, do I haaave to wear 'em?" His childish voice echoed around her in the hall. He hadn't been keen; reckoned they pinched his toes, and preferred his old boots. *Made a right song and dance about it, he had.*

They had sat there since the bomb blast, almost like a punishment, but now she found their presence oddly comforting.

Eunice wandered around the house and looked for something to put her child's things in. Through the kitchen window, she spotted the grocer's wooden crate lying on the cobbled back yard. It should have been returned to Wilkinson's, but Jack had made it into a go-cart instead. She stared at the box-cart with its big pram wheels.

"Old man Wilkinson won't miss one crate," Jack had argued.

He'd always been good with his hands, Jack; good with practical things. Of course, their boy had loved it. Alfie had careered down the streets, whooping and screaming with delight, often coming back home with scraped and bloody knees, ready to do it all over again the next day. She had forgotten what it must feel like to be so carefree. In less than a year, everything she had felt certain about now seemed built on quicksand. She remembered how she'd wished Jack dead that time he came home on leave. She couldn't believe she'd said that. To her own husband.

Eunice began to yank out ill-fitting drawers, remembering how Jack used to rub a candle on the runners so the drawers ran smoothly as she hunted through them.

"Why can't you ever find anything to write with in this damned house when you need it?" she muttered.

She found the bare stub of a pencil, took out a notepad from her bag and scribbled a few sentences before tearing out the page and pinning it onto the pile of clothes. About to pick up the bundle, she paused as if she had just remembered something and picked up the notebook again. She flicked through the pages to the back as she ran her finger down the list of past monthly dates. She stopped at the last entry and made a quick calculation.

Nine days over.

She frowned.

Chapter Nine

On a precious day off from the munitions, Lizzie sat on her hard narrow bed, pleased to be alone for once and enjoying her solitude. Her battered brown suitcase was balanced on her knees as she bent her head low with concentration. How should she start her letter? *Dear Harry* no longer seemed enough now she had given herself to him. Aloud she ran through the entire gamut of romantic salutations – darling; dearest; my dearest; my dearest darling; my love; my only love; my dear brave soldier – without settling on one or another. Finally she decided she'd come back to it once she'd finished her letter and then commit herself.

The letter itself proved easy. The words gushed from her pen as she spilled out all of her feelings for him. Beside her, a pretty postcard lay on the bedcovers. Lizzie stopped writing and her eyes strayed to the card. She picked it up and touched the gossamer silk inlay with its three flowers: a poppy, a daisy and forget-me-not embroidered in the patriotic colours of red, white and blue above a Union Jack. Below it, she read the greeting: 'A Kiss from France'. This was the first contact she had had with Harry Slater since their night in the hotel a month ago.

She thought how every day she had rushed into the hall after her shift, desperate to find something from him so she would know he was safe, and also to confirm that his feelings reflected her own. Of course, the mail from the Front was often unreliable. Now she actually knew him so intimately, this card from him was somehow more special than anything else he had sent.

Having heard yesterday's disturbing news about the number of Allied casualties (another figure so mind-numbing it was hard to contemplate it was real), she was overcome by a sudden fear that he might be killed before she had a chance to tell him how she felt and it prompted her to open her heart to him. She turned the card over and read the printed message again.

Only a wish from a friend
Only a line on a card
Only a message to send
Greeting and kindly regard.

A little bit insipid, she would have to admit – even dull, and hardly a declaration of love, but she decided it meant he hadn't just taken his pleasure and cast her off. He had sent this and so was still thinking of her. And anyway, she reasoned, he had more pressing things to worry about than writing her long, flowery love letters. This card meant he was still alive; her relief allowed her to overlook any lack of passion in the sentiments. She glanced at the scribbled almost illegible signature, put the card back down on the bed beside her and returned to her love letter. She'd make sure to post it today.

When she'd finished, Lizzie glanced over at Peggy's empty bed and wondered whether she'd stayed at Eunice's again. This had started to become a regular occurrence since Eunice's son's death. Lizzie would no doubt find out later when she saw Peggy at the Holborn Empire for that evening's show, but meanwhile she wanted to put a new trim on one of her skirts so she could wear it tonight.

As she rifled through the clothes rail, she remembered her first visit to a music hall, not long after she'd started at the munitions, and how Peggy couldn't believe that she'd never been to one before.

Lizzie hadn't bothered to enlighten Peggy about the confined and constricted life of a servant. She had been absolutely thrilled by the skills of the knife thrower, sword swallower, ventriloquist and mentalist. It was all fantastically exotic, and she couldn't remember when she'd had so much fun before. She relished the interactive experience of being part of an audience who applauded the acts, shouted "Bravo" one minute and cat-called and booed the next.

"If it wasn't for the war shortages," Peggy told her, "we'd be chucking rotten vegetables at 'em. Here! Call yourselves dancers?" she jeered at some deliberately poorly choreographed comedy girls who lumbered around on the stage, out of step with each other and the music.

"Knackered old carthorses, more like!" Lizzie called, and dissolved into a fit of giggles at her own audacity.

She smiled now at the image.

At the bottom of the hall stairs, out of habit she stopped in front of the mirror and checked her face and the whites of her eyes.

"You're a sight for sore eyes," Harry Slater had said.

"Mirror, mirror on the wall."

"Oh!" Lizzie jumped and turned, surprised to see Peggy. She hadn't heard anyone come in. "I didn't expect you so soon." She began to walk towards the back stairs which led down into the kitchen. "Been at Eunice's? I haven't seen her at the munitions in ages."

"She's lonely. Missing having someone to look after." Peggy picked up a magazine from the console table in the hall and followed her. "She's taken it hard. It's my job to cheer her up."

"Two months, isn't it?" Lizzie busied herself with making a pot of tea. "Such a tragedy, to lose your child in that horrible manner."

"There's no 'nice' way to lose a child."

Lizzie caught the edge in her friend's voice and assumed it was a reference to Peggy's decision to get rid of her unborn child. She had no reply to it.

"What're you doing with this?" Peggy picked up Lizzie's skirt, which had been slung over the back of a chair.

"Putting a new trim on it for tonight."

"Oh, just buy yourself a new one." Peggy threw the skirt back over the chair and picked up the *Ladies Pictorial* magazine she had brought down with her. "Ooh, look at that." She pointed to an illustration.

"You'll get the raw edge of Mrs Spencer's tongue. You know how touchy she is about us using her things."

"She won't miss this for a while." Peggy flicked through a few pages. "See?"

Lizzie looked at the colour drawing of a model wearing a violet silk dress with dolman sleeves and a lilac chiffon and lace overdress.

"It's the latest thing. Nice price, though."

Lizzie shoved her copy of *Weldon's Illustrated Dressmaker* towards Peggy.

"No need to make that face, I'm just being helpful."

"I've got more money than I ever earned in my life at that munitions factory. Life's too short to be wasting my time on making clothes from a pattern." Peggy threw the magazine aside.

"I just thought…"

"Let's go up the West End. I fancy treating myself."

Lizzie pointed at her skirt. "I want to get this done."

The truth was, she found shopping with Peggy tiresome. Peggy always insisted on trying on as many dresses as she could, regardless of whether she could afford them or not. Lizzie was sometimes glad the choice was so limited these days, but it didn't stop Peggy: her many purchases still took up the lion's share of the clothes rail in their room.

"Aw, c'mon. Don't be such a stick in the mud. I'll get your coat."

Lizzie shook her head at Peggy's receding figure. She knew that once Peggy set her mind to something, no amount of arguing to the contrary would deflect her, so she gave in and left the sewing. On the way out, she put their landlady's magazine back to save any ructions later.

Just to kill time, while Peggy carried on with the expected routine, Lizzie tried on a few things herself. She was tempted to buy a smart ivory cotton georgette blouse, but a quick look at the thirteen shillings and eleven pence price tag was enough to help her to resist. Eventually, the fed-up shop assistant suggested the pair of them might find what they were looking for in some other store.

"Honestly, Lady Fen-wick," Peggy's voice mimicked an upper-class accent, her tone superior, "these *shop* gels. One simply doesn't know *whaare* they get their airs and graces from. Tut, tut. One's custom will be better appreciated elsewhaare." She flounced off, her nose in the air as she waved Lizzie to follow her. Out of earshot, she complained, "Stuck up little shop girls. What right have they got, looking down their noses? We earn more than them."

By now, Lizzie's feet were sore and her back was starting to ache, but she knew if she suggested a sit down, Peggy would want to go for tea and cakes – even though she was finding it more difficult these days to satisfy her sweet tooth. It bemused Lizzie that Peggy was always complaining about her figure, yet she did little to deny herself. However, this thought of food suddenly made Lizzie feel a little queasy.

She checked the time on the large wall clock on the ground floor of the department store, and calculated there would be a spare bed back at the lodging house since the afternoon shift would have already started. She was finding she needed a short nap in the afternoons these days. She suggested they take a motor taxi back; she'd pay. Peggy bemoaned her lack of purchases the entire journey.

"Well there's always Weldon's pattern option, pet," suggested Lizzie, a little wearily. "Apprenticed to Shurliker's should mean you can run something up in no time."

Peggy curled her lip. "Don't remind me of that sweatshop. That's in the past."

Five minutes later, Peggy was instructing the driver to take them back via Poplar High Street. Lizzie looked out of the window and recognised they were at the junction of Whitechapel and Commercial Road.

"Aren't we going back to the lodging house?"

"My wages is burning a hole in my pocket. So I'm taking your advice."

Lizzie sighed. *That'll be a first.*

Halfway down the wide shopping parade, which was crammed with a mix of impressive municipal brick buildings, business premises, houses, shops with awnings and individual coster stalls, and bustling with crowds of people, Peggy ordered the driver to pull over.

"Wait for us here, Mister." She dragged Lizzie out of the cab with her.

"Only if you pay me the fare so far." The driver's tone implied he was wise to this potential ruse and he wasn't taking any chances. "How do I know you'll come back?"

"Are you saying we're not honest?" Peggy pretended to look affronted.

He wasn't for turning.

"All right, I'll pay half," Peggy negotiated. "That way you won't drive off, neither."

The pair of women jostled their way down the busy High Street. Peggy stopped in front of Kaminskis, the tailor's shop notable for its ornate angled gas lamps suspended from its fascia, something having caught her eye.

"Won't be a tick." She breezed in through the door.

Lizzie remained outside, where she noticed that the original elegant applied lettering which spelled out the owner's name and business had been spoiled by large, uneven white letters – painted in a hurry and by an amateur hand, by the look of it – which proclaimed: 'We are Russians. Not German', and which also obscured the best part of the window display. She knew that even in London's East End melting pot, not having an English sounding name made a difference these days. On a whim, she decided to wander down the street and let Peggy get on with it, having had enough of her friend's shenanigans in Whiteley's earlier.

Lizzie hadn't gone far when she became aware of a sound which was just audible above the steady hum of traffic and people. The hairs on the back of her neck stiffened, and her eyes automatically panned the sky. As the crowds in front of her parted, people scattered in all directions and she was surprised to see an angry mob burst into view. Harsh and discordant voices rent the air. She pressed her back against a wall between two shops and watched, dumbstruck, as the rag-tag crowd surged en-masse up the street towards her.

"Hun baby killers!"

The cold fingers of dread ran up her spine as she watched some of the mob peel away from the pulsating centre of the hostile crowd, axes and large wooden sticks wielded aloft.

"German Spies!"

The shattering sound of breaking glass echoed up and down the street as shards of smashed shop windows spilled onto the pavement. Rioters stuffed cakes into their mouths from a ransacked Jewish baker, and two women ran out from Merkel's butcher's shop, brandishing legs of mutton like cudgels above their heads before they melted away into the maw of the mob.

"Kill the Kaiser! Death to Kaiser Bill!"

Lizzie felt a wave of disgust wash over her as she watched their faces, twisted into frightening, ugly masks of hatred. She tried to close her ears to the cacophony of loathing and detestation for anything German, alien or foreign which echoed down the street. When a large white cabbage from an overturned coster stall rolled against her foot, it spooked her. She kicked it aside and broke into a run down the street, just ahead of the rioters. Oblivious of her surroundings, she knocked over several metal buckets lined up on the pavement outside an ironmongery. The rackety tinny noise was deafening; it jarred her frayed nerves further. Just as she reached the tailor's shop, Peggy was ejected into the street by the frantic proprietor.

"Aie! Aie! Aie! What are you waiting for, Lady? Go! Go!"

He slammed the shop door shut, rammed home the bolts on the inside and began to erect makeshift wooden shutters inside his windows: he was well practiced.

"Charming!" exclaimed Peggy.

Lizzie pointed to the crowd. "Forget good manners."

"Gawd-almighty!"

Peggy grabbed hold of Lizzie's hand. They ran pell-mell across to the other side of the street, where the road was now almost empty of law-abiding citizens. Lizzie noticed a mad glint in her companion's eye, which she recognised as a precursor to some reckless act. They stood together and watched, horrified but helpless, as the shopkeeper next to Kaminski's was beaten senseless in the doorway of his shop as he tried in vain to protect his premises from the looters. Having felled him, they started on the tailor's shop. Lizzie screwed her eyes tight shut to blot out the scene, but she could still hear the sounds of the savage violence. She snapped open her eyes only when she felt Peggy's grip loosen on her hand.

She watched as her friend darted across the street and picked up a single bolt of material lying in the middle of the road. She struggled back to Lizzie with it. She was out of breath and her eyes sparkled.

"Here, help me carry it. It's a ton weight," she panted as she shoved the material she had coveted towards Lizzie.

"Peg, we shouldn't be doing this!"

"You suggested I make my own clothes. Anyway, that mob'd have it if we didn't."

As they moved off, an odd feeling of excited complicity began to take hold of Lizzie, until the pair of them rounded a corner and almost collided with three police officers. Lizzie assumed they had been called to deal with the disturbance. She heard Peggy mutter "Bugger" under her breath.

"Now then, ladies. Steady on," one said, eyeing the material under their arms. "You'll do yourself a mischief if you're not careful."

Lizzie sobered at once, but, before she realised what was happening, she felt a jolt run up the length of her arm as Peggy's end of their contraband hit the road. As she kept hold of the other end, Lizzie watched, incredulous, as her friend disappeared around a corner. One policeman clamped his arm around Lizzie, and the two others made to give chase until their colleague ordered them to leave Peggy and go and deal with the other rioters instead.

"Meanwhile, I'll deal with this one here."

Chapter Ten

Never before in her life had Eunice felt the need to use the services offered at her destination, yet here she was walking along Old Ford Road, pushing past the queues of needy women outside Sylvia Pankhurst's 'Mother's Arms' at number 438. A desperate compulsion pulled her towards the once imposing front door ahead of her.

Just like so many others in the area, the three storeyed house was split to accommodate multiple occupants and smacked of decades of neglect. She walked up the five stone steps, worn like a shallow bowl in the middle from more than a century of other visitors' feet traipsing up them, and scanned the names on the residents' sign. *Second floor.* She looked at the door; its paint was cracked and peeling, and the brass serpent's head knocker was tarnished. Seeing that the door was not shut, she pushed it open and went inside.

At first Eunice struggled to locate the stairs in the gloom after the daylight outside, but once her eyes had accustomed themselves to the scant light, she couldn't help but notice that the rug in the hall was threadbare. As she walked up the staircase, her nose wrinkled at a faint whiff of musty dampness which lingered in the stairwell.

Three identical doors confronted her. One had a makeshift notice stuck on it:

Gathering. 2.30 Today.
Please do not disturb.

She tapped on the door. Her hand was still raised when it was pulled open, as if the person on the other side had been expecting her. A large woman, dressed in a flamboyant dress of red and black, stood in front of her. To Eunice's eyes she had the long, arched, thick, dark eyebrows, intense brown eyes and black hair of a foreigner – not unlike one of the Spanish flamenco dancers Eunice had once seen at the music hall – but her accent was English.

"Enter, my dear," the exotic vision boomed. "We are about to begin." She put out her hand, and Eunice passed over five shillings without needing to ask whether this was Madame Legarde, Spiritualist.

The woman ushered Eunice into a cramped, poorly-lit room, its thick velvet curtains pulled closed. A pungent smell of incense permeated the air. Four other people sat, expectant, around an oval table which almost filled the entire space. No one spoke, so Eunice nodded a general acknowledgement. She squeezed between a middle-aged woman, who was twisting a creased handkerchief between her hands, and a well-dressed gentleman with a handlebar moustache, who reminded her of Lord Kitchener. *Perhaps he's back from his watery grave*, she thought. *Lord knows, we could do with him*. Opposite Eunice sat a pale young woman, clearly in deep mourning, and next to her an elderly lady, swathed in black and with a prominent hooked nose, making her look like a large crow.

Eunice glanced around her. There was little room for any other furniture except a narrow console table. On it was a brass candlestick holder, a jug of water covered with a holed crocheted cover and a glass tumbler. In her pocket she rubbed the fox button between her thumb and forefinger as she tried to forget the hollowness inside her. The air was thick with the same desperate sense of hope that kernelled in the pit of her own stomach.

The medium took her position in her chair as if it was a throne and commanded her subjects to pay attention. "Now, join hands with the person next to you. On the table in full view. This circle must not be broken." Her eyes swept the rapt faces around the table. "This afternoon I will be your intermediary with the spirits of those on the other side. Please do not be concerned about what happens during my attempt to contact them."

She seemed to aim this comment at the nervous woman next to Eunice.

"The power of communication from beyond can be very strong and may take many different forms. Concentrate hard on your lost loved one and the spiritual pathways will be strengthened."

With a long-nailed finger, Madame Legarde tapped a pad of paper and a pencil on the table beside her. "I also keep these to hand in case a spirit wishes to transfer their message that way." With a flourish of her left hand, she announced, "I am ready."

She closed her heavy-lidded eyes, and within seconds her head began to sway from side to side. Apparently entranced, she made a strangled humming noise just as the gas lamps on the wall dimmed and a faint tapping noise echoed around the room. In an unconscious gesture, Eunice tightened her grip on the hands of those either side of her. The spiritualist let out a loud, guttural noise, followed by a deep masculine voice in obvious pain.

Unable to contain herself, the young woman squealed, "Who is it? Is it Algie?"

"This is for...Viola? No...Vera? Yes, Vera. Tell her I love her."

The nervy woman, responding to her name, cried out, "I'm sorry, Bob. All for the sake of a shilling a day. Please tell me you forgive me, Bob!"

"The connection is very faint...his voice is disappearing..."

"NO!" The widow was hysterical now.

"Fading...What's that? You. Forgive. Her."

Eunice felt the woman's hand start to shake as a small sob escaped from her.

Madame Legarde began writhing in her seat. The brass candlestick holder toppled off the sideboard and hit the floor with a dull thud. Everyone, apart from the spiritualist herself, jumped.

She became animated again. "I can see an angel, standing guardian over lost souls. I see a small child."

Eunice tensed. The spiritualist's shoulders sagged. She slumped down in her chair, and her head drooped on her chest as if spent. The lights flickered.

"No, no, don't give up," urged Eunice, unable to stop herself. "The small child?"

"Is she all right, do you think?" whispered the elderly lady.

No sooner had she expressed this concern than Madame Legarde's head jerked up, her eyes snapped open and she stared hard at Eunice. Slowly her hand picked up the pencil from the table, and, as she held it, the lead point began to scratch across the pad next to her. Everyone leaned forward to see what she had written. Eunice's eyes widened as she looked at the childlike spidery scrawl.

Two words: *JACK. GAS.*

Eunice's eyes rolled back in her head and she slumped down in her chair.

Chapter Eleven

The warder wrote down the prisoners' details for inclusion in the gaol's register before Lizzie was herded off with several other new prisoners to the Reception Ward. Here another female warder barked at her to remove her clothes and forced her to get washed in full view of a gimlet stare. Once Lizzie glanced over and was disconcerted and confused to see how the warder appeared to be scrutinising every aspect of her body; she couldn't tell what the woman found so fascinating. Embarrassed, she attempted to cover her pubic hair with the bar of carbolic soap the warder had shoved at her and shield her breasts with one arm across them, but she was told to desist.

"I need to make sure you're not hiding anything. Now, stand up and face me while you dry yourself."

Red-faced with mortification, Lizzie did as she was instructed. Afterwards she was glad when she pulled on the brown serge dress with its branding of light coloured arrows, fastened the blue and white checked apron and pushed the white cap down on her head. She asked for some garters to keep up the thick black and red striped stockings, but was told there weren't any so she made do with knotting the stockings at the top and hoped that would suffice. When she complained that her shoes didn't match, she was told, "Be grateful they fit." They didn't. She said nothing more, as there was little point.

The warder shoved her into a dark airless cell and told her that henceforth she would be referred to by the number on her cell door. When Lizzie heard this door bang shut, she sank down onto the cold, hard floor of Holloway Prison and put her face into her hands.

After five days of incarceration, Lizzie knew the prison routine off by heart, but if she happened to forget she could always check by looking at the list of regulations stuck to the cell wall. In here, life was proscribed during the hours of a quarter to six in the morning until bedtime at nine o'clock at night. The similarities to a servant's working day didn't escape her notice. This morning, like every other day, the routine remained the same. When she was freed, she had no doubt if anyone ever asked her about her time here (although, of course, she would never admit to it), she could recite it in her sleep.

She bent over the copper basin and washed her face in cold water, using the coarse soap that made her skin tight, and scrubbed her nails – which somehow never looked clean – with the small nail brush provided. Before she would be given her breakfast, she had to fold away her uncomfortable bedding at the back of the cupboard, empty her overnight slops from the water closet and pull down the folding table attached to the wall so she could put her plate, spoon, jug and wooden salt cellar out. Despite the fact that this repast was always a thick paste of bland, lumpy unsweetened porridge, which clung to her throat as she tried to swallow it, she looked forward to putting something in her stomach at the start of the day.

In advance of inspection by the sharp-eyed warder, she cleaned the single window and scrubbed the whitewashed floor of her cell to ensure everything was neat and tidy. If her cell passed muster, she was allowed out of her confinement to do work duty: darning hessian sacks for the war effort. Only this allowed her to pretend she was doing anything useful, and, despite its monotony, it served to keep any thoughts of self-pity at bay.

That and the anticipation of a reply to her love letter waiting for her when she got out.

"What you in for then?" the woman next to her asked Lizzie during the long work period one day.

Without thinking, she said, "Stupidity," and sucked her forefinger before checking the tiny red blister that was forming.

The woman looked at her askance. "That's not normally a criminal offence, else the gaols would be bursting at the seams."

Lizzie, too embarrassed to admit to her misdemeanour, carried on darning.

"You don't look the usual sort to be in here."

She felt the woman's gaze on her, and out of courtesy glanced up from her task. She noticed the broken veins on her fellow inmate's red cheeks and the ingrained tidemark on her neck, but saw in the rheumy eyes a desperate need to connect with someone. The woman leaned closer to Lizzie, as if confiding in a friend.

"A lily-livered soldier forced himself on me."

Without meaning to, Lizzie leaned away from her. When she saw the woman's cold stare and realised how it must look, she pretended she had needed to cough and was simply being polite.

"But that's awful," she said and resumed her initial position. Nevertheless, she thought being attacked was an odd reason to be in prison. This woman was the victim.

"One of those purity patrols caught us in Victoria Gardens, didn't they. Never thought I'd ever be glad to see those wizened up high an' mighty spinsters, and that's the truth. But this officer, he told them I was giving him a four penny one, didn't he. And they called the police."

"Not for the first time, neither," cackled someone behind them.

The woman turned and glowered at the speaker, and Lizzie set to darning again, since any slacking was a punishable offence, only a little slower to alleviate the pain in her sore finger.

"I mean to say, does the Government think they're reading the Bible with those French tarts over there? Pah. First chance they get, they're doing jiggy-jiggy with our lads for money. Come back here, and Kitchener's mob think they can treat us the same."

"I thought those patrols were meant to protect women, not punish them," Lizzie ventured.

"Nah. Those titless old hags sent him off with a flea in his ear just 'cos he was an officer – although he was no gentleman, I can tell you – and I end up in here, accused of soliciting, but..." she picked up her sack and began darning in an exaggerated fashion, giving a slight nod of her head to indicate that the warder was looking in their direction "...no one believed me." The woman lowered her voice. "They put my legs in these metal stirrups, the warder held me down, and that...that doctor got this metal instrument..."

Lizzie cast a sly glance around to see if anyone else had heard. "Are they allowed to do that?"

"Makes no difference. If you're a woman, you don't have any rights. They weren't interested in my side of the story. They're just bothered about the men, the soldiers." Suddenly, she raised her eyebrows and swung her eyes to her left to warn of the approach of the warder and to indicate that they should cease the conversation.

Lizzie saw the shadow fall across the work table as the warder's bulk loomed into view. She stood rigid, like a statue, her hands behind her back.

"If you haven't met the quota by the end of the session," she barked, "it'll be hard labour." She swung an accusatory finger at Lizzie's fellow inmate. "Got that, you?"

The woman nodded meek compliance, but as soon as the warder's back was turned to move off to the far end of the room, she continued in a whisper, careless of the threatened punishment.

"Found me guilty, of course, then they checked I didn't have the pox."

Etiquette prevented Lizzie from asking the obvious question – that and the fear of hard labour if the warder noticed. Aware of the warder's gimlet scrutiny again, she set to her darning once more. As her blunt darning needle flew in and out, she decided she would just have to persevere and get through all this.

Back in her cell, she craned her neck to stare at the fading light of the late summer evening, just visible through the tiny high-up window. During her first few days of captivity, Lizzie had railed against the injustice of her position and cursed Peggy, who was getting on with life outside while she was deprived of her freedom, and had proceeded to say aloud all of her friend's perceived faults. Now, more resigned to her fate, Lizzie had come to believe that she'd brought it all on herself by going along with her companion's reckless action. The irony of being in solitary confinement, when at the lodging house she had wished for privacy, wasn't lost on her.

Unable to settle, she paced backwards and forwards in her cell. Thirteen steps long and seven wide – she'd counted them on her second night. What a palace her lodgings seemed in comparison now. She stopped in front of the corner cupboard, and from between the Bible and a hymn book, she pulled out the prayer book and sat down at the table. As she flicked through its pages, searching for strength and inspiration, her mind turned to her reputation. She began to worry what everyone would think of her.

Lizzie Fenwick? Why she's just a common thief.

And what about her soldier-sweetheart, doing his honourable duty and bravely risking his life for King and Country? She'd have to hope he never found out: no war hero would lower himself to marry a common criminal.

Suddenly, all her dreams were in a heap.

Lizzie emerged past the prison gate house, her head bowed, not wishing to make eye-contact with any passers-by. Approaching a pillar box on her left, she was surprised to hear her name called. Peggy stood there.

"Look, I know you've probably got the ache with me," Peggy began immediately, "but I just expected you to drop your end and run after me." She put her palms face up. "I still can't figure out why you didn't."

"Because I'm not as fly as you, maybe?"

Although her humiliation, shame and resentment wrapped around her like a straitjacket, Lizzie was relieved to have her freedom again, and, anticipating being without a job or somewhere to live by virtue of her incarceration, she realised she was going to need a friend.

"You've got your work cut out to get back in my good books, mind you." She took hold of Peggy's arm. "I'm dying for a decent cup of tea and something sweet."

With a smile of relief, Peggy said, "All right then. I've got an hour till my shift starts."

Inside the crowded and shabby café, Lizzie noticed the tea was an insipid straw colour. She took a sip and grimaced.

"As weak as water. And where's the sugar?"

None of her prison food had been sweetened, and she was dismayed to find that all the sugar bowls had disappeared from the tables now.

"You've virtually got to beg for the stuff," Peggy said and went to find some. "That's your lot." She tipped one sugar cube onto Lizzie's saucer, but kept two for herself, then nodded at the grimy café window, through which the grand turreted gateway, battlements and towers of Holloway Women's Prison loomed. "What was it like in there?"

Lizzie stared at the house of correction and shivered. "Awful, horrible place." As she said this, it occurred to her that once upon a time (and not so long ago) she might have fantasised that it looked like a medieval castle, where an armour-clad knight might ride through the gates on his charger with his Lady's colours fluttering in the breeze. "I don't want to think about it." She stirred the sugar into her tea, half expecting Peggy to apologise for her part in Lizzie's downfall. When she didn't, Lizzie allowed a touch of self-pity to enter her voice. "What am I going to do? I don't suppose I can even go back in service. Even a slavey won't get hired with a prison record."

"Don't suppose they would, no." Peggy took a noisy slurp of her tea to hide a smile.

"I'm glad you find it amusing." Lizzie glared at her.

"If I was you, I'd turn up at the munitions for the early shift tomorrow."

"Leave it off, Peg. I'm not in the mood for jokes."

Peggy beamed at her.

"What?"

"Just think of me as your Fairy Godmother."

"You mean…" Lizzie blew air out between her lips, then her face darkened. "How did you swing that?"

"If you must know, Eunice could see something was bothering me – it was, believe it or not – so I told her what had happened. She finally convinced me that if I went directly to Fawcett – not the Welfare Supervisor, kept her well out of it – and told him you had a sudden illness in the family and had to go north quick-smartish, then he'd more than likely let you keep your job, seeing as how you're always in his good books for being Miss Efficient, and his damned shell-filling quotas are all he cares about."

"Thanks for doing that. It's a weight off my mind."

"Well, you wouldn't know it from your expression. You're not worried about Fawcett, are you? I told you, he bought it hook, line and sinker. Anyway, who cares what he thinks?" Peggy flapped her hand in dismissal.

Although Lizzie had been thinking that if it wasn't for Peggy, she might not have needed such a favour in the first place, the truth was she was relieved the munitions manager did not know of her incarceration. "So nobody else at the munitions knows, then?"

"No."

Thank God.

"I gave the same story to Mrs Spencer and paid your outstanding week's rent, else you'd be out on your ear. You know what she's like when she gets on her moral high horse, and not paying your rent, well…" Peggy made a dramatic slicing gesture at her throat. "What? Don't look so surprised."

Lizzie always assumed that Peggy spent every penny of her earnings on enjoying herself, and that she therefore had no savings or other funds to spare.

"Oh, thank you, Peg. Really. I'll pay you back straightaway."

"Good, 'cos it's left me a bit short and I'm going out for a lark tonight."

In an effort at nonchalance, Lizzie asked, "Are there any letters for me, do you know?"

"One or two." Peggy gave her a sly look. "Expecting-"

"What time is it? Aren't you due at the munitions?"

"Damn." Peggy pulled a face and got up to leave. "Been a bit of a struggle getting in on time without you there to chivvy me on."

All the way home on the bus, Peggy chattered on, but Lizzie barely paid attention. Now that her future was no longer in the balance, she had only one thought in her mind.

Chapter Twelve

Lizzie almost fell over the threshold of the lodging house front door in her enthusiastic hope of finding a letter from Harry Slater waiting for her. All the time she had been in prison, amid her humiliation and misery, this thought had kept her going. She flicked through the pile of mail, throwing each one without her name on it back down onto the hall console table in a careless fashion.

Nothing.

Upstairs in her room, she sat down on her bed, crushed by bitter disappointment.

Why hadn't he written back?

A tiny worm of foreboding wriggled around in the back of her mind, but soon little excuses began to shine like glimmers of hope through the cracks of her black despondency. She told herself the unreliability of the mail from the Front was notorious; someone had mentioned once how it had to be put onto hospital trains carrying the wounded, if there was space, and then wait for a ferry across the channel before it got into the normal postal system. Then she remembered press reports of mail ships being sunk and all letters lost at sea – oh, she hoped his love letter wasn't at the bottom of the ocean! Or perhaps he hadn't received hers at all.

Tying herself up in knots with all her conjecture, she took her coat and tried to work off her worries by walking around Victoria Park for the rest of the afternoon, but when a military band began to give a concert she couldn't bear to look at their uniforms or remain there any longer.

By the time she went to bed, other possibilities began to erode her self-assurance. Harry Slater was a womaniser and he had used her for his own ends, or he thought her cheap now because she had slept with him. To him, she was just another one of those desperate stabs: the sort who answered every Tommy's lonely heart advertisement and put hundreds of notes in shell boxes, only too willing to give herself to any soldier who paid her some attention.

Gradually a sickening sensation lodged itself in her chest. She forced herself not to contemplate the far worse thing his silence might mean.

Lizzie was pleased that the factory manager had been absent from the munitions for the first week of her return and she hadn't had to face him, but now she had been summoned. She knocked on the door of Mr Fawcett's office and heard his rasped "Enter." She stood motionless, with her palm gripping the handle, until the second "Come in!" made her push the door open just enough to allow her to peer around its edge. There he was, behind his desk, his head bowed as he wrote in a large ledger. When he didn't look up to acknowledge her presence, she gave a little cough. When he raised his head, his lips were pressed tight and his face closed, until he saw who it was.

"Ah, Miss Fenwick?" he called out, his tone urgent but pleased.

She came into his office. With light bouncing steps, he came towards her, and for a moment Lizzie imagined he was about to gather her up into his arms, but instead he stepped behind her to close the door before he ushered her further inside his domain.

Lizzie shot a nervous glance around the room. Her first impression was one of excessive tidiness: papers were stacked in neat piles on the corner of his large mahogany desk; a selection of ledgers were arranged in a precise line on top of a set of low cupboards;

and two chairs sat side by side in front of his desk, with a uniform distance between each other and its front edge.

He didn't ask her to sit down, so she stood before him, her hands clasped in front of her, while he leaned against the front of his desk in a rather more casual manner than the pose he affected when he took time out to visit her at her workstation to praise her efficiency. In his rich gravelly voice, he enquired after her relative's health. Unconsciously she began to spin her thumbs round each other as she told him her aunt had made a complete recovery. She saw something unfathomable cross his face which prompted her to begin to stutter her thanks for his generosity in keeping her job open for her, but he raised his hand to stay her.

"I've called you here to tell you that from the end of next week you will no longer be working in the Danger Building."

Oh. I'm going to be fired after all.

"There's another big push on so you will assume the role of Charge Hand in the shell packing section."

Lizzie's eyes widened and she just stopped her mouth from falling open, but she wasn't going to argue.

"I...er...thank you, Mr Fawcett."

She knew it was rare for someone with her background to be promoted into a supervisory position.

"Miss Hawthorne will explain your new responsibilities."

As she listened, an image of herself with a new air of authority, counting her increased wages and enjoying her higher status, rose up in front of her and her back straightened a little. Eventually, unable to find any further reason to keep her there, Mr Fawcett showed her to the door.

"I'm sure my faith in your abilities is not misplaced, Miss Fenwick."

She promised she wouldn't let him down, and was moving towards the door when she heard him say, "Ah, there's just one other thing."

"Yes?" She turned and gave him a wide smile.

"Certain things have come to my notice, and given your new position, I suggest you might do well to reconsider your choice of friends."

Lizzie lay on top of the bedcovers, her thoughts pulled away from her good fortune – and hadn't she earned her promotion by her diligence and efficiency? – by the bloating of her stomach and the onset of a dull ache which had started just above her loins. She knew this usually presaged the onset of her monthly bleed. She curled her body up into a tight ball with her arms wrapped around her knees to get some relief, but soon got up, took a clean pair of drawers, a sanitary rag and two aspirins from her old suitcase – the only place she had in which to keep her personal effects – and shut herself in the upper floor lavatory. Here she pulled down her drawers, expecting to see the start of the usual dark red stain, but frowned when she saw only a spotless white gusset again.

Suddenly she cried out, "Please, Harry. Let me know you love me back."

Lizzie sat in the changing room at the munitions after her shift, a buzz of idle chatter around her as she waited for Peggy. A women's magazine lay open on her lap, but she wasn't reading it. Instead she was listening to a conversation going on behind her.

"The first match is against the Woolwich Arsenal Ladies in a fortnight. Joe Haines said we've got to practise twice a week or he won't coach us."

"Did you hear what Fred Waller said? He said him and his mates would come to watch as they could do with a good laugh."

"I might just have to let down the tyres on his bicycle for that."

"Ah, but isn't it the truth we're always having to prove ourselves to men?"

Lizzie had seen the notice that the munitions were sponsoring a women's football team, all proceeds from matches going to a charity for wounded soldiers. She liked this aspect of it, but also thought if she put herself up for it she might be able to reignite some of the camaraderie with her fellow workers that her promotion had immediately caused her to lose. She had put her name down, and quite by accident – because it had fallen off the notice board wall and she had bothered to pick it up and put it back – she saw the list of women selected for the football team. No one had told her that the date of the trials had been brought forward.

"We could go for the Munitionette's Cup."

"That'll be a lark."

Lizzie was suddenly spiked with irritation. When she had accepted her promotion, she had been a little too pleased with her luck to give much thought to the difficult balancing act required in supervising others who had once been at the same level. Since she was 'one of them', and not a middle- or upper-class woman like all the other charge hands and over-lookers, she didn't think she would have too much trouble getting them to accept her new role. But when it became apparent to her that not every member of her group was a grafter, she had to decide when to make concessions and wield her authority lightly and when to exert stronger discipline on the slackers. So far, she hadn't always got it right, and her former 'friends' were punishing her for it. She looked at the wall clock and vented her annoyance on Peggy for her tardiness.

That girl is always last bat.

She decided not to wait any longer, closed her magazine and had stood up, ready to leave, when Mary Maguire burst into the room, her face flushed.

"Have you heard?"

The room fell silent in expectation.

"Peggy Wood's been sacked!"

There was a buzz of excitement and a few cat calls which implied Peggy's input would be no great loss to the quota system. Lizzie sat back down, careless of the munitions uniform she had folded neatly on the seat. Mary sat next to her.

"Persistent poor timekeeping, Hawthorne told her. She was just terrible when you were away."

An uncharitable voice behind them muttered, "She had it coming. Everyone knew it"

"Except herself it seems, ha ha."

"That's enough crowing," Lizzie called out, annoyed at their lack of support.

"Oooh, listen to the swank pot!"

Lizzie ignored the comment. "Where is she?"

"She's already gone."

All the way home on the bus, Lizzie thought about appealing over the head of Miss Hawthorne to the factory manager's better nature, and weighed up what she could say that might persuade him. However, she kept remembering his words: *I suggest you might do well to reconsider your choice of friends.*

Her mind was still full of this dilemma as she sorted, in a cavalier manner quite unusual for her, through the lodging house mail. She noticed the scrawled 'Undeliverable. Return to Sender' across the corner of one envelope and, knowing its dreadful import, instantly forgot about Peggy: another one of her fellow lodgers had lost a loved one. Sometimes Lizzie wondered, rather despairingly, whether there would be any young men left after the war.

About to flip over the envelope to see the original sender's name, she froze. The handwriting was her own. All at once, the rest of the letters fell from her grasp and scattered about her feet. In her hand she clutched the letter, written weeks ago, telling Harry Slater that she loved him. She didn't cry. She was quite simply numb with shock and seemed unable to accept her lover's terrible fate. She went and lay on her bed, fully clothed, and stared at the ceiling, not even stirring when Mary breezed in.

"Loan us your green silk scarf, would you, Lizzie? I'm wanting to look darlin' for my sweetheart this evening."

Lizzie did not want to talk to anyone about anything, least of all a scarf, so she said she'd lost it. Mary grabbed her wash bag, harrumphed and walked out. A violent ache had begun in Lizzie's left temple and was slowly traversing her entire body. She felt unable to move her arms or legs, so she just lay there like a stiff wooden doll.

Later, in the suffocating darkness, as she lay in her cheerless bed, her grief became uncontainable and she gave in to a flood of tears which soaked into her pillow.

No. No. It's not true. It can't be true. It's a mistake. An awful, terrible mistake.

She shoved her face into the dampness of the coarse pillowcase and stifled her great wracking sobs in an attempt to conceal them from her sleeping room-mates. She couldn't cope with their pity.

"Oh, you poor thing, how terrible."

Or their commiserations.

"He died with honour for his country."

She couldn't deal with it all. Not yet.

But they didn't stir, too exhausted from their shift to be roused by her crying. Her throat burned and she could feel the inflamed swelling around her eyes. As she lay there, her raw grief twisted her into a tight knot of despair. She wondered how long it had taken for her letter to be returned.

Did he lie dying even as she was writing it? Was he already dead? She couldn't bear to think of it. Suddenly she realised, with excruciating clarity, that her unopened letter meant he had died not knowing that she loved him, and she would never know if he had loved her back.

Chapter Thirteen

Eunice let herself in through her front door and noticed the big lumpy bag of potatoes slumped in the corner of the hall. *How nice of Peggy*, she thought, while at the same time feeling a little stab of irritation that Peggy hadn't taken them into the kitchen. Of course, they would have been acquired by some nefarious means, but Eunice wasn't going to turn them down. Not these days. Then, as she removed her coat and walked towards the parlour, she noticed that the house was warm.

"Woo! It's wild out there," Eunice said as she pushed flyaway wisps of hair behind her ears. "That storm's put paid to the last of the leaves on the trees."

She immediately saw, grudgingly, that despite the coal shortage, Peggy had lit the fire in the front room. The temperature certainly warranted it, but she still frowned and said, "Bit early in the season for that."

"Cup of Rosie?" Peggy asked to deflect further complaints. "I'll make one. Here," she patted the chair she had just vacated "sit yourself down and put your feet up."

Eunice, grateful for Peggy's companionship in her empty house and glad of the peppercorn rent she paid, was pleased to see that her new lodger seemed eager to be accommodating today.

"Ooh, that'll be lovely, but don't be heavy handed with the tea leaves."

Eunice sat down, eased off her shoes and flexed her toes as she leaned back in the chair and rested her hands on her rounding belly. When Peggy returned and handed her a cup of strong, dark tea, into which she poured a splash of watered down condensed milk, Eunice wondered why she'd bothered to mention the tea leaves. Eunice drank her tea in silence as she stared into the fire and took a guilty pleasure in watching the orange and yellow flames dance in the grate, relishing the warm glow they gave off. She knew they'd have to go without another time instead.

"I bumped into Mary Maguire," Peggy suddenly piped up, unable to tolerate silence for too long. "You know? Irish girl. I used to share a room with her."

Eunice shrugged.

"Anyway, you'll never guess."

"What?" Her lodger was proving good for a bit of gossip.

"My old landlady's been fined 100 quid for food hoarding."

Eunice heard the note of triumph. She looked at Peggy, curious.

"What? Oh, all right. I admit it. I ratted on her."

"Revenge is sweet," said Eunice. "Thanks for the potatoes, by the way." She heaved herself out of the chair. "But better sort them out."

"No you don't. Not in your condition." Peggy went out and dragged the bag into the kitchen. "Don't thank me, they were on the doorstep when I got back."

"Ah." Eunice smiled, knowing the lad who'd likely left them there. He was a good boy, but he reminded her of Alfie, of her loss, and seeing him always made her sad. She was glad she had missed him today.

Peggy placed her feet either side of the bag to steady herself, and with a huge effort slung it onto the table.

"I'll give Kitty next door half," Eunice said.

"You're always giving her stuff. What does she ever give you back?"

"She's got five kids to feed," was all Eunice said as she began to count out potatoes.

Peggy watched. "There's a limit, surely, to how much we're expected to keep on denying ourselves."

"We don't have much choice these days." Eunice leaned over the sink and ran cold water over her hands to rid them of the dirt from the potatoes. "Any more tea in that pot?"

Peggy picked up the pot and swirled it around to gauge its weight before she lifted the lid. "Sorry."

"Never mind." Eunice dried her hands. "I haven't seen your friend Lizzie recently. Since she got promoted her shifts don't seem to match mine. How is she?"

"Wouldn't know."

"Still not speaking?"

"The only work I can get pays me a pittance compared to munitions work. If you hadn't made me do her that favour..."

"Oh, I think you do all right on the tips you wangle out of all those poor saps in the King's Arms. At least you've got your complexion back. You were starting to look like an oriental."

"That's the only benefit I can see," said Peggy. "You know, she could've twisted Fawcett round her little finger if she'd wanted to."

"Maybe she didn't have the nerve to try, or maybe she did and didn't get anywhere. He can be hard sometimes."

"Except when it comes to her."

"I fancy the factory manager's a little in love with Lizzie Fenwick."

"He'll be wasting his time. She's holding out for a war hero to come along and sweep her off her feet."

"A war hero." Eunice's mouth turned down.

"And Fawcett hardly qualifies."

"The only kind of war heroes seem to be dead ones." Eunice folded the hand cloth up and a pained expression formed on her features. "I went to a séance," she suddenly blurted out.

"What? A séance. What a lark!"

"Oh, I wish I hadn't said anything now." Eunice had seen the glint in Peggy's eyes. *It'll be all over the street by tomorrow.*

Peggy suddenly looked concerned. "But just 'cos you haven't heard from Jack in a while – you said he wasn't a great letter writer – doesn't mean he's gone west."

Eunice flinched at the euphemism.

"You'd have heard by now, anyway. So what happened? At the séance?"

Eunice knew Peggy was trying to temper her need to know, but that her curiosity would always get the better of her. *Oh, what the hell.* She wanted to get it off her chest: that medium's message was eating her up.

"It was Alfie I wanted to get in touch with, not Jack. But…" she began twisting a handful of her skirt round and round.

"What? What is it?"

"The message…it wasn't about Alfie. It said, 'Jack. Gas'."

I made his life hell, Peg, she wanted to add, but couldn't bring herself to voice it. *And now he's going to die on some foreign battlefield, if he hasn't already.*

Peggy stared at Eunice for a moment before flipping her hand.

"Oh, it's just a lot of old nonsense, this spiritualist lark. Don't believe it."

That was more or less what the duty doctor at the Workers' Suffrage Federation free clinic had said, only he had been angry about the medium playing on Eunice's vulnerability and had threatened to report this Madame Legarde to the police for fraud. Eunice had almost wished the nervy woman from the séance hadn't taken her there after she'd fainted.

"Thing is, I never told her Jack's name."

Peggy pursed her lips and looked stumped for a moment. "Aw,

she just got lucky, that's all," she said eventually. "Look, Eunice, I can see all this is taxing you." She opened a cupboard and took out a small bottle. "You'll make yourself ill at this rate. Here." She offered the Veronal to Eunice. "Didn't that doctor you saw say it'd help?"

Eunice held out her hand. The doctor had been kind, but he'd had a clipped foreign accent which made him difficult to understand in her flustered state that day. She thought he'd called it a hypnotic and said it would take the edge off her nervous anxiety and help her sleep. She measured out the grains, and had a vague recollection that she was to leave it out gradually when she felt she was back to normal and could manage without it.

Normal? she thought. *What was normal these days?* She'd long ago given up trying to maintain any semblance of that.

She took the barbiturate. Just the action of swallowing it made her feel better. She glanced over at Peggy, who had turned her back and started to put the potatoes she had just counted out into a brown paper bag. The lodger clearly considered the conversation at an end. *She just expects me to turn my feelings off like a tap*, thought Eunice. She was wound up by the conversation, and this made her both uncharitable and self-pitying.

"At least Lizzie Fenwick has an admirer who's decent – unlike the low lifes you fraternise with – and he's not a soldier likely to go off and get himself killed."

"Fawcett?" Peggy shot back, turning to face the room. "He's got an ammunition shell instead of a heart." Her mouth twitched, pleased with her image.

"Lucky man," Eunice replied as she snatched up the small bag from Peggy and trudged to the door.

Chapter Fourteen

Lizzie stood in Guildford Street and stared through a wide central arch at the scene before her. At a distance, girls in dull brown dresses with a full white apron played apart from boys with their dark jackets, white collars and short pants. As she looked across at the children in front of her, and at the shadow cast over them by the austere and imposing brick building behind them, the sound of female chatter reached her ears. Lizzie glanced sideways and saw a queue of women had begun to form alongside her.

She stared at them: at the women in this pitiable queue who had been let down by men, unfortunate circumstance or their own weakness, and imagined how they might feel today: Ballot Day. Their fate would be determined entirely by chance: by the picking out of a white ball over a red or black one from a velvet bag. Even as a spectator, she felt sick anticipation stir in her stomach, and could almost feel the anxiety of having to reach into the soft interior of the ballot bag, hoping for any telltale sign or sensation that might indicate she should pick one ball over another. A white ball allowed an automatic call-back; a red one meant wait and see, with three days of agonising uncertainty; and a black, instant rejection with all hope lost.

She glanced back at the entrance, and saw the wall plaque. *The Foundling Hospital. For the education and maintenance of exposed and deserted young children.* Suddenly she did not wish to be thought part of this queue, and she began to hurry away, past the line, averting her gaze from the hard and brazen stares given off by some of the waiting women.

The boisterous and noisy crowd of women surged ahead of Lizzie after the end of their munitions shift. Ahead of her she saw the unkempt gypsy woman, her face lined and weathered to the colour of a walnut from too much exposure to the elements, and she slowed her pace. Once a week this woman stood outside the munitions to sell a selection of herbs, a dirty-faced urchin clinging to her skirts. Lizzie walked past her, ignoring her, but as soon as the last of her fellow workers had disappeared out of sight around the bend in the road, she turned back.

"The juniper, please."

She felt the herb seller's gaze on her, but Lizzie kept her eyes on the money in her hand, anxious to complete the transaction. The old hag leaned towards her, as if about to let her in on a secret.

"Put it in your shoe, dearie." She gave her customer a toothless knowing smile. "It'll see you right."

Lizzie glanced at the sleeping bodies in the other two beds in her shared room. After seven days of minor discomfort, when the juniper sprigs dug into the sole of her foot and laddered one of her stockings, Lizzie knew it would not bring on her period. For once, she wished she had someone to confide her fears to. Peggy chose to avoid her these days – clearly blaming Lizzie for failing to get her friend reinstated – and she barely saw Eunice Wilson to ask after Peggy. She wouldn't dream of discussing such a matter with Mary; as a staunch Catholic, Mary would tell her she was an awful sinner and was going straight to hell anyway. Lizzie hardly knew the girl who had taken Peggy's place, but she lacked Peggy's openness and didn't invite confidences, and there was absolutely no way she was going to expose her condition to the Welfare Supervisor. So, as was her habit, Lizzie kept her own counsel, but it was wearing her down, bit by bit, into a state of exhaustion.

She fell into bed, felt the chill of the cold sheets and pulled the thin covers up to her neck, seeking comfort but finding little, so she turned over to face the wall. The sound of the even breathing of her room-mates exploded like little susurrations in the darkness. Lizzie felt the cold prickle of despair shiver along her spine as she willed sleep to come, but it did not. Eventually, she dragged herself out of bed, fumbled to light a candle, rifled through the clothes rail in the semi-dark for something to wear to keep the cold at bay and went downstairs to the kitchen.

She sat on the Windsor chair next to the hulking black range – the only source of warmth in the room – with her knees pulled up to her chest, her nightshift straining around them, and her feet balanced on the edge of the chair. She wrapped the heavy woollen coat more closely around herself, but it was not hers, and being so ill-fitting made it a poor choice. Only the flickering yellow light of a candle offered any illumination. She stared at the strange shadows it cast on the kitchen wall as a thin draught of air from some unknown chink created a macabre dance on the wall in front of her.

But then they were no longer shadows. Instead they became those wretched fallen women she had seen at The Foundling Hospital, forced to resort to giving up their children into a life of care without the love only a mother could give. Each spectre walked by her, holding the tiny hand of one of the abandoned children Lizzie had looked on with such pity in the institution's grounds. One by one, each of the ghostly women's faces dissolved and became her own, like grotesque reflections in a hall of mirrors. With a small cry of exasperation, she thrust herself out of the chair and broke the spell.

It was now clear to her that buying the juniper was a response to her experience at that charitable institution and the first tacit act of acceptance of the path she must take.

"I've a parcel here for you." Mary turned the small brown paper package around in her hands, teasing. "I wonder what it can be now." She shook it against her ear until the contents rattled.

Lizzie snatched it from her with a curt "Thank you!"

Once in the privacy of the bathroom, she bolted the door, and with unseemly haste ripped open the package. Last week, by chance, she had noticed a small advertisement in the back pages of one of the women's magazines which were left lying about in the munitions canteen. Dr Vanbrugh's Period Regulating Pills were, she had read, designed for suppressed menstruation. When no one was looking, she'd torn out the entire page, folded it and put it in her overall pocket, but she kept it for several days before she plucked up the courage to send off the order and payment.

Lizzie turned the small bottle round in her hand so she could read the instructions on the reverse. Without waiting to catch her breath, in case she changed her mind, she took a tooth glass from the sink and went to fill it with water. The tap, always stiff, refused to budge, so it was necessary to use both hands to turn it on. When it eased with an unexpected gush, she uttered a mild curse as the water sprayed a damp pattern onto her skirt. Undeterred, she filled the glass and set it down before taking the bottle and pushing her thumbs underneath its stopper to prise it off. It came out with an echoing pop, which seemed deafening in the claustrophobic space as she tipped two small white pills into her palm. *How innocuous they look*, Lizzie thought as she stared at them, fully aware of the warning on the label that these pills could cause miscarriage if taken while pregnant.

Chapter Fifteen

"You had any news?" Jack's uncle asked as he looked up from the newspaper spread open in his lap.

You could at least wait till I get my coat off, Eddie, Eunice thought irritably as she came into her mother-in-law's kitchen. *And you could say, "Hello, Eunice. How are you?" first.* "No. Nothing. You not had anything from him?"

"No, we haven't." There was misery in Jack's mother's voice. "Oh, and to think they were ever talking of peace. And now…"

"We've breached The Hindenburg Line," Eddie cut in. "Says here," he tapped the newspaper, "our latest withdrawal's merely tactical."

Ida Wilson made a dismissive noise. "You know you can't believe what you read in the newspapers, telling you it's a great victory and then you look at the casualty lists and slowly it gets out that it was really a disaster. Makes you wonder about everything else the frocks in Westminster are keeping from us."

"Not a good day for drying clothes, I see." Eunice didn't want to talk about the war. "How are you today, Bill?" she asked Jack's father, who sat next to the range listening to Eddie relaying the news. She hadn't expected a response, and got none.

Ida had two irons on the go at once and was flushed from the effort. "Tea's in the pot." She nodded at her daughter-in-law. "Help yourself."

More than usual, the smell of clean laundry – which Ida took in to help make ends meet – permeated the small kitchen. Eunice noticed that day's wash load hanging in multiple layers from the clothes airer, which was pulled close to the ceiling to make the most of the naturally rising warm air from the range, and also draped over any piece of available furniture.

"Give that here." Ida took a damp sheet from the back of one of the kitchen chairs and motioned with her swollen, red and chapped hands for her daughter-in-law to sit down. "This incessant rain and cold weather is a tester."

Eunice slung her new woollen coat over the back of the chair, patted her hair into shape to make sure none of her styling pins had come loose, and sat down. She noticed Ida eyeing her new purchase. *What would Jack's mother say if she knew just how many nice things I've treated myself to since I've been at the munitions and got a small regular rent from Peggy?*

She helped herself to a cup of strong black tea. She'd got used to making the same spoonful of tea leaves last for several brews at home, and consequently she had come to prefer hers weaker than this. She marvelled that her mother-in-law never seemed short of tea. Maybe it was because Eddie worked down at the docks, but she couldn't remember the last time she had been offered anything. She watched Ida swap a cooling iron for a hot one.

"I hope you'll be coming for Christmas dinner." Ida addressed Eunice apropos of nothing. "Like always."

Like always? Eunice felt like crying out at her mother-in-law's apparent insensitivity. *Of course it won't be like always. It's the first Christmas without Alfie. And the second without Jack.*

Ida must've seen something in her expression, because she said, "It might help to be all together, this Christmas particularly, eh? Business as usual, they say."

Bugger their 'Business as usual', Eunice thought, but didn't comment out loud. "Oh, I suppose so, but I just can't allow myself to think more than a day ahead." What she meant was she didn't want to celebrate it. To her, Christmas was a time for children.

"Any more tea in that pot?" Eddie held out his cup in an attempt to diffuse the tension.

The request was directed at Ida, but Eunice got up, took his cup from him and poured what was left in the teapot into it. She felt Jack's mother indulged Eddie more than was good for him, which made her harbour suspicions about their relationship, but then could she blame her mother-in-law? Her husband hadn't spoken a word since he came back from the South African War nearly fifteen years ago. She didn't know how Ida stood it. She listened to Eddie continue telling his mute brother about the latest war news.

"Oh, enough of hearing about this damned war," Ida interrupted him, mirroring Eunice's own thoughts. "I can't stand it. It's all about politics and power, like always. Stupid, over-privileged men, completely divorced from the reality of *our* lives, making senseless decisions, and to hell with the human cost." She glanced at Eunice.

Although Eunice was now welcome in Jack's mother's house again, back in 1914, when Ida had taken Jack's side about the war and had even accompanied him on anti-conscription rallies (oh, the arguments there had been about that between Jack and Eunice!), there had been a decided cooling in their relationship. Eunice knew his mother considered her disloyal, and that she was failing in her marriage vows by refusing to stand by her husband over his stance on the war. This was made worse once Jack had been conscripted and she had taken work at the munitions, Ida having taken a very dim view of Eunice fuelling the war effort. However, once Alfie had died there had been a rapprochement of sorts through their shared grief, but Eunice never lost the sense that she was treading on eggshells in her mother-in-law's house.

Eunice noticed Ida's eyes stray over to where her husband sat and heard her make a little clicking noise with her tongue as she carried on ironing. Not for the first time, she wondered if there was really anything wrong with Bill or whether being mute was his way of punishing his wife. She was against this war, but was that because she had made Bill's life a misery until he'd gone to fight in the last one? Just like Eunice herself had done with Jack.

"Give us a hand with this, would you?" Ida asked Eunice as she began to fold up the sheet she had just finished ironing.

Eunice got up to oblige. After the two women had folded the sheet lengthways twice and once again in the middle, they walked towards each other, Eunice averting her eyes from her mother-in-law's gaze. She took the folded sheet from Ida and laid it on top of a previously ironed pile of sheets.

"Would you mind putting them in the parlour, out of the way? Make sure you put them in a separate pile from the others."

Eunice took the newly ironed stack and went into the front room. Every seat had piles of ironed bed linen and clothing on it with names pinned onto them – evidence that Ida had probably been up since dawn. The only space she could find was on top of the china cabinet, but she had to move the silver trophy which had pride of place on top of it first.

As soon as she picked it up, a lightning bolt of melancholia hit her. It was one of Jack's boxing trophies. She turned it around in her hand, noticing its well-polished sheen. Her husband had been a gifted amateur, everyone had said so, and he had just turned professional during their early courtship. She remembered his first paid engagement earned him eighteen shillings and his last 300 pounds. In that one he'd had the crowd on its feet, but it was a precarious living.

"He was good box office."

Startled, Eunice turned to see Eddie in the doorway, another newly ironed sheet in his hands. She remembered Jack's matches were always dramatic; that's what had made watching him so exciting, and was why he drew the crowds. He either knocked out his opponent or was knocked out. There were no half measures with Jack, but she had found she couldn't bear to see him down on the canvas.

"Had a cracking straight right." She saw Eddie had a faraway look in his eye, as if he was back at Holborn Stadium. "He could've given Kid Lewis a run for his money, you know."

She thought of her husband's boyish enthusiasm in the ring; how he always kept going forward at his opponent, allowing him no quarter yet retaining his good manners and sportsmanship. She smiled at the memory.

"Put that lot on here." She heard Eddie's voice. Blinking hard, she saw he was indicating for her to give him the laundry she was balancing over one arm. She put the trophy down, noticing the smudge from her fingers marring the shine (Ida would have something to say about that), and hurried back to the kitchen.

Eddie followed her in, resumed his seat and picked up the newspaper again.

"That last anti-war rally you was at, Ida," he remarked. "Says here it drew quite a crowd – bigger than last time even."

Eunice turned her head to look at her mother-in-law, surprised. She thought once Jack went off to war his mother had given up on her anti-war activism. She saw Eddie look across at Ida with a touch of pride, being well aware that demonstrating against the war required considerable bravery. However, there was a definite note of disappointment when he said, "Looks like people's patriotism is wearing a bit thin these days."

"Hardly a shocker, is it?" Ida shot back. "Three and a half years. For what?" She lifted up the new sheet she had been ironing, folded it and began on the other side. "The men, and us with the air raids, are paying in blood. I don't think people can take much more of it."

Ida kept on with her task, the dull thud of her heavy iron on the ironing board suddenly the only sound in the room. She stopped ironing and looked at Eunice.

"I hope you don't mind my saying so, love, but you look done in. All this uncertainty, this grief and separation, well, it takes its toll."

She came from behind the ironing board. "This war's pushing us all to our limits, and sometimes beyond, but if there's one thing I know, it's that I have to believe that our Jack will come home safe and sound at the end of it all. It's the only thing that keeps me going. That and"– Ida reached over and placed her hand flat on her daughter-in-law's rounding belly –"this little 'un in here."

"For me as well," Eunice whispered.

Chapter Sixteen

Coming out of her swoon, she recognised the male voice addressing her. "Goot afternoon, Lizzie."

She opened her eyes and looked into the face of her erstwhile employer.

"You fainted in my waiting room," he explained as he helped her to sit up. "It is nice to see you again, but I would prefer it in a less professional capacity, *hein*?" He smiled benevolently at her. "Let me have a quick look at you." He peered at her eyeballs and then asked her to stick her tongue out. "So, this is fine."

She felt reassured by the familiarity of his mildly clipped foreign accent as he encouraged her to swing her legs off the side of the examination couch.

"Can you sit over here?" he asked, his arm presented for support as he led her to a chair. From behind his battered and worn desk he pulled out another chair, put on his pince-nez and sat down beside her. "Now, what is the trouble?"

She kept her head down and couldn't meet his gaze. "Erm… ah…"

"The munitions, you know, it is an unhealthy place to work."

She heard the underlying gentle reprimand for leaving his employ and this made her blurt out, "My periods seem to have stopped."

He asked her when she last had a bleed.

She hesitated. "The beginning of July, I think."

"This TNT, it has a very bad reputation…"

"I don't think it's the Trotyl."

In her line of vision she saw only his crossed legs, and noticed his right foot stiffen and then drop back to its original position.

"Then I need to examine you."

As he palpated her stomach she saw him cast a quick glance down at her unadorned wedding ring finger. He finished his examination and she returned to her seat.

"It is so. You are with child."

Her face flushed crimson.

"The father, he is not willing to do the right thing by you?"

"He was killed." Her lip began to tremble.

"Ach. The war, the war," he said with a note of despondency. "I am sorry to hear about it. So. You are compromised."

She hung her head, fearing the flames of shame might engulf her.

"Lizzie?"

From out of her pocket she took a bottle and handed it to him. "I took two a couple of months ago to…to…then I changed my mind. They had no effect in that way, but I have been feeling feverish and a bit light-headed recently."

He read the label, frowning, then looked at her in a stern manner.

"You know, most of these quack remedies are useless, but some of them are dangerous ecbolic drugs which can do irreparable damage to your uterus and your general health, as well as to your unborn child. With sometimes fatal results."

"Yes," she whispered.

"I know it is often unavoidable," he said with weary resignation, "for women round here to use abortion as a form of birth control, but it is a human life inside you, Lizzie." His voice softened. "But I think I know you well enough to see that you must have been desperate to try such a thing as these abortifacients."

She chewed the corner of her lip. Right from her first day in service with him, when he had taken her in, employed her and brought her to live in London after the mining tragedy, he had always seemed able to read her.

"Your symptoms may well just be a reaction to your condition."

Lizzie gave him a weak smile of relief.

"But you know that the stigma and the need to support yourself as a single woman with an illegitimate child will make life exceptionally difficult, if not impossible – for you both."

Lizzie pressed her lips together. She knew that already.

"In the circumstances, would the paternal grandparents not take the child in? Often they can find great comfort in having a physical reminder of their lost son. And it is quite usual for…" he hesitated, "…such children to be absorbed into the wider family."

Lizzie cast her eyes downwards. "I don't know them."

"I still haf one or two connections which might be of use. High class women who cannot conceive a child of their own."

Her eyes flitted between his face and the floor.

"But you must understand that you will be giving your child up for good and you will not be able to see him again."

This child was her last remaining link to Harry Slater; giving him up would tear her heart out, but she gave an almost imperceptible nod of her head.

"I will make enquiries. Meanwhile, there is nothing for you to do now until you give birth." He patted her arm. "And another thing. You ought to consider finding alternative employment. Working in a munitions factory is not good for you, or your little one. Although I must say, you do not look like a canary." He made the standard joke about female munitions workers. "Take some aspirin, but leave 'Doctor' Vanbrugh well alone."

She pulled on her coat. "Thank you, Dr Keppel."

"One thing more, Lizzie." He looked embarrassed. "My name. It is no longer Keppel. I haf changed it to Carroll. Some people aren't willing to wait for me to explain that I am Swiss born before they wish me dead. So, I felt it wise to anglicise my name."

"Like the royal family." She gave him a weak smile, but she realised now why he no longer lived in the beautiful house in Lansdowne Place, where she had been in service, and had gone to earlier when she felt unwell, but was dispatched to Commercial Street, E1. His respectable, well-off patients had shunned him.

"Just so."

Outside she stopped and leaned against a wall, but paid little attention to the dampness which seeped out of the blackened bricks into her coat. Now that she had talked about her impending motherhood with someone, the reality of her situation loomed up in front of her like a giant advertising hoarding. There was her image, a baby in her arms. At once she knew that she would keep this tiny, helpless little thing, with its barely-there heartbeat, nurtured within the protection of her womb for the past five months, come what may.

It bound her in love to Harry Slater and allowed her to have a part of him still.

Chapter Seventeen

Lizzie sat on the wooden lavatory seat lid, the four walls around it still her single refuge in the lodging house, but she only managed to let out the waistband of one skirt before a fellow lodger knocked on the door and asked, irritation peppering the words, whether she had taken up residency in there. The implied rebuke made tears prick Lizzie's eyes, and for a moment she felt as if a huge sob might surge up from the depths of her soul and she would just cry and cry and cry, and not be able to stop.

"Well?"

"Give me a minute, can't you?" she croaked, afraid the emotion in her voice was all too obvious as she hauled herself up from the seat and wished she could also be rid of the ever-present dull ache in the small of her back.

"You're looking bockety," Mary said as Lizzie returned to her room and collapsed onto the bed.

"I don't feel well. It's these stomach cramps," she feigned, her voice low so as not to wake the room's other sleeping occupant.

"And what kind of stomach cramps might they be?"

"The monthly sort."

"Shut up, you two," a sleepy, irritated voice broke in from the next bed. "I've not slept properly for weeks now thanks to Jerry's bombs."

They all suffered from broken sleep these days, and it gave Lizzie an excuse to stop any further conversation, but she saw in Mary's expression a vestige of the coldness which she felt had developed between them recently.

"And are ye sure they're the monthly sort now?" Mary hissed.

"I can still hear you, you know."

Lizzie took out a three penny bit and showed it to Mary to indicate she was going to have a hot bath, hoping it might help. "Tell Mr Fawcett I'm not very well, will you?"

She had not taken a single day off through personal sickness since she started the munitions. Even more recently, when she felt a little under the weather she had gone to work because her new life away from service and her recent promotion made her happy and fulfilled, but also it took her mind off her predicament. Today her spirit was wearied and the burden of concealing her pregnancy weighed more heavily on her than usual.

"I'll do it this once," Mary said.

Suddenly, Lizzie thought how much she missed Peggy's easy companionship since her friend had gone to lodge with Eunice Wilson.

Before she eased herself down into the welcoming heat of the water, Lizzie dropped her payment into the box provided for the purpose. She relaxed back and allowed herself to luxuriate in the enveloping warmth and comfort of her newly drawn bath. Out of habit, she placed her hands on her stomach and looked down past her full breasts at the small mound of her belly that just breached the water like a tiny atoll in the ocean. Her weariness dissipated as she lay there, cocooned with the steam and hot water, and stroked her thumbs up and down over her tightening skin, allowing herself a little smile.

"Here, I hope you haven't used up the last of the hot water!" an exasperated voice called from the other side of the door.

Lizzie thought she probably had, but the guilt was momentary:

she'd had to take plenty of cold baths in similar circumstances.

Back in her room she climbed into bed and immediately fell asleep.

Just before seven o'clock she awoke and turned over to face the room and two empty beds. Her bathing and sleep hadn't refreshed her and a great swell of loneliness washed over her. Her eyes were drawn to the attic window above her, rimed with December frost. She gave a little shiver. Beyond the glass pane, Lizzie looked up at the sickle moon and the bright stars, silhouetted against the inky sky. It occurred to her that she ought to pull the blackout curtain, yet as she watched, the start of a fiery orange glow spread across the window pane. Suddenly a sound like a loud thunderclap echoed in the distance, powerful enough to rattle the attic window and her room door. A brilliant light lit up the whole of the visible sky and dimmed into an angry red haze.

"Another air raid? That'll be the third in as many weeks," she grumbled to herself as she reached up and pulled the curtain closed. *Well, I am not going down into that stinking underground station again, crammed together like sardines in a tin.*

The next morning Lizzie was intrigued to discover no air raids had been reported the previous night. She only knew something was amiss when Mary and the other girl didn't return from their shift at the munitions.

Chapter Eighteen

Eunice got off the bus, rushed along sleet-drenched streets and tried to avoid the grey slush and puddles which would ruin the leather on her boots. The leaden sky cast an ominous shadow across her back as she hurried to get her front door open. Even in such a short distance, her outer clothes were soaked through and clung to her legs like a wet sheet on wash day, causing her to berate herself for forgetting her umbrella despite knowing how changeable and unsettled the weather had been recently. She shook herself down in the hall before she peeled off her dripping coat and hung it on one of the wall pegs along with her hat. She grumbled a little more when she realised she had stamped all over a swathe of envelopes scattered across the doormat.

Warily, she bent down and gathered them up, unable to breathe until she had checked each one. These days there was no escape from the sensationalist headlines which screamed news of yet more casualties and shocking revelations about the thousands of British soldiers who had been taken prisoner in one month alone. In moments of black depression Eunice had even contemplated blocking up her letterbox to prevent any bad news coming through it. *What the eye doesn't see, the heart can't grieve over.*

They were all Christmas cards: at least DORA hadn't outlawed these. Relieved, Eunice started to turn away to give her frozen feet a quick warm in front of the gas oven, but a series of loud, unexpected knocks stopped her in her tracks. Her heart missed a beat. She took a deep breath and opened the door, hoping against hope that it wasn't the telegram boy. *Thank God*. It was the tally-man, come to collect his next instalment.

For once she broke with her usual custom and invited him into the hallway, watched him with narrowed eyes as he closed his umbrella and made a mental 'tut' when she noticed he hadn't bothered to shake off the excess water, but instead let it pool all over the floor. She tried to avoid his gaze: she always found it very uncomfortable, the way he looked her up and down as if she was goods for sale. She had heard the gossip that he accepted payment in kind from some women if they were unable to pay an instalment.

"Filthy day, Mrs Wilson. At least it might keep the Hun bombers away for another night, eh?"

As she paid him, Eunice agreed that would be a blessing, but pulled her hand away quickly as he grasped her fingers along with the proffered money. She caught the look of disappointment on his face as she showed him out into the wild weather, glad to be shot of him for another week.

She stared down at the small puddle of water from his umbrella and made a little moue of annoyance. As she turned to go and get a mop from the kitchen, she happened to glance at Alfie's shoes, still in their designated place by the front door. Her heart lurched: sticking out from between the shoes was the edge of a plain brown envelope with an unmistakeable stamp. The narrow hall seemed to contract around her as the walls tilted and she was forced to put out her hand to steady herself, but instead grasped the sodden material of her coat on the wall pegs, oblivious to the tiny rivulets of water which ran down her arm.

Eunice had no idea how long she had been sitting in the parlour, staring at the brown envelope that was propped up against Jack's photograph on the mantelpiece. His image looked out at her above the envelope, accusation in his eyes as the medium's prediction swirled in her head. Eventually she dragged herself up from the settee and stood in front of the fireplace. At once the memory hit her of her knees buckling on the day the truth about The Somme emerged, long after the battle itself. Eunice experienced that weakness in her legs now. Had Jack marched towards the same horror?

She pushed her trembling thumb between the glued edges of the flap, but misjudged it and it tore. *Oh, how could she have had so few qualms about believing he should go?* Her chest tightened, and she felt a pain in the pit of her stomach. In the silence of the room she heard the echo of her own shallow breathing as she took out the sheet of folded paper, which was a numbered form. She let out a little cry.

Missing, Believed Wounded.

Eunice went to say it again, but her throat constricted and it came out as a dry croak. She felt the anguish of these three words almost as much as if they had told her he was dead. They offered no certainty, just increased her fear and doubt a hundredfold. Her eyes moved to Jack's photograph and her chin began to quiver. For a fleeting moment she experienced a strange feeling that he was in the room with her and the hot tears burned her eyes.

He was a good husband really, she told herself, better than a lot she could name. After he gave up the precarious and dangerous life of a professional boxer to become a husband and family man, he had been in regular work, gave up the majority of his wages to her each week, didn't squander his money on drink or gambling, and didn't knock her about or go off womanising. Yet she had called him a coward for not enlisting; for being true to his principles and remaining his own man. And so her intransigence about the war had built an impenetrable wall between them, brick by stupid brick.

Hadn't he told her men didn't always enlist for patriotic reasons? She only had to look at the eldest son of Kitty next door, who'd joined the rush to the colours as soon as he found out his girl was in a certain condition, for the truth of that one. Perhaps it was braver to do what Jack had done. He'd gone anyway when he got the notification; had even earned an extra stripe for going beyond the call of duty. Not like Jim Humble over the road, who'd volunteered then deserted before he got anywhere near the Front. A month later she heard he'd taken his wife and four children away and that they'd changed their name. Eunice knew they would always be in fear of the knock at the door.

Maybe she was the coward, not Jack. She had joined in all the jubilation and flag waving the day war was declared, certain in her belief that it was Great Britain's duty to honour her pledge to Belgium in the face of German barbarism. At the time she had convinced herself that she just wanted to feel a part of it all and be proud of a husband who joined up to fight, but now she knew part of her had wanted to be able to crow about it like her friends and neighbours. She had begun to resent how Jack's refusal to enlist determined people's attitudes towards her as well. Yet now, with the notification grasped in her hand, a vision of Alice Tranter's husband rose up before her. He came back a basket case: a broken man with only one limb intact.

A stark white edge formed around her bloodless lips as her trembling fingers tore the form into pieces, smaller and smaller, until with one brisk flick of her wrist she sent them cascading into the fireplace. Mesmerised, she watched them flutter, like falling snowflakes, down between the blackened bars of the empty grate.

Chapter Nineteen

Lizzie stood looking at the enormous crater carved into the ground, around which stood the three burned out towers of the flour mill, the remains of the fire station and the jagged and destroyed walls of once adjacent factories. Here the munitions works had exploded in a dramatic fireball without any help from German bombs. Mary Maguire had died in it, and so had other people she worked alongside.

There but for the grace of God.

But Lizzie's livelihood had also been blown to smithereens.

She trudged past the fifth rate houses and tenements which had stood cheek by jowl with the munitions factory. Gaping black holes replaced windows and doors, and she stepped gingerly over slates, ripped away from roofs, which lay scattered in the road. She stopped and looked at the wrecked gable end of a house where, like limp and dislocated piano keys, the exposed loose edges of the bedroom floorboards dangled in a precarious fashion and shattered pieces of furniture jutted out from the smashed lower floor.

As Lizzie walked, she watched people scurry like ants as they picked over the rubble with their wheelbarrows and handcarts balanced on pyramids of debris. At first she assumed, with a sickening lurch in her stomach, that they were looking for bodies, then that they were thieving scavengers, but as she saw a woman hoist a teacup aloft like a trophy, she realised they were also searching for possessions whose sentimental value now far exceeded their original cost.

Even without taking a circuitous route to avoid the rubble, Lizzie's feet became harder to lift as the realisation that she had lost her means of earning a living began to take hold. How would she be able to support herself and a child? A great wave of wretched self-pity was about to overtake her when she heard a motorised van pull up not far away. She edged her way along the street, being careful not to trip, and when she realised the van was an improvised canteen she stopped and offered her services. At least helping others would be a temporary respite from her own misery.

"Cut the bread thinly," she was commanded by a harassed woman with an upper crust accent, "and only a scrape of butter. This lot will have to go a terrifically long way."

Lizzie prepared sandwiches with scant fillings, topped up large, heavy urns with weak tea and coffee and packed crumbling cakes and broken biscuits for the troops, police and other rescue workers engaged in clearing up the disaster zone. Squeezed into a small space with six other volunteers, she completed her work like an automaton, barely aware of the occasional elbow in her side, the muttered curse and garbled apology, but it wasn't long before her legs and back started to ache and her head throbbed. Her numbed mind glossed over collective stories of miraculous escapes and bravery and terrible tales of personal loss and catastrophe.

After three hours with one break, Lizzie eventually admitted defeat, but her shoulders sagged automatically when she contemplated her cold, cramped and uninviting attic room, where she knew her mind would start to run riot with nightmarish images of her blown apart future.

As she plodded back towards Albert Road, her head lowered, Lizzie heard a buzz of voices. She spied a line of people ahead of her, standing two deep. Her first thought was that it was some sort of food queue, and she was surprised to discover it was a line of ex-Silvertown munitions workers. Down towards the far end of the queue, Lizzie could just make out a makeshift sign on a wooden hoarding, but it was too far away to be readable. She approached the end of the queue where a conversation was going on about how the munitions manager had gone back inside the factory after the main explosion to get people out, careless of the danger to himself, and how the fire had taken hold by igniting more TNT, its huge roaring flames destroying anything in its path.

"Never have had that Fawcett down as a hero."

"Me neither, God love him."

"You come to put your name on the list, Lizzie?"

Lizzie had no idea about any list, but her spirits rose a little as she felt once again the old camaraderie of the munitions: of people coming together in adversity.

"If you ain't dead, you need to put your name on the list. Otherwise you won't get any help."

She supposed she would be in need of such help now, so she joined the back of the queue and was glad of the other women's company.

"Maybe the King and Queen will pledge money like they did with the *Titanic*."

"Your Majesty." A big, florid-faced woman held out her skirts and made a clumsy curtsey to an imaginary monarch. "Any spare beds at Buckingham Palace?"

"You been practising your curtseying for when you come out at the next Court, Hilda?"

"Ooh, don't 'come out' in front of the King!" cackled a voice behind her. "He doesn't expect that sort of thing from posh young ladies."

A ripple of laughter ran around the women until, as if on cue, an impressive looking motor car drove slowly past them. Its chauffeur manoeuvred the vehicle carefully around the piles of rubble as its finely dressed male and female passengers stared at the queuing people, appeared to make comments behind their gloved hands and pointed excited fingers at the devastation in front of them.

"Bleedin' gawpers!"

"What d'they think this is, London Zoo?"

Three men joined the back of the queue, engaged in some kind of debate about the explosion itself. They gave a cursory nod to the women.

"They should never have let that factory handle Trotyl so close to where us poor blighters live," moaned one.

"Didn't hear you complaining when you got your wages at the end of the week, Reg."

"We all knew the risks."

"Odds of staying alive were still better than *Over There*."

The line gradually shortened until Lizzie stood at the door of the temporary office. A shiver ran through her body: she hadn't realised it was so cold outside. She started to bang one foot against the other and hugged herself. A man's voice she recognised as Mr Fawcett's repeated the same message in a mechanical fashion to each former employee.

"Name? Here. Hand in this ticket at the Town Hall. After two o'clock. Not before. They'll see to you. This is for distress payments only. If you're looking for compensation, try the Ministry of Munitions. Here's the address you need to apply to for a claim form."

Lizzie was suddenly surprised to find little beads of perspiration on her top lip in spite of her shivering. She shuffled forwards when it was her turn, and she saw the munitions manager. He smiled when he saw her, but when he stood up he swayed from side to side. She called his name and reached out for him, but he dissolved into an unfocussed blur.

1918

Chapter Twenty

Somewhere an argument was going on between a man and a woman.

"I felt it was my duty…"

"Duty?"

A heartbeat of silence.

"Has she played you? That factory girl. Taken you for a complete fool?"

Lizzie recognised the male voice as Mr Fawcett's, but wasn't sure whether she was dreaming it, and got the vague impression the argument was about her.

"Don't be absurd, Charlotte!"

"I thought your head was full of ammunition quotas, and all the while you were…"

"If you had seen the devastation, you might not be so hard hearted. Besides, it would be uncharitable to turn her away in her time of need."

"Really? Oh, what a terrible way to start a new year."

Lizzie heard the bang of a slammed door as it echoed around her before a stultifying silence seemed to descend.

Later a plain girl with fair curly hair and a noticeable Cockney accent roused Lizzie from her indolent fugue and offered her a blue and white bone china teacup which contained a warm almond smelling liquid.

"What is it?" Lizzie's head seemed stuffed with cotton wool.

"Tincture of meadowsweet, miss. It'll help you sweat out your fever."

Lizzie felt disoriented. She knew she was no longer in the line of munitions workers, but in a large comfortable bed in an unknown place. The fire was lit in the grate and weak January sun shone through a large sash window.

"Sweat what out? Where am I?"

Seeing the patient struggle to lift her head, the girl helped to raise her up and put the cup to her lips. Lizzie took a wary sip.

"East Ham, miss. You collapsed and Mr Fawcett brought you."

Lizzie sank back onto the pillow. A vague memory of an argument came back to her. "I hope Mrs Fawcett doesn't mind."

The maid put the cup aside and started to straighten the bedding. As she tucked in a wayward sheet edge she gaily told Lizzie that there was no Mrs Fawcett, just Mrs Dearden, his sister – a widow.

"I see."

"They normally rub along nicely together, but I'm afraid you've put the cat among the pigeons a bit."

Lizzie registered the maid's indiscretion, but didn't have the energy to care very much.

"What a to-do yesterday, I can tell yer. I had to go in an' clear up his study. Everything was all over the floor – papers, a broken whisky glass and all sorts. Dunno what he was thinking, I'm sure." The girl gave Lizzie a sly smile. "He don't normally get so aeriated."

Lizzie tucked this image of the munitions manager giving vent to his emotions away in her memory.

"Just got to do this now." The maid began sprinkling a powder over the carpet. "Mrs Dearden insists."

Lizzie recognised the bug powder from her own time in service. "And have you got to lock up the silver as well?"

*

Lizzie adjusted the feather bolster between her knees again, but turned over after five minutes – her back still ached and her belly was heavy – to repeat the routine. She sighed. Now she could feel the weight of her child pressing on her bladder and knew she would have to get up to go to the lavatory. Afterwards, she waddled flat-footed back across the carpet on the landing, where she became aware of the claustrophobic silence of the house. All at once she felt the faint fluttering deep within her of a new life reminding her of its presence.

She knew her time was approaching.

Chapter Twenty-one

"Tray's over there," said Mrs Ryder, the cook, and nodded at the kitchen table, where the tea things were laid out, as she continued rolling some grey looking dough. "The delivery boy's late, so Martha's gorne to queue up at The International. There's no way I'm taking it upstairs, not with my old pins." She stared pointedly at Lizzie.

Lizzie usually remained below stairs, doing light work. This arrangement seemed the line of least resistance and suited Mr Fawcett's sister, who preferred to pretend the interloper didn't exist.

"You'll just have to do it this one time."

This was the first instance of the cook pulling rank, and it served to remind Lizzie of her position. Although grateful for Mr Fawcett's kind intervention, this quasi-servitude was starting to seem far worse than being a paid domestic servant, for she now had even less control over her own destiny, reliant as she was on Mr Fawcett's and his sister's charity until her child was born. A further difficulty was her awareness that both Mrs Ryder and the maid, Martha, seemed unsure how to behave towards her (a servant didn't sleep in the guest bedroom, as Lizzie did, but neither did a guest receive the same treatment as a servant) because they were suspicious of Mr Fawcett's intentions towards her. This latter issue was also the reason for Mrs Dearden's cold animosity, Lizzie assumed.

"Go on, then!"

The cook stood, one hand on her hip and the rolling pin in the other, so Lizzie pulled on Martha's spare apron, barely managing to fasten the ties at the back, and struggled up the stairs with the laden tray. Just outside the morning room door, she stopped and took a deep breath to give herself courage.

"Dear God!" She heard Fawcett's voice from the other side of the door. "Haig is saying we've got our backs to the wall."

"Really, Edmund! Must you be so dramatic?" His sister's exasperation was clear.

What struck Lizzie as she heard this brief exchange was that she'd had no idea that Fawcett's Christian name was Edmund. At the munitions, he had always been 'Mr Fawcett', 'Fawcett', or, more often, something much worse. *It's a little old-fashioned*, she thought, but decided it quite suited him.

She knocked and went in, but to her dismay she could see no uncluttered surface on which to place the heavy tray. She looked around helplessly, sour thoughts about Mrs Dearden's untidiness passing through her mind until Fawcett put his paper aside, got up and took the tray from her. Lizzie noticed how his eyes crinkled at the edges behind his glasses and that his usually closed expression brightened at the sight of her. She was quite taken aback to hear him apologise, sotto voce, for the mess.

"Thank you, Lizzie. That will be all." His tone was a little abrupt, but not unkind. She guessed it was to facilitate her quick escape.

"Ask Mrs Ryder if my Fortnum's hamper has come," his sister commanded, determined, it seemed, to have the last word and establish her authority in household matters.

Lizzie acknowledged the order with a brief nod and began to retire, wondering how, with all the food shortages, it was still possible for those with money to get hold of the choicest cuts of meat and savouries and delicious desserts.

"A strange sense of priorities, if I may say so, Charlotte." Lizzie heard the unusually terse tone in Edmund Fawcett's voice, and she sensed his eyes following her all the way to the door. "Everything's in the balance on the Western Front and all you're concerned about is your damned Fortnum's hamper."

Lizzie hid a smile.

"There's no need to take that tone with me, Edmund. I am simply fulfilling my patriotic duty by leaving the cheaper foods to those who can't afford anything better." Her virtuous tone changed to one with a hint of slyness in it. "And I am perfectly aware that this outburst is nothing to do with my Fortnum's hamper – or the desperate state of the war, come to that. Perhaps that explosion at the munitions has affected your judgement."

Lizzie pulled the door shut.

At Mr Fawcett's insistence, Lizzie was allowed to have a short nap in the afternoon, but as she started up the stairs to her bedroom, she heard the noisy hum of the newly acquired electric housemaid suction cleaner. This new contraption had at first scared Martha, and then delighted her once she realised how much it reduced the back-breaking nature of some of her work, but Lizzie groaned inwardly that she would have to listen to the racket it made.

Halfway up the stairs, she noticed it had stopped, and as she passed Mrs Dearden's room she saw Martha in there with her back to the door. Lizzie leaned against the doorframe as she watched the young girl flick through a book. Martha must have caught sight of Lizzie in the reflection from the dresser mirror, because she spun round and put her hands behind her back to conceal what she was looking at.

"Gawd!" She put one hand to her chest. "You frightened the life out of me!"

Lizzie walked towards her, made as if to go past her, and instead snatched the book from her hand.

"*Married Love.*" Lizzie read out the title and looked for the author's name. "Dr Marie Carmichael Stopes." She raised her eyebrows, vaguely recognising the name as having some scandalous association.

The maid's features contorted in panic. "Please don't tell."

Lizzie flicked through a few pages, almost expecting something salacious to leap out at her, but saw only dense, scholastic prose. Rather disappointed, she was about to say she didn't see what all the fuss was about when her eye fastened on the words 'the sex act' and 'birth control'. Her face coloured immediately.

"Bit racy," she mouthed and dropped the book onto the bed covers as if it was a bomb which might go off at any minute.

"She's got this an' all." The maid went over to the open wardrobe and brought out a box, which she presented to Lizzie, her eyes twinkling with mischief. "Universal Douche." She shrugged her eyebrows and lowered her voice, as if she was drawing Lizzie into some great conspiracy.

Slaveys know everything, Lizzie thought. If she was ever in a position to afford servants, she didn't think she'd employ any. She looked at the box, puzzled, and turned it over in her hands.

"What's a 'douche'?"

"After you an' a bloke, you know, have done it" – Martha mugged a leer – "it stops a baby."

Lizzie's face reddened again: her ignorance about these sorts of sexual matters had certainly played some part in her own predicament, and she felt the maid was showing it to her to make a point. While this birth control device didn't seem respectable somehow, in spite of herself Lizzie found it a little titillating, and she asked Martha how she knew all this.

"Looked at the picture what came with the instructions, of course," Martha said proudly and showed her.

Lizzie looked at the diagram, both intrigued and a little appalled.

"I know, looks disgusting, don't it." Martha giggled.

Lizzie screwed her face up, but it was less to do with the

strangeness of this birth control device than with the unusual sharp pain which followed hard on one of the usual fluttering sensations in her belly, which she had become used to of late.

"You all right?" Martha asked as she gathered up the box and the book and shoved them back into the bottom of the wardrobe.

"Just a twinge." Lizzie automatically put her hand on her stomach. "So what happened to her husband then?" Although not really interested, she asked this to take her mind off the queer sensation rippling through her body.

"Dunno. Before my time. Mrs Ryder said he never came back from some foreign war and she was on her uppers. That's why she had to come and live here."

Without warning, a strong contraction forced Lizzie to bend over and cry out in pain. During the night she had felt some strange physical sensations, like someone clenching a fist and releasing it inside her, followed by one or two sharp stabbing pains. Afterwards she dozed fitfully as each cramp lessened, until by morning they seemed to have gone.

"Is this it? God, this is it."

Lizzie's body sagged onto the bed. She rubbed her stomach, the circles increasing commensurate with the pain. She felt her chest tightening as if in a vice, and a little spike of fear struck her; she couldn't sit still. She walked away and paced up and down the length of the landing, shooing Martha's concerns away. Another contraction bent her double. All at once, Lizzie felt as if some unknown force was trying to pull her feet up through her head. She began pressing herself up and down on a small chair near the top of the stairs, left there so Mrs Ryder and her 'gammy knees' could take a rest before attempting the next flight of stairs. Lizzie didn't care if she made a ludicrous picture. Beads of perspiration formed at her temples and on her top lip. To cope with the pain of the contractions, she found she had to take deeper and deeper breaths.

Martha seemed to find the spectacle both comical and frightening at the same time.

"Bloody blimey, you must be sucking all the air out of the entire world the way you're going on!"

But when Lizzie let out a frightened "Oh!" as a puddle of amniotic fluid formed between her feet, the maid seemed rooted to the spot with fright.

"Divvent stand there like one o' clock, half struck!" Lizzie shouted, careless of her accent. "Get us some help."

Lizzie heard the maid as she thudded down the stairs, crying, "Blow me. Mrs Ryder! Mrs Ryder! I'm never doing it with no man, ever!"

Hallucinatory faces loomed in and out of focus and dislocated voices with slurred speech and elongated vowel sounds floated all around Lizzie, while someone dabbed her burning forehead with a cool, damp cloth. Suddenly, a piercing scream, which she barely recognised as her own, scythed through the hubbub. All she knew was that the agonising pain came from deep inside her lower body, and some visceral instinct told her to keep pushing to bring it to an end, but with each push she had a sense it might actually consume her instead.

Then it was all over.

Lizzie heard her child's plaintive cry and felt his reassuring weight as she touched his peach-soft skin and inhaled his distinctive newly born smell. She sensed a needle-like pricking in her breasts, and could hear a distant voice telling her it was her milk coming in. Someone put her baby to her breast; she enfolded him with her arms, and enjoyed the pleasurable closeness and the sensation of him suckling her. A weary happiness washed over her.

After what seemed only a very few minutes, somewhere nearby she heard a vaguely familiar voice say, "I haf given her a strong sedative. She has had quite a bad time of it, and she will need to rest. Best to get it over with now."

As she was gradually enveloped by a warm and pleasant glow, dulling her senses, she hardly registered her baby being taken from her arms.

Chapter Twenty-two

Eunice balanced the baby on her hip.

"Look, Alfie. Look who I've brought." She hunkered down over her elder son's grave as she fussed over the arrangement of some wild flowers into a small vase.

It had taken three hours from the first painful contraction to the time Eunice had given birth to her new son on the floor of her small kitchen. She had leaned against the sink, amid the messy detritus of his birth, still linked to her baby by his cord, and held him close in her arms while she waited for her placenta to come away. She knew from past experience that it might take ten minutes or one hour, and was in no hurry to clamp the cord and cut the physical link to her child. Mother looked at baby and gently traced the blue veins beneath the translucent skin of his tiny hairless skull. She kissed away the splash of a tear which fell onto his forehead. Later, she swaddled him in a shawl and put him in Alfie's old baby basket.

After conceiving five children during her marriage, Eunice knew the routine well. She washed the floor clean of amniotic fluid and blood, wrapped the afterbirth up in newspaper and put it in the rubbish bin in the back yard; she would take it out and burn it later.

When Peggy came home, Eunice had been singing lullabies to her child, like she used to do with Alfie, she said, and wasn't he the spitting image of Jack? Peggy had to agree, but prised the child from his mother, placed him in the perambulator and took the unusual step of getting the pair of them to a doctor.

William began to grizzle. "Oh, I'd forgotten what hard work babies are," Eunice grumbled. "I don't remember you being this difficult, Alfie." Eunice jiggled the child up and down for a few minutes while she chattered to her dead son and fretted over individual flower stems until she was finally satisfied with their placement.

"Peggy thinks he'll take my mind off you, you know. As if you can replace one child with another. Then she's never been a mother – well, she never let it get that far – and never had a mother neither, so I don't suppose I can expect her to understand." Eunice paused and stared at the child on her knee before her gaze was pulled back to her dead son's grave. "You know, Alfie, I'm almost afraid to love him, just in case." Her voice began to falter. "I loved you with all my heart, and look where it's got me."

She bowed her head as if in prayer – only Eunice didn't pray anymore – and looked down at her son's grave in silent contemplation. The bond formed with him extended beyond death: a huge piece of her heart was buried with him. Even this new bundle of life, with lungs like bellows, could not replace that missing part.

On her way home, Eunice thought she was seeing things: barely a queue outside the butcher's shop. The lines had been getting shorter ever since the Government had introduced proper rationing. Gone were the days when she queued outside Brown's for the best part of half a day, when there was nothing else for it because you had to eat, and you had to try your best to avoid any confrontations or fights when frustration got the better of some people. She rummaged around in her bag for her ration coupons. *Fat. Sugar. Where's the meat one?* The thought that she might have left it at home made her suddenly want to cry.

A voice next to her made her blink back the tears. "Oh, look, such a little poppet!" The speaker, a middle-aged woman, peered into the perambulator and began to speak to its occupant in the silly voice adults seemed to reserve for talking to babies. Eunice didn't know whether to laugh or cry.

"He looks just like you."

Of course he doesn't.

Eunice smiled graciously at the woman, but in reality she felt wrung out, like an over-used dishcloth. Some days she felt so exhausted she could barely move, and she had to supplement her breast milk with watered down condensed milk to satisfy William.

"Morning, Missus!" boomed Tubby Brown, rubbing his red-raw hands down his blood stained butcher's apron, his odd head and hairstyle – which reminded Eunice of a large cauliflower – almost obscuring the hand-written sign that proclaimed 'No Tick' on the wall behind him. "D'you want the good news or the bad news? Bad news is I've only got half rations of beef or mutton for you, but every cloud has a silver lining and I've got plenty of bacon. How's that for some good news, eh?"

Eunice had heard him repeat this virtually word for word to the woman ahead of her as the prelude to setting about another carcass with his meat cleaver. Not that long ago, frustrated, disappointed and tired customers would mutter under their breath where they'd like to stick Tubby Brown's meat cleaver. Truth was, Eunice was sick of bacon, but she supposed it was better than nothing.

As she walked home, down uniform streets of mean-looking cheap terraced houses, she passed older women sitting outside on wooden kitchen chairs, the younger ones standing beside them as they killed time by gossiping and swapping bomb stories. Eunice sometimes wondered whether they thought it was some kind of competition to see who could relay the worst tale of devastation, but she stopped occasionally and engaged in some banal pleasantries with them.

Further down the street, she saw Mrs Baxter from across the

way down on her hands and knees, whitening her front step with a donkey stone, likely donated by the totter in exchange for a few unwanted goods. Eunice knew she carried out this regular routine not because she was house-proud, but because it enabled her to keep an eye on the goings-on in the street. It was common knowledge that she was usually the source of any malicious gossip doing the rounds, especially about Jack.

At this thought a provocative voice in Eunice's head urged her to run across the road and give a well-aimed kick at the woman's upturned backside, but she was diverted by the shout of her next door neighbour.

"Hey, Eunice!"

Eunice could tell by the woman's bright eyed expression that she was bursting to tell her something, so acknowledged her with a begrudging wave of the hand. All Eunice wanted to do was put her feet up, not listen to gossip.

"Your Jack's name's in the PoW lists."

Eunice, her aches and weariness immediately forgotten, abandoned William's perambulator in the middle of the road and dashed over to her neighbour.

"PoW? Are you sure?"

"Sid Blythe picked up a copy of *The Times* off the bus. Took it home to use for lav paper, as usual, and that's when he noticed it."

Eunice bumped the perambulator along the uneven road in the direction of the newsagent's shop, in her haste not bothering to avoid any holes or dents, all the while feeling as if she might cry. William rolled from side to side, and he soon began to wail.

"Hush, now. I said be quiet. Shut up!"

She arrived at her destination, her hair flying loose from her pins, and carelessly grazed the baby carriage against the shop window. Inside, her chest heaved up and down as she took out her purse. In other circumstances she would have baulked at 4d for a newspaper which told her the same war news she could get for 1d by choosing a different title, one which she didn't need a dictionary to read, but Jack's name was in this one. Her hands trembled as she handed over the coins.

Outside, William's cries of distress continued to bludgeon her brain. She accepted the half folded newspaper from the vendor, but its edge tipped her purse up and sent coins scattering across the floor. A handful of customers helped pick them up. A woman held up something small and looked at it with curiosity. Eunice snatched back the fox button, took the newspaper and dashed out of the shop.

She ignored her child's crying and scanned each page. Finally, she found the list of PoWs. Until she saw it written down in black and white, she knew she wouldn't believe it. There! There was his name. It was now official. Lance Corporal Jack Wilson was a prisoner of war. No longer missing, and definitely not dead. She threw back her head and let the relief waft over her like a warm breeze, then she put the newspaper into the bottom of the baby carriage and pushed William all the way home with a little spring in her step, oblivious to the boy's distress. All Eunice could focus on was the fact that Jack was alive.

As soon as she was home, however, a desperate need to know exactly where he was overcame her. How could she find that out? The War Office, she supposed. She didn't even know where that was. Oh, why didn't the Government tell you these things? Send you a letter to explain everything. Like they did, quickly enough, when they wrote and told you your husband wouldn't be coming home anymore. She offered up a mild curse that the frocks at Westminster didn't give a damn about the relatives left at home, worrying themselves sick.

Chapter Twenty-three

Martha cleared yet another morning's untouched breakfast tray away and muttered about waste and lack of appetite. Lizzie ignored the maid, closed her eyes and lay back against the pillows. She automatically put her hand on her stomach, wanting to feel the comforting roundness of her skin stretched tight as a protective drum around her unborn baby. All she felt through her nightgown was the thin, slack folds of deflated skin that wrinkled her stomach, and her face crumpled.

Martha relented and sat down on the bed beside her. "It's for the best, you know."

No. No, it isn't.

The taking of her child felt like an open wound into which poison was poured every day, and she couldn't shut out the cruel echo of Mrs Dearden's cold and unfeeling words, telling her that she must consider her baby dead to her now. Worse torture arrived when it was time to change her lochia soaked sanitary rags, and she watched the stains progress from deep red to pink to brown to yellowish white, each fading colour lessening her connection to her child, and to his father.

Edmund Fawcett had now taken to coming up to see Lizzie after dinner. Some evenings he sat with her and read to her from a novel he had brought with him. It was another side of him she had never

142

imagined at the munitions factory. At first she barely registered his presence, but with each encounter she came to appreciate more and more his warmth and kindness towards her, and because he so obviously liked her, she found she began to like him in return and look forward to his visits. He slowly drew her out of herself, yet remained respectful of her grief. Once, she did open her mind to the possibility that her benefactor might be in love with her, but her status as a fallen woman rose up before her and snuffed out such a flight of fancy. She did, however, feel indebted to the munitions manager for taking her in, and out of a sense of gratitude did nothing to discourage him.

These past two evenings she had noticed he seemed restless and distracted, and had broken off his visit, disappeared for an hour and come back, fleetingly, to say, 'Good night'. As Lizzie remained in her room, preferring her own company and relishing her freedom from the work of a servant during her recuperation, she was unaware of the growing crisis in the household. During the night she was woken by the sound of subdued voices, talking in hushed yet anxious tones, outside her door. The next morning, when Martha brought in her breakfast tray later than usual, she told Lizzie that Mrs Dearden had taken to her bed two days ago, and that last night her face had turned lavender and blood had come out of her nose. Without further explanation, she rushed off to attend to the extra work the incapacitation of her mistress was causing.

This news made little impact on Lizzie, who didn't care for the woman, and she kept out of the way for the rest of the day. In the early evening, however, Martha burst into her room again, clearly agitated.

"Come quick. Mr Fawcett's taken to his bed. He's turning blue. Oh, miss!"

Lizzie was galvanised into action, her own misery temporarily forgotten. At the open door of his bedroom, she hesitated, Martha so close behind her she could feel the girl's hot breath on her neck.

"Mr Fawcett?" She peered into the dimly-lit room and could make out an inert figure on top of the bed. Receiving no reply, Lizzie ordered Martha to stay outside and hurried to his bedside.

She was quite relieved to see that Fawcett was fully clothed, but when she leaned over him, she saw the blue-hued face which had so frightened Martha. He seemed barely conscious, and Lizzie's stomach lurched. She took hold of his hand, which felt clammy to the touch.

"Mr Fawcett?" She whispered closer to his ear, "Edmund?" but there was no response. She felt the start of a rising panic in her chest, and she called out to Martha to call for the doctor at once.

The physician looked sombre when he spoke to Lizzie. He told her a nurse would be required to look after Mr Fawcett, and that since Mrs Dearden's condition had improved he had recommended she get away from the stresses of London. It pleased Lizzie to hear Mrs Dearden wished to go and stay with an aunt in Folkestone, freeing her of the woman's presence in the house.

"Since all the nurses are dealing with the war casualties," Lizzie said, "I can nurse Mr Fawcett myself." In truth, she was suddenly selfishly grateful to have something important to do to fill the chasm of emptiness which had taken hold of her.

The doctor took his top hat from the table in the hall and said he would look in again tomorrow, but he left behind him a sense of futility in the household. He gave Lizzie the impression that all the salves in the world wouldn't help. She was sure she heard him say, under his breath as he left, that the best they could do was pray.

Lizzie was relieved when Charlotte Dearden, and a hired nurse the doctor had conjured up from somewhere, left the next afternoon and she could look after her patient without any interference, but instructions were left that she telephone Folkestone each day, without fail, to provide news of Mrs Dearden's brother's condition.

The doctor had no medicine other than aspirin to offer by way of relief for this un-named infection, so he gave Lizzie some instructions for relieving the congestion on Edmund's lungs. At first she was a little shy about unbuttoning his shirt to apply a hot poultice to his naked chest, but when it released the congesting greenish-yellow pus blocking his lungs and brought him relief, she put aside her prudishness, told herself she must behave like a proper nurse, and looked after her patient with dedication and without complaint.

By the fifth day of sitting by her patient's bedside, only allowing herself to fall asleep for a few hours at a time, tiredness and exhaustion were starting to get the better of Lizzie, but she wanted to have Edmund Fawcett to herself; to take on this burden of care alone. Didn't she owe him this at least? He stirred, and she gently sponged his brow with a damp cloth and touched his lips with little drops of water. The intimacy of these acts made her feel increasingly tender towards him.

Suddenly a commotion started up downstairs, and she looked up just as Martha appeared in the doorway of the bedroom.

"It's some sort of Spanish flu, that's what's going round!" Martha cried.

Lizzie put her finger to her lips to quieten Martha and nodded at Edmund. Martha dropped her voice to an excited whisper.

"I heard it at the chemists…" Martha's voice dried and she began to cough. "They're dropping like flies in Madrid. But there's no cure for it. You live or die. Oh my."

Lizzie went over to her. "Are you all right?"

The maid looked sheepish. "Got a bit of a sore throat, truth to tell."

"Go and gargle with some permanganate of potassium at once, and then again every four hours, like the doctor said. Have the rooms been disinfected with Jeyes Fluid?"

"Did it this morning."

"Good. Now go to bed and rest."

When Lizzie looked in on Martha later, she feared the worst and called the doctor.

"Is it this Spanish flu?"

"We can't be quite certain yet," the physician admitted, "but from various reports we've had, I'm afraid it does look like a very virulent form of influenza, which, oddly, is proving most fatal to healthy younger people."

Martha deteriorated at an incredible speed as the thick fluid blocked her lungs. She gave up the fight at three o'clock in the morning. Dazed, Lizzie closed the young maid's cold and staring brown eyes and pulled the sweat-soaked bed sheet over her lavender face. She sat down in the little wicker chair in the corner of the attic room and stared at the slim, girlish shape under the covers, hardly believing what had happened.

Later, she sat at Edmund Fawcett's bedside in his darkened room – for too much light still seemed to hurt his eyes – and willed him to live. For the second time in her life, she felt completely alone in the world.

The next morning, her patient's eyes fluttered open, and with an effort he turned his head to look at her. Instinctively she grasped his hand and put it to her cheek.

"Edmund?"

He forced his head up from the pillow, indicating he wanted to say something to her. She leaned her ear towards his dry and cracked lips.

"I adore you, Lizzie Fenwick," he whispered. "Marry me?"

Chapter Twenty-four

Eunice walked through the forbidding arch in Whitehall and stood in the quadrangle to face the imposing classical stone building which housed the War Office. Ahead of her, two young women unfurled home-made anti-war banners and began to harass any man in uniform who passed them, telling them they should be ashamed to support such mass slaughter. Soon enough the women were manhandled away. It made Eunice think of her mother-in-law, who was still sporting a black eye and a cut head after being roughed up at an all-women peace march yesterday, and who was looking after William in her absence.

It's busier than the munitions at the end of a shift, was her first thought as she walked into the impressive but grim entrance hall and saw messenger boys, other personal enquirers like herself, Government staff and men in uniform coming and going in their droves. One of two indifferent officials, in some sort of fancy livery and a top hat, asked her what her business was.

When she told him, he re-directed her towards Carlton House Terrace, where the Red Cross Central Prisoners of War Committee were handling PoW enquiries. After a short walk, Eunice entered yet another grand building, which looked like it had once been an aristocrat's home. Eunice found a spare chair and sat down, her handbag on her knees and her hands clasped over the top. Her eyes darted from one face to the next. At once she sensed the oppressive mix of barely suppressed hope and an air of desperation which hung like a miasma above the crowd in here. It was, she thought, like watching an ocean of shipwrecked sailors, clinging to a tiny piece of jetsam amid a storm-tossed sea: any promised morsel of information about their loved ones was like sighting longed for land.

Eventually she was told to fill out a form specifying the nature of her enquiry and to give her name and address. When she had finished, Eunice watched with interest as others approached the enquiry desks in their turn. She saw an alert mouse-like man listen to the clerk, get up calmly and walk away towards the door, where he smashed his fist into the wall and muttered obscenities under his breath.

"My only brother's been missing nine months."

Eunice turned to look at the source of the comment. Her immediate thought was *you got dressed in the dark*, for the woman's attire was ill-matched.

"They still reckon they can't tell me whether he's alive or dead. Barely twenty, he is. But I come every day, just in case he's found in a PoW camp somewhere."

"I'm so sorry," Eunice replied, admiring the woman's fortitude and feeling a little chagrined for her first uncharitable assessment. She didn't know what had come over her these days; she struggled to find something good to say about anything.

"Who've you come to find then?" the woman asked.

"My husband."

"Lost my husband at first Ypres. The date's etched on my memory: 20 October 1914." The woman folded her arms in front of her chest. "Of course, there's no body. And no grave."

Eunice winced. How terrible it was not to have anything tangible to fasten your grief onto.

"Shame, that. I would've danced on it."

Eunice's mouth fell open, unsure whether this was an attempt at a joke or not, but she was saved from having to find an appropriate response because the woman immediately turned away and began repeating the story to the man on her other side. Eunice decided it must be her party piece and was designed to shock. She put it out of her mind.

When it was finally Eunice's turn, the female clerk read her completed form and flicked through a box of index cards, unable to stifle a yawn. Without warning she scraped her chair back, setting Eunice's teeth on edge, stood up and disappeared through a door behind her. Eunice looked to her left and right: she supposed she was to sit there until the clerk came back.

Waiting, she thought after five minutes had elapsed. *All I seem to do these days is wait.* She started to drum her fingers on the desk. The clerk eventually returned to give Eunice the information that Lance Corporal Jack Wilson had recently been admitted to a German military hospital at Aachen with a knee wound, and was now interned at the German PoW camp at Soltau in Lower Saxony. No, she said in a monotone, she had nothing further but she gave Eunice an information booklet about PoW's and recommended Eunice read it. As she sat on the bus on the way home, Eunice unconsciously fretted away at a small hole in her glove. Her relief that her husband was alive began to give way to a little worm of worry about what a 'knee wound' really meant for Jack. It had required hospital treatment, but was that a good thing or a bad thing? Any damage might be lessened with early treatment, but what if the injury was so severe that...

Oh!

An image of a returned soldier, both legs missing, loomed up in front of her. Her head suddenly became full of myriad anxieties. That place they'd taken him – where was Aachen? She knew Jack had an Atlas at home among all his political and history books; she'd check it when she got back. The clerk had said he'd been taken somewhere else, though, hadn't she? What was that other name? Sounded like a condiment – salt, or something or other. In Lower Saxony. Where were these places? They sounded so foreign, alien and far away from what she knew.

Eunice remembered all the times she had skipped past articles in the press about the hardships endured by prisoners behind German lines: they hadn't interested her. The newspapers were also full of advertisements, asking for more donations to help fund the food and clothing parcels sent regularly to the camps. She had largely ignored them. Neither had she given much thought to those munitions workers whose husbands were prisoners of war when they started grousing.

"'S all right for them officer wives. Doesn't matter to those la-di-dahs what prices these so-called authorised shops charge. I've only managed to send Bert one parcel so far in six months."

Eunice had dismissed such petty gripes as insignificant compared to the anxiety and fear she felt for Jack's safety: he was actually risking his life at the Front, not holed up in some camp or other, away from the fighting. Even when he was reported missing, and she suffered the sheer hell of not knowing what had happened to him, she paid scant regard to the plight of PoWs or their families at home. Now she realised these women's concerns would also be hers.

She caught sight of her gloved hands in her lap and saw the large hole in the fabric. Eunice sighed and turned her gaze away to look out of the grimy bus window, only to discover she had missed her stop. Not for the first time, she wondered what her life had come to.

Chapter Twenty-five

Lizzie stood in a crowd which lined the streets of London to cheer a great procession of American troops as they marched past and waved their national flag, the Stars and Stripes, on their way to France. There was a strong scent of jubilation and victory in the air, because it was generally believed that the tide had turned in the war in the Allies' favour. It made her think about the return of peacetime and her acceptance of Edmund's marriage proposal. A renewed sense of hope and optimism about her future swept through her and she determined to be the best wife she could and to take full advantage of everything her new life with Edmund offered.

She returned home to discover that Charlotte Dearden had decided that a life in London would be too deleterious to her health. This secretly delighted Lizzie, and she felt as if she could now truly throw off the shackles of her previous servitude and that her position as mistress of the house was free of competition. She immediately cemented her authority by assuming responsibility for finding a new maid to replace Martha without any recourse to Mrs Ryder, and she set about her first household management task with relish. Lizzie knew which agency to go to, but she also knew that the lure of war work meant that her choice of servants was still limited. However, she had liked Elsie Thomas immediately for her youthful enthusiasm, despite her lack of experience – and

Lizzie had enough nous to realise that such a young girl would be easier for her to manage and a blessed counterweight to the well-established Mrs Ryder.

For want of any friend or other female acquaintance to accompany her, Lizzie took the new maid along to help her choose a wedding dress. In the bridal gown shop Elsie was like a child in a well-stocked sweet shop; any casual observer might rather suppose she was the future bride, but when Lizzie tried on the first wedding gown – made from cream tussore silk with floating lace panels down the sides and bodice and with a fashionable V-neck – her eyes lit up at the wonder of her own transformation. She chose a lace mob cap and a floor length veil to complete her outfit.

Elsie clapped her hands to her mouth. "Oh, miss, you're like a fairy tale princess!"

Carried away by the romantic image, Lizzie imagined all the single girls from the munitions being jealous of her now: choosing her wedding gown and getting married. Immediately she decided this first dress was perfect and she determined to make her future husband proud of her.

"These shoes, miss." Elsie pointed to a pair of pale satin shoes with cross-over straps, pointed toes and Louis heels in one of several boxes of bridal shoes the assistant had brought out. "These'll go beautiful with your gown."

Lizzie, who until recently had been more used to wearing boots than shoes, and who knew her ankle length wedding gown would show her shoes off to good effect, rather thought they would.

At the florist the young assistant told her she must have white carnations because they represented true love. Elsie almost swooned. After a pause, Lizzie ordered them.

*

The pair were married on 3 August, the day before the fourth anniversary of the war. Aware of the need not to be too showy or frivolous, since deaths from influenza and the war meant that amid the new hope an underlying grief was still pervasive, Edmund and Lizzie made sure their wedding was a small and intimate celebration in the local church of St Mary Magdalene in East Ham. None of the bride's few friends, or even fewer distant relatives, attended. Even Peggy did not show up, although an invitation was extended as an olive branch (but also, if Lizzie was honest, maybe just to allow a little crowing). No one gave her away. Although this was not how, in her days before her romantic illusions were so heartlessly shattered by Harry Slater's death, she had imagined her wedding day would be, she saw Edmund's mile wide grin as she lifted her veil and knew she was loved. A wave of tenderness and affection for him washed over her and she allowed him to claim another little piece of her heart.

Lizzie, who had never had a real holiday or stayed in such opulent splendour, gazed with delight at the marble and ornate plasterwork, cleverly illuminated by the new electric lights installed everywhere, of the Metropole Hotel in Brighton. Her heart fluttered a little as the newlyweds took the electric lift to their third floor bedroom. Once inside their large room, with tall windows that offered a clear view of the sea and esplanade below, Lizzie knew Edmund was showing her what kind of life he could offer her. For a second time, then, a man had brought her to a certain place hoping to impress her. A brief shadow of a Lyon's Corner House passed over her mind, but in order not to disappoint her new husband on their honeymoon, she swanked around the room, admiring everything her eyes fell upon.

"Oh, it's really lovely, Edmund!"

"I'm glad you like it, my love."

As she swept past him, he caught hold of her and she saw the dark desire in his eyes as he folded her in his arms. He kissed her on the mouth with an intensity that surprised her, but she was overcome by a storm of unexpected warring emotions. Her life suddenly seemed like a roller coaster. She pulled herself free with the excuse she would like to take a walk on the esplanade before dinner.

"I fear it might be too breezy." Lizzie heard the note of disappointment.

"We might find it rather stirring."

She shot him a coquettish glance as she headed for the door.

"Very well." He seemed prepared to indulge her for the time being.

They walked, arm in arm, to the Palace Pier, where they lost themselves in the splendour of the amusement and pleasure emporium. Edmund moved away from her for a few moments and left her gazing out to sea, protected from the elements by the glass sides that ran the length of the pier. On his return, he had his hands behind his back, obviously hiding something, but she teased him by pretending not to notice. Eventually he brandished two tickets for the Palace Pier Theatre that evening. She took his arm and gave it an affectionate squeeze.

As they walked back to the hotel, Lizzie thought, *it has been too long since I felt I might be happy again.* On the way they passed the bathing stations on the beach. She glanced at her husband to see if he was looking at the women in their bathing suits, but he kept his gaze steadfastly ahead of him. She hid a little smile of satisfaction.

In their marital bed that night, Lizzie sensed a little uncertainty in her husband. She saw the hunger for her in his eyes, but she was surprised to find he was rather a constrained lover towards her. Afterwards, she lay next to him in the darkness, his body folded around hers like a shield. As soon as she closed her eyes, on the back of her eyelids she saw an image of herself intimately entwined with Harry Slater as he took possession of her body and her heart. She tried not to make comparisons; it would only make her unhappy again.

She was inclined to blame herself, this first time with her husband. Her own sexual feelings had been a revelation to her when making love with Harry, but she had been afraid to admit her desires to Edmund for fear he might think her utterly wanton. She considered the possibility that her new husband had never made love to a woman before – she had no idea about any past relationships he might have had, if any – rather than that he thought only of satisfying his own needs. This impression seemed to make it even more important to her that she did not hurt his feelings. She would be patient.

The appearance of her monthly period the next day, however, put paid to any further marital relations on their honeymoon. Neither party mentioned it: she was overcome with embarrassment, and Edmund made no sexual overtures to her for the remainder of their short honeymoon.

During the rest of the long weekend, Lizzie gave herself energetically to playing the role of Mrs Edmund Fawcett, spurred on by the newness of her situation and finding her husband a most companionable partner. Although she noticed he could be a little stiff and formal in his manner, he was sociable when the occasion demanded, and she was pleased to see that others found him convivial. She discovered that, other than work and the war (but who wasn't affected by that?), he seemed to have few interests. Nevertheless, she made the effort to appear attentive when he enthused about classical music and stamps. She made a little joke about the King's famous stamp collection, which made him laugh.

After dinner, Lizzie wanted to dance. When Edmund confessed that he had two left feet, her expectations were very low as he led her out onto the dance floor. She was left quite breathless after a brisk one-step and rather dizzy after a more than competent waltz.

"I think you led me on, husband," she whispered in his ear.

Edmund Fawcett was constantly surprising her.

Lizzie was sorry to leave Brighton and its cosmopolitan gaiety behind when they moved on to Folkestone for a few days, where Edmund planned to visit his sister and the aged aunt she had decided to live with. They arrived at their hotel, which was far less impressive than the Metropole, somewhat late after a fractious journey, dined in relative silence and then retired early to bed. The next day the sky turned an ominous dark grey and the heavens opened. The ensuing deluge delayed their plans to go out. Edmund, newly in charge of a large and profitable chemical factory in West Ham, was forced to occupy himself with some paperwork, so Lizzie wandered about the visitor rooms downstairs. However, there seemed to be very few guests whom she might engage in conversation.

"Still at your work?" she asked later, a deliberate note of boredom in her voice.

"Almost done, darling." He continued to read the document in his hand.

She threw herself down into an armchair and stared at the unadorned plaster ceiling. Eventually he dragged his eyes away from the sheaf of papers he was reading and looked across at her. Feeling his eyes on her, she perked up, hopeful.

"Oh, can't we go out?"

"Do you think it wise to go out in this rain? You might catch a chill."

"We'll be home in two days' time and I won't have seen anything of Folkestone." She pursed her lips into a little pout in the hope he wouldn't be able to resist her plea.

"The weather's meant to improve tomorrow." He put his sheaf of papers down, and seeing the downward tilt of her mouth, said, "Tell you what: how about a game of cribbage?"

She swallowed down a little scream of frustration, but he had already called for the cribbage board and cards: a fait accompli. She slumped back in her chair and stifled a yawn: card games had never particularly interested her. She told him she had no idea how to play. He said he'd soon fix that.

"Oh, very well then," she sighed.

Edmund ordered some drinks and set about instructing his new wife. As he showed her how the pegs in the board indicated each player's score and explained how to play, Lizzie stared at the wooden board, with its tarnished metal top punctured with groups of holes, and pretended to look interested. Edmund unsheathed the cards from their packet and placed the deck on the table in front of them.

He told her it was customary to cut the cards to determine who dealt first.

"Lower card deals."

Lizzie assumed she was to keep her card to herself, so she put on what she considered to be a poker face. He seemed to find this amusing as he made his cut and showed her the two of diamonds. With a huff of annoyance, she revealed her card was the Queen of Clubs. She caught the brief smirk as he told her she could peg three points on the board as compensation. That pleased her. He shuffled the cards, then asked her to cut them again and deal out five cards each.

"The first to score sixty-one points or more is the winner," he explained. "Now let's see."

He described the rules as they went along. At first Lizzie played carelessly, as if indifferent to the score, but when she began to win points she became increasingly engaged in the game. Edmund ordered two more drinks. Various residents came and went, unnoticed by them.

"Oh, I've won!" she cried, her eyes sparkling when she was the first to reach sixty-one.

"Beginner's luck."

"Maybe I have a flair for it."

His eyes crinkled with pleasure. "I'll concede that as a possibility if you win the next one."

Each time she moved her peg ahead of his, she allowed herself a sly grin and sneaked a wary look at him, but dropped her gaze almost immediately he returned the look. As their game progressed, they exchanged playful glances and flirted wildly with each other. This was a side of her husband she had never guessed existed. When her score again took her past sixty-one, she leaned her body towards him in a provocative fashion.

"So much for beginner's luck, Mr Edmund Fawcett." Her eyes challenged him.

He met her gaze and she knew he had not really been trying to win; but she also saw something else dancing in his dark eyes, which excited her. She shot him an inviting glance, and then remembered she had her period.

By the next morning, the weather had not improved. Edmund's suggestion that a taxi cab ride, via the town, to his aunt's house would at least allow Lizzie her wish of seeing something of Folkestone was greeted with a lukewarm response, but she agreed. As they travelled, Lizzie didn't bother to look out of the vehicle's windows because the driving rain, which ran in torrents down the glass, obscured any view. She didn't think she could remember a wetter summer. She sat with her left hand on her temple, her eyes lowered, until they reached the aunt's house. Immediately she decided she couldn't face her sister-in-law.

"Edmund, I hope you don't mind, but I seem to have a bad head. It must be the weather," she apologised. "Would you mind if I went back to the hotel?"

After waving away his concern and insisting he visit his sister and aunt as arranged, Lizzie instructed the driver to take her into the centre of Folkestone. She reasoned with herself that it would improve her mood more than having to make polite conversation with the unfriendly Charlotte Dearden, or spend time in the hotel alone.

As she got out of the cab she put up her umbrella against the rain, which fortunately had now eased to a light drizzle. She was shocked to find the streets filled with crowds of soldiers embarking and disembarking for France. Many were maimed and wounded, bandaged up like ancient Egyptian mummies. They didn't seem part of her world.

Lizzie stood and watched them, unsure whether she was fascinated or repulsed by them. Almost without realising it, she began to look closely at them, and her eyes darted from one face to another. Once she started forwards, convinced she had seen the lop-sided grin, the barely tamed black hair and the blue-grey eyes, but stepped back in abject disappointment when the soldier turned around and she became the subject of lascivious whistles, gestures and cat calls by his fellow Tommies.

"Now there's one of the jammiest bits of jam!"

Lizzie walked off and headed along the harbour wall, where she stared out to sea. A sudden whiff of fish hit her nostrils from the rows of fishing boats lining the shore. The smell reminded her of the stink of the razor clams her elder brothers used to dig up from the wettest parts of the beach at Tynemouth, and of the dead crabs and seaweed they would thrust in her face to tease her. She had pretended not to be scared, just to show them.

The sudden screech of a seagull, which stood watch on the harbour wall nearby, made her start. She eyed it coldly as the bird began to walk towards her. She stamped her foot, cried, "Shoo!" and flapped a hand in its direction before turning on her heel and hurrying off, fearing retribution.

"It's called a 'bob'," she informed her husband later as she stood in front of him and turned her head first this way and then that, plumping up the style with her hands.

She had passed the hair salon on the way back to the hotel, she told him, and on a whim she had gone inside. She noticed her husband seemed out of sorts: the result of an afternoon defending his actions in marrying her, no doubt, but he refrained from questioning her sudden recovery from her headache or rebuking her for going out in the rain. However, she did see a flash of disappointment cross his face: he had adored her long hair.

"I suppose it's the fashion these days."

She leaned over and kissed him and he brightened up immediately, pulling her down onto his lap where he put his arms around her to hold her close.

She didn't tell him her new hairstyle had nothing to do with fashion and everything to do with putting her old life behind her.

As they journeyed back to London, the train was crammed with men in uniform heading for leave in their home towns along the way. Four young officers got into their carriage. They smelled of the trenches and war, and Lizzie tried to ignore them. They alighted after only a few stops, and were replaced by a nervous bird-like woman, who seemed content to take out some knitting and pay no attention to Edmund and Lizzie.

Lizzie watched her new husband opposite as he fell into a gentle doze, his newspaper spread open on his lap. When she saw that the newspaper might slip down between his legs, she leaned towards him, gathered it up, folded it and placed it on her own lap for safekeeping. Out of the window, the patchwork colours of the countryside gradually gave way to a more familiar, industrialised and darker urban landscape, and Lizzie fell to musing about what awaited her back in London.

Suddenly she became aware of the hypnotic clicking of knitting needles and she looked across at the woman opposite. Although her head was bowed and her eyes focused on her task, Lizzie felt the woman carried an aura of sadness about her. Lizzie watched her nimble fingers moving rhythmically backwards and forwards and noticed she wore no wedding ring. *Is that by choice or circumstance?* Lizzie found herself wondering.

Edmund stirred and she looked at him from under her eyelashes. He opened his eyes – dark and handsome and full of reassurance – and, seeing her looking at him, he winked. This small yet intimate connection was so uncharacteristic of her husband that it made Lizzie blush and she threw an embarrassed glance at the other occupant in the carriage. The woman was staring at her, the knitting temporarily halted. Something about her expression made Lizzie shift uncomfortably in her seat before she turned her head away and looked out of the window again. The clicking of the woman's knitting needles started up again.

Lizzie had the impression that she had been silently judged.

Chapter Twenty-six

"God's sake," muttered Eunice as she heard the front door bang and unsteady leaden footsteps tramp up the stairs to the room next door. Her eyes half closed, she squinted at the clock on the bedside table. *Twenty after midnight.* As if on cue, the baby started to whimper in his basket next to her bed. This soon turned into a grizzle, which she knew would become a full-blown wail if she didn't pick him up and feed him. As she rarely undressed properly these days, due to a morbid fear of being caught in an air raid in her night attire, she struggled to undo her layers of clothing to enable her to put the child to her breast. When he latched greedily onto her nipple, she winced. She knew she wouldn't be able to get back to sleep afterwards; that she would toss and turn until daylight unless she took her sedative.

Next morning the sound of her child's frustrated crying broke into her pleasurable fugue. Downstairs she could hear the faint strains of music and Peggy singing along. Eunice sighed. *Blasted gramophone.* It was still a novelty, she supposed, but it must have woken the baby up. Eunice got out of bed, picked William up and trudged down the stairs, the insistent beat of the music marking each step. She went into the front parlour and took hold of the gramophone arm. In her vexation, she scraped the needle across the surface of the shellac record. A dull silence descended on the room.

"Ooh, someone got out of bed the wrong side this morning."

Peggy's cheery voice grated. Eunice turned to face her. *There she stands, Miss Happy as Larry.* She shoved William at her lodger's outstretched arms and went into the kitchen.

"You know when you come in really late?" Eunice picked up the teapot, realised from its weight that it was empty, harrumphed loudly and put it back down.

"Hmm? What's that?" Peggy had followed Eunice into the kitchen and was now bouncing the mesmerised infant up and down on her lap while she flashed her eyes open then shut at him.

"You always wake him up," Eunice snapped.

Peggy tickled the child under the chin, which made him pedal his pudgy little legs with excitement.

"It's just that it takes me ages to get him back off again."

"This little piggy went to market," Peggy assumed a silly voice and made a face as she tweaked the child's big toe, "and this little piggy stayed at home."

Eunice couldn't rein in her exasperation. "Then it's difficult to get through the day."

Peggy looked at her; two frown lines appeared between her eyebrows.

"The doctor gave you something for that." She nodded at the kitchen cupboard. "You're not regretting having this little 'un, are you?"

Eunice closed her eyes and rubbed her temples in little circles.

"'Course I'm not. It's my last chance, I expect, so don't think I'm not grateful, Peggy. I am. 'Course I am. But, what if Jack...?"

Her companion put up a hand to silence her.

"We're not going to talk about that again, are we? We agreed. It's for the best all round."

"And if..." Eunice tailed off as she looked at Peggy's disapproving expression. "It's just I couldn't go through..."

"Oooh! You're an absolute peach, aren't you." Peggy picked up the boy and jiggled him from side to side. "I could just eat you up. Yes, I could!" She stopped and looked at Eunice. "Listen, I'm not on for a couple of hours. Go back to bed. Get some beauty sleep and I'll take his nibs out in his carriage. Slap on some of that new Pond's cold cream I bought while you're at it."

Eunice caught the tone: *you look like you need it.*

"For God's sake, Peggy. I don't care what I look like!" Eunice suddenly exploded. *And if you hadn't put that bloody gramophone on, I'd still be asleep.* She collapsed onto a kitchen chair and closed her eyes.

"Well perhaps you ought to."

Eunice didn't move or say anything.

"What's your Jack going to think when he gets back?" Peggy fussed the baby into his carriage. "You owe it to him not to let yourself go – keep yourself nice."

Eunice opened her eyes and looked at William in his carriage. Peggy seemed to relent and offered to make some tea when she got back after her afternoon shift.

"Let's have Scotch salmon, asparagus and fried potatoes with fresh white bread."

"Ha, ha."

In truth, Eunice struggled to think as far ahead as the next meal, particularly since she had to force herself to be interested in food these days. Occasionally she had tried out the suggestions from a cookery lecture she had once attended, courtesy of the munitions works, or she used to cut recipes out of newspapers and magazines, but she couldn't summon the interest anymore, so usually made do with cobbling together something from whatever she had to hand.

"I'll eat anything as long as there's no bean fritters or barley rissoles involved. Here." Peggy took the Veronal bottle down from the kitchen cupboard. "Dose yourself up a bit."

Eunice accepted the bottle, put it on the table in front of her, and waved 'Bye, bye' to the boy, glad of a bit of peace and quiet. Her hands trembled as she unscrewed the top from the little medicine bottle. *Just half a measure to tide me over*, she told herself. She stretched her arms out in front of her on the table top and looked at her wedding ring. She touched the plain gold band and moved it around easily – she'd almost lost it down the sink last week – before she folded her arms and laid her head on top of them. Eventually she closed her eyes and waited for the welcome blanket of oblivion.

Somewhere between wakefulness and sleep, visions of happier times came to her. Eunice saw a younger Jack in the boxing ring, his body the subject of lascivious glances from all the girls who crowded round and cheered when he gave his opponent his deadly right hand treatment. As she watched him, she felt a decided lightness in her chest. At other times she observed him shyly from afar as he joked and shadow boxed with the kids in the street: their hero showing them a few feints and jabs.

She was in the crowd outside Shurliker's garment factory when he'd turned up, stood on a chair and stridently argued the case for joining the clothing workers' strike, encouraging them all to believe they deserved better pay and conditions. She saw the passion and fervour in his eyes, and how the small crowd of workers responded to him. When the other girls found out she was his sweetheart, at first she resented the loss of the inner pleasure that keeping the secret had given her, but soon found compensation in talking about him openly at every opportunity. Eunice remembered the first time he asked her to dance, their bodies pressed close, her heart thumping in her chest, hoping he'd offer to walk her home at the end, and then praying he'd kiss her when he did; his proposal, in front of a crowd after winning a fight, down on one knee. How her pulse raced! She was giddy with love for him.

Then four lost babies: Ada and Freddy, barely formed but given names; Mary and Jimmy, absolutely perfect yet lying dead in Jack's arms; his consoling embrace after each one. At last Alfie, and Jack's wide smile as he hoisted the baby up in the air, all their hopes and dreams invested in him. Jack's refusal to join the rush to the Colours. Eunice shrugging him off when he touched her…

An infant's piercing cries, followed by an echoing thud, partly roused her from her stupor. Peggy always managed to bang the front door flat against the hall wall in her attempts at getting the baby carriage inside the house. *That'll be another mark to clean off.*

"Sshh! Here's your ma now." Peggy was trying to mollify the hungry boy. "Sorry, Eunice. Bumped into Pearl Jacobsen, you know how she gossips. Got to fly. I'm going to be late for my shift. Don't wait up."

Eunice stood up shakily and went to feed her son. She didn't think she could be bothered with making any breakfast for herself, even though it was now past one o'clock.

What did it matter?

Chapter Twenty-seven

Lizzie stood outside the terraced house. Decayed plants hung in desiccated tangles from the single window box. Further up the street a woman swept the road in front of her house, casting occasional furtive glances at her. Lizzie rocked on the balls of her feet, and eventually she raised her hand and knocked on the door.

She thought back to her shared history with Peggy and the early camaraderie of the munitions. She missed it. Her new life was comfortable, but dull. Her husband coming home from work was the highlight of her day, and managing a household of two servants was hardly time-consuming. There was only so much embroidery and fancy needlework a sane person could tolerate, Lizzie felt. Ladies' magazines became repetitive and boring if you read enough of them, and she was convinced she had read every novel in Edmund's modest library. She had made no new friends because she hardly went anywhere or met anyone. It was time to mend fences.

The door opened. Lizzie found she was pleased to see a familiar face, but tried not to stare at the woman's soiled and grubby apron.

"Well, I never," Eunice Wilson said, and at once began to wipe her hands on her apron, leaving red streaks across it. "Lizzie Fenwick."

"Hello, Eunice."

"Didn't expect to see you round here again. Peggy's at work. Come in and wait, if you like. I'm skinning a rabbit," she indicated her apron, "but I'll put the kettle on."

Lizzie, keen to connect with someone – anyone – from her old life, followed Eunice inside.

In the kitchen the carcass of a rabbit lay beside the sink, half-skinned, its separated feet and head lying in a tiny pool of coagulating blood. Lizzie guessed it hadn't come from a butcher's. She averted her eyes.

"Tea?" Eunice turned on the gas hob and opened a box of matches. She gave an irritated "Tut!" when the only match left in the box failed to light as she struck it. "Another dud." She threw the empty box aside and began to search in a drawer for another one.

Lizzie smelled a faint hint of gas. "Eunice, do you think you should turn the gas off for a minute? It's ticking off your allowance."

"What? Oh." Eunice sounded annoyed with herself as she eventually lit the gas and it burst into flames like a small explosion. She put the kettle on to boil and busied herself getting cups and saucers down from a cupboard. Only the hissing gas jets under the kettle interrupted the silence.

"I heard you got married to Mr Fawcett," Eunice said over her shoulder. "Congratulations. Gadding about to fancy places and all that now, I expect."

Lizzie took this as an invitation to chatter on about her honeymoon at the Metropole in Brighton, how she had heard Bizet's *Carmen* at a promenade concert at Queen's Hall and been to see the new Albert de Courville musical comedy at the Apollo.

"My husband's a PoW." Eunice strained the tea leaves and reused them.

"Oh." Lizzie at once felt guilty. "Well that must be a relief, and with all this talk of peace I suppose he might be home soon."

"There'll be no peace until Germany admits defeat – until they're forced to agree that we've smashed them." Eunice plonked the teapot down on the table between them and Lizzie watched her eyes blaze. "Otherwise Alfie…and everything we've suffered will have been for nothing."

It seemed as if Eunice was about to cry and she turned away to retrieve the teacups and saucers. Lizzie saw how the woman wore her heartache and misery for her lost child like a close-fitting garment. Since her marriage, Lizzie had made a promise to herself that she would try not to dwell on her own personal loss. It only left her physically wasted and emotionally spent, but her heart went out to Eunice.

"I send Jack food parcels now and again." Eunice sat down opposite Lizzie, her equilibrium regained. "But it's not easy with rationing. At least the Red Cross sends regular parcels out. I help out now and again, collecting with the tins. But we're always short of volunteers and funding." She allowed her gaze to linger on her visitor's smart clothes.

"I don't seem to have any proper order in my life without a job these days," Lizzie said, without irony. "Edmund suggested I might try volunteer work."

It was, she knew, a way of supporting the war effort, but he suggested it might also be a useful way to gain introductions to other women in her position. However, she associated charity work with the likes of Charlotte Dearden, and it didn't appeal.

"I'm sure the Red Cross would be pleased for another pair of willing hands. Tea should be brewed. No sugar left, I'm afraid." Her companion nodded at the teapot. "You can be mother."

At once Lizzie felt the tears prick her eyelids: despite her best intentions, those last four words almost undid her. Blinking hard she focused instead on the task of pouring the tea.

"I wish Peggy would make a good match," Eunice said. "Or any match, come to that. She might have a long wait for Mr Right after the war."

Lizzie blew on her tea, which was too hot to drink yet, and remembered how Peggy used to flit from one romance, one soldier, to the next. Lizzie was never sure whether it was by choice or because the war claimed them or because they let her down.

"She'll get left on the shelf."

The cardinal sin.

Eunice placed her cup down on its saucer. "I think she's afraid. It takes courage to love someone." She pushed a lock of stray hair behind her ear and her eyes misted over. The action drew Lizzie's attention to Eunice's tangled bird's nest of hair, barely held by loose pins applied without too much care. "Then one day you close your heart and mind to the person you love over some foolish thing, and before you know it," Eunice drew a tiny droplet of blood as she picked, absent-mindedly, at her cuticle, "that love flows away."

Lizzie had the impression Eunice was talking about her own marriage and that she had just laid her soul bare. Lizzie didn't know how to reply and was quite relieved when Eunice returned to the rabbit. An awkward silence fell on the room again. Lizzie watched with a gruesome fascination as Eunice pulled off the rest of the rabbit's skin, like pulling a stocking from an anaemic leg.

"What's Peg doing these days?"

"Oh, she couldn't get any more munitions work. The Welfare Supervisor discharged her without a Leaving Certificate, you see, and no other employer would take her on and risk a fine at that time. She's a barmaid at the pub on the corner."

Lizzie remembered walking past it; she now wished Eunice had directed her there earlier. She watched the woman pick up a knife and take hold of the rabbit to make a neat cross-like incision in the animal's belly.

"It was good of you to take her in."

"Ever since we worked alongside each other in the sweat shop I've tried to look out for her, what with her being a foundling an' all." Eunice tugged out the rabbit's innards and carefully put aside the liver to use later.

"A foundling?" Lizzie hadn't known this.

"Abandoned by her mother on the steps of the workhouse."

A terrible vision rose in front of Lizzie of an abandoned infant left to its fate at the hands of a charitable institution. In her head she thought she could hear a baby's low keening. She stared at the weak brown tea in her cup until the clatter of a knife being banged onto a surface made her look up. Eunice let out a heavy sigh and cleaned her hands, said she'd be back in a minute and hurried out of the room.

Puzzled, Lizzie looked around the kitchen, her gaze avoiding the rabbit carcass. Her eyes settled on the wooden clothes horse in the corner and saw it was adorned with tiny baby clothes. She hadn't noticed these when she came in. *Of course. Eunice has had her baby.* She leaned over and picked up a pair of blue knitted booties, their little laces made from ribbon and tied over the rail to dry, and ran her hand over the soft wool. A sob caught in her throat. *You promised not to do this*, she admonished herself. *You promised.* Her own child would be more than five months old now. She thought how lucky Eunice was.

Worried that more than ten minutes had gone by, Lizzie opened the door to the front parlour in search of her host to find Eunice slumped on the settee, her eyes closed and head thrown back against the antimacassar, with a child at her breast. A sudden wave of sadness and envy washed over Lizzie at this intimate scene of mother and baby.

Eunice's eyelids snapped open and she jerked her head up. "Oh. You gave me such a fright!" She disengaged the baby from her breast and covered herself up. "Must have dozed off, I expect."

"Boy or girl?"

Lizzie moved compulsively towards the infant, risking stirring up her own longing, forced to step over piles of baby clothes and unironed squares of grey cloth which littered the floor, but Eunice put the child into his perambulator and stood in front of it like a guard.

"Boy. William."

Stranded in the middle of the room, Lizzie said, "A King's name," and then the first pleasantry that came into her head next: "You've got it nice here."

"Thanks for saying so, but it's hardly a palace – it's a struggle to keep on top of it."

Self-consciously, Eunice moved away from the baby carriage and began to pick up a handful of scattered toys from the floor. Lizzie couldn't help a glance towards the child. A loud knock at the front door made Eunice freeze.

"Shall I see who it is?" Lizzie asked.

"Please."

Lizzie returned and said it was a Mr Sowerby come for the weekly rent.

Eunice seemed relieved. "Now where's my purse?" She cast a furtive look at the baby carriage and then at Lizzie before she left the room.

Lizzie noticed a pawnbroker's ticket had fallen onto the floor. She picked it up and popped it back into Eunice's bag, resisting the strong temptation to read it. Raised voices in the hall made her snatch a look at the parlour room door before she let her gaze wander over towards the perambulator once again.

Where's the harm? Just a quick peek.

Lizzie saw the infant's milky-white skin and wide, inquisitive blue eyes. She noticed a flushed red patch on his left cheek, and instinctively put the back of her finger on it and rubbed gently in little circular motions.

"Ooh, those nasty toosie pegs trying to come through, are they?" she crooned.

She knew she shouldn't, but she lifted him up into her arms and held him gingerly as if he was the most precious thing in the world to her. He gurgled with pleasure, his alert eyes never moving from her face. She smiled down at him. *Oh, how right this feels.* She put her finger out and he grabbed hold of it: at his touch, she thought her heart would break. She gently moved her finger up and down, watching a tiny smile start at the corner of his lips then move across his whole mouth. Instantly she had an unbearable yearning for her own child, and a dull leaden ache settled on her heart.

Lizzie walked around the room with the child still cradled in her arms until her eyes settled on the line of photographs on the mantelpiece. She stopped dead.

"Are you all right?" Eunice asked as she came back. "You're as white as a sheet! I say..."

She caught hold of William as Lizzie planted him into her arms, pushed past her and slammed the front door behind her.

Chapter Twenty-eight

Lizzie's face was a mask of concentration. "A, s, d, f," she said through gritted teeth and thumped the typewriter keys one after the other "a, s, d, f," as she worked away at the rows of practice exercises in the Pitman instruction booklet. In the empty hope the servants wouldn't hear her efforts, she had locked herself away in Edmund's sister's old bedroom these past several days, determined to master the Corona portable typewriter she had bought in Whitechapel High Street five days ago. To ensure she didn't have to ask Edmund's permission, she had cashed in two of her War Bonds so she could afford its £13 0s 0d price tag. On its seller's recommendation, Lizzie also sent off for a correspondence course in shorthand and typing: anything to keep her mind occupied.

She stopped typing and looked at the undersides of her fingers. That was definitely the start of a blister on her left index finger. She needed a lighter touch. She glanced up and caught the image of herself, with her little Corona in front of her, reflected in the dresser mirror. Just as she was deciding whether she looked business-like, the image of a man in a khaki uniform with a neat moustache, blue-grey eyes, black wavy hair and a lop-sided smile appeared behind her in the mirror. Her head shot round, a flurry of butterflies in her stomach.

"Mrs Fawcett?" Elsie's voice brought her back to normality. She saw the maid glance at the typewriter. "Sorry to disturb you,

M'm, but there's a Miss Wood downstairs asking for you. Are you at home?"

Flustered, Lizzie asked Elsie to put her visitor in the morning room and to bring some tea; she'd be down presently. She tried to marshal her thoughts while she smoothed her skirt and blouse and patted her hair into shape, making sure to put the typewriter away in the bottom of the wardrobe before she walked calmly down the stairs to greet her old friend from her munitions days.

Peggy stood in front of one of the twelve paned sash windows, a cup of tea in her hand, her back to the garden outside. "You definitely played your cards right."

Lizzie didn't say that little in this house was to her taste, or of her choosing. Her visitor gave a quick nod over her shoulder at the neatly planted rows of vegetables in the garden. "Nice war patch."

"Yes. Pity about the flowers, but the vegetables come in handy."

Peggy walked over to the mantelpiece, picked up a small statue and looked at the maker's mark on the bottom. Lizzie smiled to herself: her friend hadn't changed.

"I'm glad we're on speaking terms again."

"I came because Eunice asked me to give you this." Peggy handed over a piece of paper and emptied her teacup with one noisy slurp.

Disappointed at her friend's lack of reciprocity, Lizzie looked at Eunice's neat hand. *Miss Preston, British PoW Food Parcels and Clothing Fund, Packing Dept., 4 Thurloe Place, SW7.* She felt her chest tighten.

Recovering herself, Lizzie made light of it. "Couldn't she just have posted it?" She folded the note and put it in her skirt pocket and indicated the teapot. "Help yourself to another."

Lizzie watched Peggy pick up a biscuit with one hand and pour another cup of tea with the other. As she nibbled on the biscuit, she seemed to relent.

"All right. I came 'cos Eunice told me about your funny turn." She sat down opposite Lizzie. "Said you looked like you'd seen a ghost. I got worried."

Lizzie knew that Peggy would also not have been able to resist seeing what kind of house she lived in, but she didn't mind; she felt it was just as if they'd seen each other yesterday, and she realised how badly she had missed her old friend's easy camaraderie – and even her capricious nature.

"What's it like, then, being a lady of leisure?"

"A bit dull, to be quite honest."

There was a moment's silence before they both began to laugh, although Peggy's expression told Lizzie that she didn't believe a word of it.

"So, what was that all about at Eunice's?"

"Oh, that." Lizzie hesitated. She wasn't entirely sure she was ready to unburden herself.

Peggy leaned towards her, eyes bright with interest.

"The picture on the mantelpiece. Of the man in uniform."

"Jack. Her husband."

"I assumed that's who it was."

"What of it?"

"It upset me." Lizzie paused. "It reminded me of a soldier I knew."

Peggy's posture and face invited a confidence.

"Oh, I did what the rest of you did, that's all. I put a note in a box of shells…and I got a reply. We wrote a few letters to each other." She didn't know why she had kept it a secret; all the other girls passed their letters around and boasted of the many Tommy Atkins they wrote to. "Then I met him, Harry Slater, one weekend when he got leave."

"Aha! I knew you were too good to be true." Peggy nodded at Lizzie's hand. "You'll break that expensive china cup if you keep on stirring it at that rate."

"What? Oh."

"Mind you, I'm a bit miffed you never let on. What are friends for if you can't share stuff like that? So, what was he like, then, this here Harry Slater?"

Typical Peg, eager for all the salacious details.

Peggy laughed suddenly. "Look at your face! My, oh my, Lizzie Fenwick." She made a show of searching behind her as if she'd lost something.

"What are you looking for?"

"Your halo. It must've fallen off."

"He was killed almost as soon as he went back."

Peggy sat still, her teasing having fallen flat, and rearranged her expression. "Oh, you poor lamb."

Lizzie rubbed the rim of her cup with her finger. "There's something else."

Peggy leaned towards her and placed a sympathetic hand on her knee. "Three guineas to get rid? You did the right thing, else you wouldn't have this nice life you've got now."

Lizzie was only partially shocked that Peggy had anticipated what she was about to confess. "I had the baby, but he was taken away." Lizzie felt her lower lip tremble. "I need a cigarette. Have you got any?"

Peggy obliged, and Lizzie took a long drag on the cigarette before blowing out a coil of smoke to veil her distress.

"In my experience a knitting needle and a quart of gin is a better option by far than growing up in an institution."

Even as she remembered Eunice's revelation about Peggy's background in a charitable institution, Lizzie couldn't help saying, "Please don't say that. I can't bear to think of it."

She felt the sofa sag as Peggy sat down beside her and put an arm around her. The pair sat in silence.

"Have to ask," said Peggy eventually, "how did you manage to pull the wool over Fawcett's eyes?"

"I didn't. He let me stay here until I had the baby."

Peggy leaned away from Lizzie and looked at her, as if appraising an unknown yet suddenly interesting object. "Soiled goods, and he still married you?" She let out a long, low whistle. "I might have to revise my opinion of old Fawcett then."

"Don't call him that. He's not old."

"Saves you the aggravation of keeping up the pretence, I suppose, an' the fear he'd find out." Peggy stared at her. "So, a convenient marriage. Do you love him?"

Lizzie leaned forwards and stubbed out her cigarette in the ashtray with short, sharp movements. "I'm really very, very fond of him."

A crafty smile spread across Peggy's lips. "'Very fond'. Hmm."

Lizzie felt the flush move up her neck. "I loved Harry Slater. I can't just forget that – flick a switch, and it's all transferred to another man in exactly the same measure. And there's something..."

"Lor', is that the time?" Her visitor suddenly leapt up. "If that clock's right, I'm late for my shift."

"Peggy..."

"Sorry." She was at the door. "Don't be a stranger, now. And remember, there's nothing to be gained from being soppy over this Harry Slater. He's nothing more than a ghost. Forget him."

But, Lizzie wanted to say, he's not a ghost and I can't forget him, because the man to whom I willingly gave my virginity, and my heart – the man who fathered my child – is in the photograph on Eunice Wilson's mantelpiece.

Chapter Twenty-nine

Over breakfast Lizzie casually mentioned to Edmund that she was going to help out at the Red Cross, packing parcels to send to British prisoners of war.

"Very admirable, my darling," he replied, but wondered aloud whether she wouldn't find the trip to SW7 five days a week rather tiresome on a full-time basis.

She wanted to do something useful for the war effort, she told him. It would give her some purpose. Didn't he support that? He apologised, kissed her on the top of her head and wished her luck with it.

On the underground, moving towards her destination, a little kernel of excitement grew inside Lizzie. She had gone to have a look around a week ago, and had been amazed at the interior size of the rambling Red Cross building at Thurloe Place, particularly its cavernous basement piled high with vast amounts of goods destined for PoW camps. A woman volunteer had showed her round. She would have to learn to distinguish between officers' parcels and those of ordinary soldiers and learn the rotation cycle of standard parcels very quickly because of the sheer volume of parcels they handled.

"Each prisoner needs to be sent parcel A, B, C or D in strict rotation," her guide explained. "You also send each newly captured prisoner a special pack with a complete change of clothing as soon as his address is known, and this must be renewed every six months."

"And what are these used for?" Lizzie asked as she pointed at stacks and stacks of postcards piled on a desk.

"A postcard has to be put in with each pack for the prisoner to sign and send back to indicate he has received the parcel," her guide informed her. "Sometimes they attach a little thank you note as well."

Lizzie picked one up.

"Mrs Fawcett?"

"Sorry, what? I was just imagining what it must be like to get a reply. Make personal contact."

"I always think that's what makes this job so worthwhile."

"Yes, I should think so."

Her guide had laughed. "Well, if you're that keen, you can 'adopt' a prisoner through our Adopter's Bureau if you like. You know, take a personal interest in one particular chap and keep his spirits up, that sort of thing. Now, what do you think? Feel like joining us?"

Lizzie packed her first parcel in a stout cardboard case, filled round the food items with paper shavings and bound it securely with string.

"Oh, how does this contraption work?" she exclaimed, exasperated as she tried and failed to make the addressograph print off the special Red Cross label she required to address the parcel.

"There's a knack to it. You'll soon get it. Oh dear, I'm rather afraid you've filled out the wrong form too. It needs to be absolutely correct for the records. Here, I'll show you again."

Lizzie had so wanted to make a good first impression.

"Don't worry. It'll become second nature soon."

It was hard and arduous work, reminding Lizzie a little of the munitions in its monotony and routine, and she suffered many painful paper cuts, but back home she laughingly told Edmund they were her 'war wounds'.

As she worked, she chatted with some of the other women and got to know one or two of them. She realised most of them were married to Army or Navy officers, and that they had never had a paid job.

"They're absolutely beastly to our chaps, and it's awfully hard in these places because I'm rather afraid the German camp guards hate the British the most, more than the French or the Russians," said Emma Raythorne, a well-spoken and carefully groomed young woman, whose husband was a prisoner of war and who was keen to share her superior knowledge. "Most of the ranks are sent out to work away from the camps to replace all the German men who are fighting."

Lizzie didn't think that sounded too bad.

"Unless, of course, you get sent to the salt mines," Emma said. "I've heard Soltau is absolutely ghastly. The thought of it." She gave a mock-shudder. "The commissioned officers don't get sent out to work, of course, so my husband Gerald won't...ouch!" she cried. "Another beastly paper cut. Sometimes I regret not learning to type." She sucked her injured finger. "Then I could get a jolly easy number over in the secretarial department." She seemed to find this amusing for some reason and laughed.

At home at the end of her first week, over a lunch of mutton chops and fried potatoes, Lizzie relayed the gist of her conversations to Edmund. He was pleased that she was so animated and her work had given her some purpose, but he took only a mild interest in how she actually spent her volunteer days until she told him the number of British prisoners of war held in German camps.

"Forty-nine thousand? Good God, I had no idea they had so many of our men."

"The Red Cross also runs the Adopter's Bureau," she said, her voice casual. "Individual benefactors can 'adopt' named prisoners, so as well as extra food parcels they can get other privileges, such as money orders. You need tokens to exchange for basic items in the camps, but to buy the tokens prisoners need money."

Edmund nodded, but made no comment and carried on with his lunch. She continued, fully aware that her husband's silence meant he knew she was building up to something.

"I bumped into Eunice Wilson the other day." She flashed him a look. "Remember, she used to work at the munitions?"

"Wilson? I recognise the name, but I can't place the woman herself."

"She lost her son in the school bombing of Upper North Street."

"Ah. Dreadful business."

"She told me her husband's a PoW."

He paused, a forkful of mutton between his plate and his mouth. "One of the unfortunate forty-nine thousand." He carried on eating.

"Well, I was thinking it might be a nice gesture if we adopted him through the scheme." She reached out and placed her hand on his arm. She saw him tilt his head slightly to the left, and when the little crease appeared between his brows, she knew he was giving the matter serious consideration.

Finally, he said, "So, Mrs Wilson's husband is about to become your pet project, is he? Very well. If it pleases you. It seems this war will end soon, by all accounts, so I foresee it will be a short-lived project."

"Oh, thank you, Edmund." She squeezed his arm and surprised him by leaning right over towards him and kissing him full on the mouth. She saw the mix of astonishment and pleasure on his face.

"I only hope Mrs Wilson appreciates it when you tell her what you're doing on her husband's behalf."

She didn't think she need bother telling Eunice.

"But please don't feel the need to try to best the other adopters' efforts by sending him anything of quality, or appropriating one of my favourite suits for your war prisoner's parcel." He smiled.

She knew his tone was partly a mild admonishment and partly a joke, so she nodded and assumed a mock-grave expression, but she couldn't conceal the tiny grin of satisfaction at the edge of her mouth.

"I'll instruct Mrs Ryder at once."

She had got her way and she had told no lies.

Chapter Thirty

Lizzie looked at the table in the hall where that day's post lay. On top of the pile of envelopes she saw the card with the unusual postmark. She snatched it up. Her hand trembled as she turned it over.

Soltau, Hamburg, Germany
30 September 1918

Dear Mrs Fawcett (Kind Adopter)
Thank you for your welcome parcel and money order. I am most grateful.
Yours sincerely,
L Cpl J. Wilson

Short and to the point. She felt a small stab of disappointment. But really, what else had she expected him to say? To all intents and purposes she was a stranger to him; just another charitable do-gooder who had sent him some food and money. He was 'most grateful'. No more than that. And anyway, she had put a note in with the food parcel because she wanted a written reply: the handwriting was more important than the content.

In her bedroom, from the top of the wardrobe Lizzie yanked down her battered old brown suitcase. She had no idea how it came to be here; someone must have gone to her lodgings to retrieve it along with her other possessions, but she had never thought to ask about it. She dumped the case down onto the bedcover, not caring that it rucked the cover up, and took out the thin bundle of letters and cards with French and Belgian postmarks on them. Lizzie looked at the words from Harry Slater and she was immediately transported back to the Buckingham Hotel and the electric shock of his naked body against hers; his sweet words of love and encouragement swirling in her head. She sighed and closed off the memory. She held her postcard from Jack Wilson next to the letter from Harry Slater and compared the sloping handwriting.

Of course, immediately after her shocking discovery at Eunice's, Lizzie had cursed and scorned Jack Wilson for his deceit. Whenever she found herself alone, she'd pace around the room and talk to herself like a madwoman, trying to convince herself how much she despised and hated the man who had deceived her. This man had taken her greatest treasure. Why, he wasn't even free to love her properly, because he already had a wife. She couldn't bear to think about Eunice. He had betrayed her too, of course, which simply made it even more hurtful. Then she thought about their son. By his actions, Jack Wilson had denied her child the chance of a father, and also her the chance of being a mother.

Gradually, however, Lizzie had started to wonder about the identity of Harry Slater, and whether you could claim to have loved someone if they were not who you thought they were. Who was Harry Slater? Had her correspondent and lover been Jack Wilson all along, and he had merely used this other man's name? Or was Harry Slater himself actually her correspondent, and Jack an imposter who had turned up at the Corner House and opportunistically seduced her? She didn't want to believe any man could be so cruel, but recalling how she had first been exposed to the decidedly un-romantic nature of some of the munitions women's relationships with men, she knew it was a fact of life.

Now, as she looked at the handwriting, she had her answer: Jack Wilson and Harry Slater were one and the same man.

She tapped the edge of the postcard against her lips. Perhaps he had begun their correspondence as she had: as a bit of light-hearted fun amid the horrors of the war, but by the time they met, sentiments had already been expressed between them which could not be unsaid or unfelt. It was there in their exchange of glances, his evident joy in her company, his inviting lop-sided smile, his touch on her skin, the press of his warm lips on hers and in his last words, thick with longing and regret: *I only wish I could stay.* These things clung to her memory, and in spite of herself Lizzie found she could not prevent a tingle of creeping joy whenever she left off her harsh condemnations and contemplated the inescapable fact of his existence. He was not dead, but very much alive.

Lizzie sat down on the bed. She should be satisfied; she had her answer. There was now no need to continue the correspondence via the food parcels. No, she would get on with being a dutiful wife to a husband who was honourable and upright, and who loved her.

In keeping with these intentions, she felt she should show the postcard to Edmund, who glanced at the message and said that Lance Corporal Jack Wilson showed just the right amount of formality and gratitude for his wife's efforts. He handed the card back to her.

"Rather bad luck that he's in one of the worst camps."

"What?" She hadn't paid attention to the actual postal address when she stuck the label on his food parcels, nor had she noticed the location on the postcard. All her thoughts had been on her intended goal.

"He'll need more than a few food parcels to…Lizzie? Are you all right, my love?" Edmund moved towards her when he noticed the colour had drained from her face.

"Yes. Yes," she replied through numb lips as she feebly swatted him away.

Later, she took out her collection of letters and postcards, reread every one and gradually persuaded herself that she should continue with putting notes in his food parcels. After all, she could hide behind her married name, and it gave her a little thrill to think that her duplicity mirrored his own.

One afternoon, Emma Raythorne noticed Lizzie wincing as she fastened up parcels, forcing her to admit she had been teaching herself shorthand and typing and that her fingers were suffering as a result.

"Goodness, why on earth have you been doing that?" The cut-glass accent oozed condescension.

Lizzie was confused. "Why, to get a job in the secretarial section. You said yourself it was a jolly easy number."

"But you're married." It was said as if that was that. Lizzie realised the woman had not been serious when she had bemoaned her lack of shorthand and typing skills.

"Being married doesn't mean I can't learn how to do new things."

"Won't you feel rather bad depriving the poor unfortunate spinsters of an income? And besides, Miss Davenport's a slave driver and a frightful old dragon."

Lizzie felt she had gone down in her new acquaintance's estimation.

"However, I do happen to know that her permanent typewriters are dropping like flies because of this new wave of influenza, so you might give it a go if you like."

Lizzie looked at the pile of work left on her desk while she had been on her tea break.

"Oh-oh," warned the fresh-faced girl who sat next to her and was typing at a furious pace. "The lisping serpent's on the warpath."

186

Already from the top copy, Lizzie could see the myriad errors ringed in Miss Davenport's angry red pen and her shoulders sagged. Perhaps she had been too ambitious; her home-taught typing skills were not up to it. It was clear that the typing pool supervisor would never have taken Lizzie on had she not been so desperate for staff.

"Don't worry, her hiss is worse than her bite." Her colleague laughed. "You'll thank her for her high standards, I promise you. It'll help you get a jolly good placement after the war."

Lizzie began on her long list of corrections.

She didn't confess her trials to Edmund. Instead, Lizzie told him she was doing well in her new role. He said he was pleased she was out of what he obviously considered to be no better than a factory packing department, but his enthusiasm seemed lukewarm at best.

"You encouraged me," she said, pursing her lips in a petulant fashion.

"In the interests of supporting the war effort, of course I did," he countered. "But I wonder whether all this effort you're putting into your shorthand and typing won't be rather wasted after the war."

She didn't want to think about that.

"And Mrs Ryder will have her own way in managing the household if you don't pay sufficient attention to domestic matters." He looked stern, before smiling and saying, "And I'd much rather take my orders from you, my darling."

She knew he was being facetious, but she understood instinctively that he was concerned where her new skills might lead her.

Lizzie swiped the foreign postcard up from the hall table, unaware of the presence of Elsie, who watched her mistress almost break into a run to get into the morning room to read it.

Dear Mrs Fawcett,
Your continued kindness cheers this terrible life of
grinding frustration, where it is not possible to
contribute anything worthwhile. I am sorry to say
that your last parcel was ripped open and one or two
items were taken. I think we're not the only desperate
ones here. You can have no idea how welcome they
are.

And your notes.
With grateful thanks.
My best wishes,
L Cpl Jack Wilson

The 'And your notes' was clearly an afterthought. She tried to interpret this, but gave up. Instead, she skipped downstairs to rifle the kitchen cupboards for little niceties to include in her next food parcel.

At the kitchen door, Lizzie heard Elsie mention her name. She froze.

"I'm sure I dunno what's up with Mrs Fawcett. Nearly knocked me over just now to get to the post. And only last week she gave me a day off without me asking for it, then she nearly took my head off the next day for not clearing a tray away quick enough." Lizzie heard the maid mimic her voice. "'I swear the food on this tray has grown a coat, Elsie, the length of time you've left it here'."

"Cares more about prisoners of war than she does about her own husband, that one."

Lizzie's face reddened and a wave of guilt washed over her.

*

Mid-morning on 11 November 1918, the other typists stopped their work, their fingers poised above their keyboards, and looked at each other. Lizzie got up and threw open a window and peered out into the rain-sodden street to see what the sudden commotion was.

"What's happening?"

A gaggle of women crowded behind her, eager with anticipation.

"Steady on, I'm getting wet here!"

Hundreds of people began to emerge from their offices and premises. Someone shouted something, and the street erupted into a frenzy of cheering and jubilation.

"They've done it!" cried Lizzie. "The war's over!"

A tumultuous cheer went up behind her.

"No more fighting?"

"I can hardly believe it."

Immediately, shrill voices began to echo around the room.

"Four years, now it's all over. How marvellous!"

"Can it really be the end?"

Suddenly all the women began to hug each other, some crying with joy and others with remembered sorrow for a lost loved one. Lizzie and another girl linked arms and danced round and round until they staggered against a desk, dizzy from their exertions. The pair of them laughed hysterically.

The resonant, jubilant peal of church bells rang out above the din, and the sound of distant cannon fire boomed in through the open windows. As soon as one of the women decided to go outside, they all ran out after her. Lizzie hurried into the street to be greeted by a surging crowd, shrieking with joy and waving flags, no one caring about the drizzle. *It had been like this at the start of the war too*, she thought, *yet so much has happened in between.*

Somewhere the faint strains of a military band came floating above the mêlée. Out of the corner of her eye, Lizzie noticed a woman whose figure was young, but whose face was old, standing back from the crowd, an umbrella over her head, swathed in mourning black like a rebuke to show she hadn't forgotten the dead of this war.

Lizzie turned her gaze away and was glad to be swept along by the crowd. She joined in with the patriotic songs, started up conversations with unknown people and even allowed herself to be kissed by a complete stranger. Later she tripped gaily home, intoxicated with a sense of euphoria, and wondered how long it would be before the prisoners of war came back home.

1919

Chapter Thirty-one

Eunice bent down and picked up the official looking postcard from the hall floor. It informed her that Jack Wilson had arrived back in Britain three days ago on 3 January, and was at the Prisoner of War Reception Camp in Ripon, Yorkshire. The relief which flooded her body was spoiled only by a little kernel of anxiety in the pit of her stomach. Nevertheless, she smiled as she walked off down the hallway, still looking at the card, only to turn around to see who was letting themselves in through her front door.

She was quite unprepared to see her husband standing there.

"Jack!"

Eunice moved towards him and embraced him, wincing at the feel of his bones through his clothing. She smelled the alcohol on his breath and guessed he'd stopped off at the King's Arms on the way home, but was unaware that he'd needed a few pints of Burton's just to give himself enough Dutch courage to walk the seventy-five yards to his own house.

"Thank heavens."

Since the war ended and the first reports began to flood in about the release of prisoners from the camps in Germany, she had thought of this moment with an almost painful sense of anticipation. *Will he still find me attractive?* Her reflection in her dresser mirror told her how much she had aged these past two years: the strands of grey hair at her temples and the lines on her face testament to that. Can he love me still? After everything we've been through?

"Hello, Eunice," he mumbled into the side of her hair before he clasped her close to him and lifted her up so her toes barely touched the floor.

She released herself from his grasp and put her hands against the side of his face: she wanted to take him all in, to make sure she wasn't imagining it. However, when she looked at his sunken eyes, his hollow cheeks and the unhealthy grey pallor of his face, scarred and pitted with tiny red weals, she couldn't help an intake of breath.

"No oil painting, eh?" he said sheepishly before he limped off down the hallway.

While he had his back to her, she quickly wiped away a tear with her sleeve. Ever afterwards, she would torment herself with memories of the day of his return, berating herself for not holding on to him; for not saying she was sorry; for not telling him she loved him; for not taking him to bed.

"You look like you need feeding up, Jack Wilson," she said over-brightly, while she fussed round him and made sure she used fresh tea leaves for his cup of tea. He gulped it down and asked if there was any chance of another one. She obliged and offered him a thin slice of bread, a scrape of butter and jam on it.

"We're still on rations," Eunice apologised as she watched him eat, pleased to be fulfilling the role of a wife again.

If she was waiting for him to tell her anything about his experiences, she was disappointed. All he said was he was glad he had run into some American Red Triangle workers who gave him food and clean clothing until he got transport to the Belgian coast and a ferry back home. When he saw her looking at his right leg, heel resting on the floor, knee unbent, he said simply, "Shrapnel" and left it at that.

To fill the awkward silences, Eunice chattered on about rationing and food queues, about how Peggy had been lodging with her until she knew he was coming back, and other domestic matters which had absorbed her during his absence. He nodded now and again when she paused to allow him time to respond, but eventually his failure to take part in the conversation forced a feeling of awkwardness.

The ghost of Alfie, their dead son, hung between them like an invisible yet impenetrable curtain. Jack seemed preoccupied, a vacant expression etched onto his face. She wondered whether he felt the presence of their lost child, as she did, all the time. Should she speak of Alfie? The last time they had seen each other it had been a source of bitter rancour – that and the war. Perhaps she should say nothing; best not to get off on the wrong foot so soon.

She stared at her husband. This wasn't how she had expected it to be.

How had she expected it to be?

She didn't know.

But not like this.

She had heard from some of her neighbours that their husbands' returns had not been unalloyed joy, but Jack didn't even seem relieved to be home, or glad that the war was over. After a little while he got up and excused himself.

When she heard the click of the latch on the back door, she went into the kitchen and stood at the sink, looking out at the yard. He stood in the middle of the small walled space, smoking. He gave her a cursory glance as she watched him through the window. She couldn't shake the memory of the last time he had stood there, eighteen months ago, when they had argued and he had walked out. She could barely imagine what had happened to him in between, but she'd heard the horror stories. It made her feel unworthy.

Eunice watched her husband and noticed how thin he looked; skin and bone, if she was honest. He looked as if he was contemplating something, then he lifted the latch on the back gate, but seemed to think better of it and instead disappeared into the outside lavatory.

She stood at the bottom of the stairs, looking up them. She became aware that Jack had come back into the house and she glanced at him, nodding her head in the direction of the landing above.

"That's our son, hungry as usual after his nap, I expect," she said to explain the low grizzling sound.

She moved over to her husband and automatically took hold of his hand to lead him up the stairs, but on the first step, when she heard his wince of pain, Eunice stopped and turned towards him, unsure whether to continue. His hand slid from hers and gripped the banister instead so he could better pull himself up onto the next stair. On the landing she waited for him before she beckoned him to follow her into Alfie's old bedroom.

He got as far as the doorway and remained there. Eunice followed the direction of his gaze and saw him looking at the tank-shaped money box, his eyes moist. She turned to the whingeing child and picked him up.

"Alfie, here's your daddy." The words left her mouth before she realised her mistake.

Jack's brows knitted together. "Is that some kind of cruel joke?"

"William. It's William. I named him after your father. Call him Billy if you like. Or Bill, or..." Eunice floundered. "Take him." She shoved the boy at Jack. "Please."

Her action forced him to put out his arms to receive the child. Father looked down at his son, cradled in his arms. In return, the child's inquisitive eyes looked at this stranger, taking him all in.

"He looks like you," she said.

A small tear rolled down Jack's cheek and she felt a thickness in her throat.

Without warning, the boy let out a piercing cry. Jack instinctively went to clamp his hands over his ears, forgetting about the infant who bounced out of his opened arms. Eunice just caught William mid-fall.

"My God, Jack, what the hell…"

She could already hear the staccato machine-gun-like tread of his boots on the stairs and his attendant cry of pain. The front door slammed. She rushed out onto the landing and looked down over the stair rail. Her heart pounded in her chest. William was rigid in her arms, stunned into silence. Eunice placed him back into his cot.

"Now look what you've done," she said.

Suddenly she had a horrible premonition that the Jack Wilson she knew before the war was gone forever.

"You in love with that one?" Peggy asked Jack.

She looked down at his still quarter-full glass of beer. For the past five minutes she'd been watching him from behind the bar, thinking his looks had definitely suffered. Although she would no longer call him handsome, she still considered he had something about him. He'd been nursing the same glass of Burton's for an hour now, slumped in his seat, wrapped up in his own thoughts. The landlord, Vince, had sent her over to encourage him to buy another one.

"All right. Give me a whisky," he rasped like an order.

"Yes, sir!" she saluted him, mimicking his tone. "Coming right up, sir." *If we've got any.*

Whisky had been in rather short supply recently, and Vince had his preferences over whom he served it to. Peggy knew allowing Jack Wilson and anti-conscription cronies to use his upstairs room at the start of the war had brought the pub landlord to the attention of Special Branch, and he'd had to keep his nose clean ever since. No, he probably wouldn't have any spare whisky for Jack.

"Enjoy your stay in that German holiday camp, Wilson?" someone asked as they passed.

Ignorant sod, Peggy thought, but Jack pretended he hadn't heard and tossed back his beer in one rare gulp. This surprised her, for usually Jack Wilson could make a glass of beer last for an eternity.

"Peggy?"

She got the idea that his voice had something of the confessional in it, so she arranged her face into a serious expression, but unconsciously her body affected its usual flirtatious pose when she was talking to punters: one hand on her thrust out hip, giving her full attention. Disappointed, she noticed he didn't even bother to lift his gaze from his empty glass.

"I hope you won't be reporting back to Major Wilson."

"It'll be our little secret, Lance Corporal," she said archly.

Her tone made him finally glance up at her. She tapped the side of her nose before she walked off.

"I'm not half seas over yet," he called after her. "And even if I was," he said under his breath, "I'm prepared to risk it."

Peggy thought she'd be sure to tell Eunice about it later.

Chapter Thirty-two

Lizzie stifled a yawn as she pretended to be interested in her friend's eulogy about a new lip colour in a stick. In her head she was trying to work out how to turn the conversation round to Jack Wilson.

"Want your eyes back?"

Peggy's harsh voice snapped her out of her interior world, but it took Lizzie a moment to realise the comment had been aimed at a horribly disfigured war veteran who sat at an adjacent table. She gave him an apologetic smile before she glared at her companion.

"You can take that look off your phizog, an' all." Peggy took a sip of her coffee and immediately relented. "I'm sorry," she lowered her voice, "but look what the war's done to the flower of our English manhood. They give me the willies."

Realising the air had soured, Lizzie almost didn't pursue her intended aim, but found herself asking how Eunice was.

Peggy shrugged. "Getting used to having her husband back."

Lizzie's ears pricked up. After the chaos of the German surrender, even via the Red Cross it had been impossible to ascertain Jack's whereabouts.

"I had to move out." Peggy put her elbows on the table and cupped her hands round her face, an expression of self-pity forming on her features. "Vince's let me have use of a poky room over the pub."

"How is he?"

"Who, Vince?" Peggy shot Lizzie a curious glance, then realised her mistake. "Oh, Jack. Could be better, I suppose."

"What d'you mean?" Lizzie began to play with her teaspoon.

"He's in the King's Arms most days."

Lizzie's teaspoon clattered onto the table top. "The pub on the corner of Eunice's street? Where you work?"

"Although I wish I didn't, but it's still the best I can hope for these days."

Lizzie knew the returning servicemen expected their old jobs back, and women were being turned out of their positions in their droves: they were now surplus to requirements.

"Be grateful you don't need to work."

"Frankly, I don't want to lead a life without some purpose at least. Drinking tea all day, simply improving my needlework skills is very dull." She shook her head. "So I taught myself to type…"

"You're a tartar," Peggy laughed. "I'd give my right arm to sit around doing nothing all day, spending my old man's money, and here you are trying to improve your non-existent employment prospects."

"If I start up my own little business, I won't be beholden to anyone else or taking work away from the men coming back in need of a job. Doing nothing's not very satisfying."

"Is that the only thing that's not very satisfying?" Peggy gave a sly grin as she took a sip of her coffee.

"Marriage is only one sort of fulfilment."

The two fell silent for a moment. Peggy rummaged around in her bag for something, until Lizzie couldn't help herself.

"What was Eunice's husband like before the war?"

Peggy looked at her, perhaps a little surprised at the question, but answered willingly.

"Oh, he was always his own man, was Jack." She had one final rootle around in her bag. "Look, I've left my purse back at…"

"Have another." Lizzie pointed at her cup, desperate for her to stay. "My treat."

"You paid last time. And the time before, as I recall. I'm not one of your charity cases yet." Peggy bristled. "If you come back with me, I'll get my purse and pay you back. It's not far."

It wasn't the promise of repayment that made Lizzie agree.

Outside Peggy linked her arm through Lizzie's as they walked off towards the King's Arms.

"I suppose it's hard for Eunice. For wives, I mean," ventured Lizzie. "You must have to get to know your husband all over again after he's been away."

"Most marriages are a mystery to me, even without the war." Peggy shot a furtive look at Lizzie. "Eunice reckons her Jack had someone else during the war. In France."

Lizzie's heart missed a beat.

"I told her he most likely wants to forget about France now he's home. And so should she."

Chapter Thirty-three

Awoken from her slumber on the settee, where she had been resting to try and fight off yet another headache, Eunice slowly opened her eyes. Her head jerked up from the antimacassar.

"Oh, Jack. I nearly died! You frightened the life out of me."

Since his return, her husband never slammed the door, and instead she had got used to listening for the dull thud as it was pushed gently shut. He stood in the doorway of the front parlour now, both hands on the frame as if to support his weight. Almost unconsciously, she noticed the thin sliver of green, just visible beneath his shirt cuff, as she asked him if he'd like a cup of tea. It was impossible to be around him without busying herself with some task or other these days.

"There's a letter come for you." She pointed at the mantelpiece. "Looks official. How did you get on at the Labour Exchange?"

"Over an hour and a half in the damned queue," he said in a dead voice as he picked up the letter, looked at it and turned it over and over in his hands. "They're saying there's half a million out of work already."

Eunice hadn't thought her husband would be one of them. He had gone to his old employer to see about getting his job back, but was turned away with apologies and excuses. She suspected his anti-conscription activities had had something to do with it, but she didn't say so. Instead, she mentally calculated their income without his old job. They were already several weeks into the twenty-six allowed by the Out of Work Donation Policy. If Jack hadn't found work after that, her meagre income alone wouldn't be enough for three of them to live on. His injury pension award was still pending, but a gammy knee wasn't worth much. A depressing vision of the pawnbroker in Gainsborough Road flashed across her mind.

She felt a sudden twinge of disappointment. Her Jack, the Jack who went away to war in 1916, wouldn't have given up so easily, but this Jack – she didn't know him at all, and, to her own discredit, she wasn't even sure if she liked the stranger to whom she was married.

Ever since the fourth night home, he had followed the same routine. In the early hours he sat bolt upright in bed, as if he heard something of which she was unaware.

"What's wrong, Jack?"

He remained silent and threw the bedclothes off as if they were attacking him. Within minutes the landing light would cast its dim glow under the door. Her instinct was to follow him downstairs, but she had heard too many stories from other wives of their husbands' strange behaviour as they re-enacted some unfathomable drama which terrified them, and she chose to remain huddled underneath the bed covers with her knees pulled up to her chest, her arms wrapped around them tightly. *What you don't know doesn't hurt you.*

Even if he came back to bed, there would be no intimacy between them. That first night she had almost cried out with relief when he turned to her, but just as quickly he turned away. In the darkness she could sense his frustration and humiliation. She told him it didn't matter. For the next few days she got into bed and put one arm around him as she spooned her body to his shape, but made no sexual overtures towards him and received none in return. Yet she loved the musky, manly smell of him, and yearned for physical contact, but she was afraid to take the initiative, scared of the effect any further humiliation might have on him.

But one night when she had begun to get undressed in the perfunctory way she had now assumed, she noticed him watching her for the first time since he had come back. Encouraged, Eunice thought she'd chance it. She started to disrobe in the slow, seductive fashion she knew had served their relationship well before the war. She took her time to roll down her stockings provocatively, because Jack had always admired her legs, and she knew they, at least, were still good, before she slipped off her undergarments. Holding her breath, her heart beating a frantic rhythm in her chest, she had bared herself to him. He reached out and touched her breast; she closed her eyes as a wave of relief and pent-up desire flooded through her.

"Jack?"

He had let his hands drop back down onto the bedcovers, uttered a pitiful moan of distress and left her alone. Afterwards, Eunice had looked at her slackened stomach and no longer full or firm breasts and blamed herself that he didn't love her anymore.

Now she watched his hands as he opened the envelope and unfolded the letter. He crumpled it into a ball and threw it into the fireplace.

"Who's that from?" she asked, frowning.

"The King."

Eunice pushed past him and leaned into the fireplace to pick up the ball of paper from the cold ashes in the grate. She had used the last of the coal yesterday, otherwise the fire would have been lit and the flames would have destroyed the letter. She dusted it off and smoothed out the creases before opening it.

> *The Queen joins me in welcoming you on your release from the miseries and hardships which you have endured with so much patience and courage.*
>
> *During these many months of trial, the early rescue of our gallant officers and men from the*

cruelties of their captivity had been uppermost in our thoughts.

We are thankful that this longed-for day has arrived, and that back in the Old Country you will be able once more to enjoy the happiness of home and to see good days among those who anxiously look for your return.

George R

"It's written in his own hand!" Her eyes were wide with pleasure and surprise.

"It's a lithograph," he said matter-of-factly.

"Well, I'm going to keep it," she announced.

Here, at last, was recognition from the King himself that her husband had done his duty as well as anybody, and the fact that he had been taken prisoner was a misfortune: it wasn't his fault. She knew that the Government was not sympathetic to prisoners of war, and that this attitude filtered down to their neighbours too. Well, she'd show them the letter. *They could stick that in their pipe and smoke it.*

He shrugged. "As you like." He turned in the awkward manner made necessary by his knee wound and began to walk out of the room.

"Off to drown your sorrows again?" Her voice was sharp with irritation.

"Something like that."

Chapter Thirty-four

Lizzie wondered whether Peggy's reasons for bringing her to the King's Arms had less to do with paying her way than with a need to elicit some sympathy for her current circumstances. Her room above the pub was not dissimilar to the poky little attic room they had once shared as munitionettes, with its camp bed and thin mattress, bare floors and dull brown walls, but here the tangy and acrid smell of hops permeated everything, and there was no inflated wage to compensate. At least she was near her work, Lizzie said, trying to find something positive in her friend's situation, glad that her good fortune meant she didn't have to live here.

"Maybe you could lend me your typewriter to better myself?" Peggy laughed. "Your face! You'd think I'd asked you to give me your best jewels."

Lizzie wasn't parting with the Corona: she had plans for that typewriter.

Peggy found her purse and paid what she owed, ignoring her friend's reluctance to accept it. Having accomplished what she had set out to do, she led Lizzie back out past the saloon bar.

"Back later, Vince." Peggy stopped and called out to the landlord, who stood behind the bar. Lizzie gave her a hard shove in the back, pushing her towards the door.

"Ow! Where's the fire?"

"Sorry. Just wanted some fresh air."

"Ha! You won't find none of that round here. Fancy coming to Petticoat Lane market, then?"

Lizzie declined her offer, claiming a prior engagement.

"Don't be a stranger!" Peggy called over her shoulder as she walked off.

Lizzie waited until her friend was out of sight before she turned around and went back inside the pub. She took several deep breaths as she approached the counter. The man, whom Peggy had acknowledged on the way out, watched her approach with wry interest and kept throwing odd glances at her as he poured her a drink. As she waited, Lizzie cast a furtive look to her left. Her pulse fluttered when she saw the familiar side profile which had made her so eager to get her friend outside.

Aware of several male eyes on her as she walked to a booth, Lizzie positioned herself in her little cubby-hole so she gained a vantage point without easily being seen in return. She took a sip of her drink and looked at Jack Wilson. She put her hand on her breastbone and allowed it to rest there in an attempt to still the rise and fall of her chest, and didn't immediately notice the approach of a man with a rolling gait until he sent sour fumes into her face when he addressed her.

"Fanshy shome comp'ny?" The fair haired man, tall and not unattractive, slumped down in the seat opposite without being invited.

Taken aback, Lizzie tore her eyes away from Jack. "No, thank you. I'm waiting for someone." Her tone was excessively polite.

"I'm shure he don't desherve a peach like you." The man grinned at her.

Lizzie looked down at her drink, an action which the inebriated man took as a brush off.

"Oh, not good enough for you, ish that it?" He leaned over the table towards her. "No one wantsh to know ush now the warsh over.

King and Country? Fat lot o' good that done ush. All you women, encouraging ush to go." His voice suddenly dropped to a whisper. "Pity you don't want to look at the conshequenshes."

Lizzie almost felt sorry for him.

"Leave the lady be, Stan."

At the sound of the familiar voice her heart did a somersault in her chest and the gooseflesh came up on her arms. She lifted her head and looked straight into Jack Wilson's blue-grey eyes. She saw a flicker of uncertainty, followed by a spark of recognition, before he put his hands under the demobbed soldier's armpits and gave him a rough shove in the direction of the door.

"Get yourself home and sleep it off."

The drunk staggered towards the door, crying, "Where'sh thish land fit for herosh we wash promised then?"

"You'd better take that up with Lloyd George," Jack Wilson called to the man's receding back before turning his gaze on Lizzie. In his eyes she fancied she saw a reflection of their brief passion and all her past feelings for him began to run away with her.

"You'll have to excuse him. He forgets his manners when he's in his cups."

The drunk was already a distant memory as the thumping of her heart threatened to overcome her.

"Thank you," she managed to whisper, unable to take her eyes off him.

"Elizabeth Fenwick."

She didn't bother to correct his use of her maiden name.

Close up, she was jolted into pity at the change in him. His clothes hung off him, his once masculine presence shrunken away. His handsome blue-grey eyes were bloodshot and red-rimmed and his hollowed cheeks gave him a haunted aura.

"You look very solid, for a ghost."

Her tone was arch to try and conceal her shock at his appearance.

It was also an act of unconscious self-preservation, to give the impression that he meant little to her now.

As if in surrender, he raised his arms – which barely filled his loose sleeves – and ran his hands through his hair; a familiar gesture which made Lizzie feel giddy. It was then that she saw it: the remnant of green cuffing his wrist. A lightning surge of excitement grabbed hold of her. Light-headed, she stood up with a lurch, thinking only that she might fall rapturously into his arms, until she realised with a pitch of her heart that he was fighting back tears which threatened to un-man him. Suddenly afraid of the power of her own feelings, she pushed past him and hurried out. After a few paces, she slowed and looked over her shoulder. The street was deserted. She was disappointed that he had made no attempt to follow her.

Lizzie walked all the way home in a state of numb excitement, oblivious to houses, shops and people. She no longer knew what she thought or felt. She spent the rest of the day restlessly wandering from room to room in the house, unable to settle. Eventually she ran upstairs, ignoring Elsie filling the linen press on the landing, and threw herself onto the bed she shared with Edmund. As she lay there, Lizzie replayed in her mind all that had taken place between Jack Wilson and herself. Thoughts of him burned in her memory and she felt a delicious tug at her heart as she pictured her green scarf fastened to his wrist.

Minutes after she had left him behind in the room they had spent the night in, back in July 1917, she realised she had forgotten it – her favourite scarf. It had been expensive, and so she reasoned she ought to go back to get it. She could almost feel the sensation all over again of her heart hammering in her chest as she hurried up the stairs and along the corridor; how she had stood still, her hand raised to knock and about to call his name, when she heard the heart-wrenching sound of her lover keening behind the door. Her first instinct had been to rush in and embrace him, to utter comforting words of tenderness and commitment, but some heavy article had thudded against the other side of the door and made her take a shocked step backwards. The sound of her own breathing became deafening to her ears; she took fright and ran back down the hotel corridor.

Her scarf was not lost – had never been lost – and why else would he have kept it except as a dear memento of the union which bound them together in love? She felt a surge of pure ecstasy to think that, whatever his reasons for pretending to be someone else, he had not simply taken his pleasure and used her for his own ends then forgotten her. He had kept her scarf.

Wrapped in the tumult of her emotions, tears suddenly welled up in her eyes, but her feelings were so confused she didn't know whether she was blinking back tears of frustration, anger, love or guilt. Gradually she desisted. She sat up and swung her legs over the bed edge and rested her hands on the counterpane. She knew she was looking into the abyss.

"Mrs Edmund Fawcett," she said in a cracked voice. "Mrs Edmund Fawcett." She said it louder to remind herself of her commitment to her husband and her good fortune. "Mrs Edmund Fawcett!"

This last was so loud that Elsie knocked on her door to see if she wanted something.

Down on her knees in front of her husband's sleeping form, Eunice held the kitchen scissors in front of her face as if hypnotised by their shape and weight. She reached out, unable to resist touching Jack's wavy black hair, but he stirred and her hand froze. Laid out on the settee, he was sleeping off a drunken stupor, his head on the fancy embroidered cushion she had carefully crafted. She stared at his face: she barely knew what thoughts and emotions went on behind its facade; what unknown passions it hid. She waited until she heard his lips start to make little popping noises again before she recommenced her task.

His left arm dangled listlessly over the edge of the settee. His shirt cuff was pulled up and exposed both his wrist and the sliver of green material which had begun to obsess her. Eunice leaned in closer and noticed it was faded in patches and starting to fray at the edges. All this time she had wanted to ask him why he wore it. What did it mean? But she hadn't. She was afraid to know the answer. Now her fingers gently touched the material. Silk! Her heart twisted into a tight knot and a fountain of bitterness washed over her at an unwanted vision of Jack, cavorting with some lovely French village girl possessed of an unblemished alabaster skin, a taut stomach and firm, young breasts.

Slowly she slipped the scissor blades underneath the piece of green silk, and found her task made easier by the material having slackened over time. A sublime shiver of satisfaction ran down her spine when the green fragment slithered to the floor.

This is sacred to that girl's memory, she thought. *Now I have exorcised her ghost.*

Back in the kitchen she sat at the table, the scrap of green in front of her as she measured out her Veronal.

Lizzie turned left out of the King's Arms and leaned into the strong breeze as she walked a few yards, halted suddenly to put a hand onto her hat to stop the wind whipping it away, did an about turn and set off in the opposite direction. Within minutes she found herself at the far end of a familiar street. She paced back and forth.

A few minutes before, the demobbed soldier from last week had watched her eyes scan the customers of the saloon bar and laughed. "If you're looking for Sir Galahad, he had one over the eight last night. He's probably still sleeping it off at home."

A small part of her was disappointed at Jack's absence, but

a greater part of her felt a dangerous thrill as her unchecked imagination recognised the possibilities in finding him home alone.

In a fizz of nervous excitement, Lizzie counted the gates as she walked down the narrow, weed-infested alley until she came to the one she sought. She pulled up the latch and stepped inside the rear yard. Just as she made to rap on the back door, the wind slammed the gate shut behind her. She jumped and her hand shot to her chest, where it remained as she tried to even out her breathing while she waited to see if anyone came to find out what the noise was. No one did. She leaned sideways to take a quick peek through the sash window and saw Eunice at the kitchen table. *Damn!* It simply hadn't occurred to her until now that Eunice might be at home. This brought Lizzie to her senses. She berated herself for her foolish actions and turned to leave, but something stopped her. The image was all wrong.

She peered in through the window again, using her gloved hand as a shade to help her see more clearly. Jack's wife was slumped forwards with her head resting sideways on one arm and her eyes closed. Her other arm dangled by her side. She looked like she was asleep. Suddenly the hairs on the back of Lizzie's neck pricked up. She grasped the door handle and pulled it open. Immediately a rush of gas fumes enveloped her. She slammed the door shut again. A sickening wave of panic rose up in her chest, but she had to do something. Lizzie took a deep breath and yanked open the door again. Inside the gas-filled kitchen, her first instinct was to get Eunice out, so she put her arms around the unconscious woman's middle and tried to pull her sideways off the chair, but she was a dead weight.

"Eunice! Wake up! For God's sake, Eunice! Help me! WAKE UP!" Lizzie could hear herself screaming in her head. She didn't dare call out for fear of inhaling the gas.

It was hopeless.

Despite her best efforts, the noxious smell of the gas was

beginning to overpower her senses. In her panic she didn't think to turn off the gas tap. Instead she made one last effort to dislodge Eunice by grabbing her clothing with both hands and pulling. Eunice's inert body toppled sideways into her and sent her staggering backwards. As she fell, Lizzie caught the side of her head on the edge of the enamel sink. The room blurred and faded out.

The kitchen door, which had been swinging on its hinges in the wind, banged shut.

Chapter Thirty-five

Peggy sat and observed Edmund Fawcett as he paced around the small hospital waiting room, his brows knitted with concern. He stopped on each circuit to stare out of the window above the half-nets for a few minutes before he commenced his pacing again. She'd just arrived, and he told her in a flat voice that his wife was undergoing oxygen therapy to try and purify her blood of the coal gas toxins. Peggy asked about Eunice, who was the main reason she was here, not knowing anything about Lizzie's part in the drama, but he said he didn't know what had happened to Mrs Wilson – only that her husband had apparently found them both unconscious and had dragged them out. No, he didn't know where Mr Wilson was.

Peggy sat down, glanced around the clinical and oppressive room and automatically started to bite her nails. *How is Eunice? Is she all right? But what on earth had happened? Why was Lizzie Fenwick round there? Where was Jack when all this was going on?* Peggy twisted these thoughts around in her head until Fawcett's pacing began to get on her nerves. *Can't you sit down?* she wanted to say. *You're making me dizzy going round and round.*

As if she had spoken aloud, he sat opposite her. He leaned forwards with his hands clasped and rested his arms on his knees as he stared at his shoes. Every now and then she noticed him raise the toes of his shoes and put them back down flat on the stone floor. She wanted to say something about that as well, but she was pre-empted by the waiting room door swinging open.

"Jack?" Peggy leapt up and faced him, her voice a mix of concern and confusion. "How is she? What's gone on?"

Eunice's husband stood with his head bowed. She saw the veins pulse in the backs of his hands as he ran his fingers through his hair. He remained silent for a moment. She watched him as he tried to compose himself, but she could contain herself no longer.

"Is Eunice all right?"

Jack put his hand up to quieten her and said in a strained voice, "They couldn't save her." His eyes flicked away from Peggy and back again.

Peggy's hands flew to her gaping mouth as she let out a small, strangled cry.

Edmund Fawcett, saddened by the news but realising that this must be the man who had rescued his wife, shot to his feet and put his hand out as he introduced himself.

"Please accept my most heartfelt condolences. A terrible, terrible tragedy."

Jack Wilson looked stunned and confused as he accepted the other man's proffered hand.

"But I am completely indebted to you, sir, for rescuing my wife in those very unfortunate circumstances."

"Your wife?" Jack looked blank.

"Mrs Elizabeth Fawcett. She was with Mrs Wilson, I believe, in your home."

Jack repeated her name, and Peggy watched two deep lines appear between his dark eyebrows before his expression lifted and he muttered something about food parcels. "She isn't..."

"I'm told there is still hope for her." Edmund gave him a weak smile before he turned to the window, his back to the room.

"I need a smoke." Jack turned to leave and jerked his stiff leg round, not bothering to excuse himself.

"Me an' all," said Peggy and hurried out after him. She didn't want to be alone with Fawcett a moment longer, and she had things to say to Jack.

Outside Jack fumbled with the pack, trying to take out a cigarette. When he eventually succeeded he inhaled the smoke deep into his lungs before blowing it back out into the crisp spring air and offering the pack to Peggy. She gave him a watery smile as she pulled out a cigarette and put it between her lips. He struck a match, and as she cupped her hand around his to get a light, she noticed how the match flame wavered. She glanced up at him and saw him staring at her with vacant eyes before he shook the match out and cast it down to the ground. They stood in silence, side by side as they dragged hungrily on their cigarettes.

The clanging of an ambulance bell as it arrived at the hospital broke the heavy atmosphere. Peggy noticed how Jack's body stiffened. She watched him and saw the thin line of sweat glistening on his top lip. A sudden recollection of what Eunice had told her about his reaction to William's scream the day he came home made her move and stand in front of him in case he bolted. She could see the effort it took to control himself, but she persisted: she hadn't finished with him yet.

"I just can't understand it. Why was the gas on?"

He kept his eyes focused on the ground, but the cigarette wavered between his lips as he took a long drag on it. She saw a flash of something like shame cross his face. She'd seen him reel out of the King's Arms the night before, properly three sheets to the wind for the first time since he'd come home. She remembered how she'd wondered what had provoked it, and how it had amused her to think of the reception he'd likely get from Eunice when he got home.

"The door was shut, and when I opened it…"

"You were in the house all the time?" She suddenly realised he'd been sleeping off the effects of the previous night's binge. "You must have smelled the gas."

"I lost my sense of smell in the trenches."

She'd heard about the stench of the putrefying bodies strewn over the battlefield and in the trenches themselves, and for a moment she pitied him.

"I saw her in a heap on the floor." He shook his head in disbelief. "I turned the gas jets off and opened the back door to get the fumes out. I carried her out into the back yard."

"But you don't think she meant to do it, do you?"

He stared at her for a second and shrugged, as if to say that these days he had no idea what went on in his wife's head.

"Not with William." She looked at him in panic. "William?"

"He's all right. He's with my mother."

He started to shuffle from foot to foot, wincing occasionally, but he kept on. Eventually he threw his cigarette butt down onto the road and ground it to nothing with the toe of his left boot.

"It was hell for Eunice, you know," Peggy blurted out.

"What do you know about Hell?" he snarled. "I could tell you about Hell, all right. About…" He stopped abruptly and shook his head as if to indicate he wasn't going there.

Peggy kept on, her thoughts with Eunice. "I think she was desperately unhappy." She intentionally made it sound as if it was entirely Jack Wilson's doing.

"Happiness?" He rammed his hands deep down into his coat pockets and stared off past her into the middle distance.

"Look, I don't know what went on between the two of yous…"

He shot her a look that told her it was none of her business. He started to rock from foot to foot, wincing as if hot coals were burning through the soles of his shoes. Peggy could see it pained him; she gained the impression he was punishing himself.

Jack pulled the Veronal bottle out of his pocket.

"Did you know about this?" He shoved it at Peggy.

"It's her knock out drops. She needed something to get her through the day – after Alfie."

"I was told she was drugged up on this when she gassed herself." He turned the bottle around in his hand. "It was on the kitchen table." He stared at it for a moment, then he looked at Peggy, his expression a mix of sorrow and blame. "You were her friend. You should've helped her."

"You were her husband. You should've protected her."

They squared up to each other, but Jack broke eye-contact first, put the bottle in his pocket and busied himself with lighting another cigarette.

She gave him a sly glance. "It's funny, though."

"What is?"

"Lizzie, being round at yours like that." It hadn't gone unnoticed that Jack didn't mention her in his description of getting Eunice outside.

"Lizzie?" He looked at her blankly.

"Mrs Fawcett. We all worked at the munitions. She married the factory manager." Peggy nodded over her shoulder in the direction of the hospital waiting room. "Why was she round at yours?"

"Elizabeth." She saw something dark flash in his eyes.

"Elizabeth? Don't you be giving her airs and graces. She was always plain old Lizzie to us lot."

"The manager. Fawcett," he repeated, his eyes focused on something beyond Peggy. Suddenly his head snapped round towards her. "Is he a good man? A kind man?"

Peggy eyed him. That was a strange question from someone who didn't know either Fawcett or Lizzie, and shouldn't be of the slightest concern to a man who had just lost his wife. She pulled a face.

"Bit too square rigged for my taste. But he'd go to the ends of the earth for her." She removed a flake of tobacco from her lower lip. "Anyway, she was grateful to him, I suppose. Rode to her rescue when her soldier lover got himself killed, and…"

She watched him as he chewed his lip. "And what?"

"Nothing. Now she's got reason to be grateful to you as well."

"I don't deserve her gratitude."

"That's up to her. She set out to make the best of this war. I did an' all. I don't think either of us got what we expected, and nor did Eunice." A tear started at the corner of her eye. She let it fall all the way down her cheek without attempting to wipe it away. She waited for a reaction from Jack, but when she got none, she said, "After Alfie…"

He stopped his rocking and stood stock still at the second mention of his dead son. He turned away from her to face the building, put his arm up against the wall and leaned his head on it.

"Jack?" She sniffed and made to touch his shoulder.

"Leave me be!" His voice wavered and cracked as he shrugged her off.

"Oh, please yourself, then." She turned and flounced off in the opposite direction.

To hell with Jack Wilson and his moods.

Chapter Thirty-six

As soon as she turned into the street, Lizzie saw the removal cart, with its jumble of belongings and furniture piled onto it in a haphazard fashion, outside number fifteen. She hastened her pace until she stopped right outside the Wilson's house, the door of which was wide open. She stepped inside the hall. Above her she heard the creak of bare floorboards as the removal men's footsteps echoed through the empty shell of a house.

Lizzie knew she should not be here. She was meant to remain at home to recuperate from the toxic effects of the gas, but she seemed unable to stay away. Edmund would not approve. He already seemed anxious and concerned about the circumstances in which she had found herself, resulting in him becoming a little tetchy and perhaps even suspicious of late. Maybe it was just her own guilt she felt, but he had forbidden her to attend Eunice's funeral on the pretext of her health.

She walked down the hall towards the back of the house and stood in the doorway of the kitchen where she stared at the money-in-the-slot New World gas cooker, with its door now firmly shut. The image of Eunice, slumped over the kitchen table, unconscious and perhaps dead even then, flashed into her mind. She herself had nearly died in this room. Now empty of furniture, only a ghostly trace of what had played out between its walls remained.

Lizzie stepped back out into the hall where two hefty men were hauling a set of drawers through the front door, too busy discussing German reparations to notice her.

"Squeeze 'em till the pips squeak, that's what they're saying."

She flattened herself against the wall until they'd gone out, after which she slipped into the front parlour. Once in the room, which was now stripped bare apart from the array of photographs on the mantelpiece, she went to the fireplace and picked up the photograph of Jack – the one which had tilted her world dangerously the last time she had looked on it here. She took the photograph with her and went back into the hall. She stood at the foot of the stairs and looked up at the faded shapes on the wallpaper, where pictures had hung so recently.

"Sorry, missus." The removal men had come back in and wanted to go upstairs. "Got to get the beds shifted."

She asked where the occupants had moved to.

"No idea, missus. All's I know is this lot is being repossessed."

Lizzie entered the King's Arms and immediately saw Peggy, who sat with her elbows on the bar, her face in her hands and a downcast look on her face, which was replaced by a wan smile when she saw her friend approach. Peggy eased herself off her stool, looking as if she had the body of a fifty-year-old, came around the bar and embraced her friend. She sniffed loudly and ushered Lizzie to a table in a quiet corner while she went to fetch a couple of stiff drinks.

Lizzie's eyes scanned the sparsely populated saloon bar.

"On the house." Peggy knocked back half of her double gin in one go. The spirit made her eyes water, but Lizzie had already noticed they were red-rimmed.

"I know. I know." Peggy put her hands to her puffy and blotchy face. "Vince says I'm putting the punters off and it's affecting the takings." She took another large swig of her drink. "Anyway, *you* look a damn sight better than when I saw you in that hospital bed. Recovered now?"

Lizzie caught the slight accusatory tone behind the obvious sympathy, but she hadn't come here to talk about herself. After the shock of seeing the removal men she wanted to know about Jack, but she knew she'd have to approach her friend carefully. Peggy wasn't daft and could sniff out any subterfuge a mile away, but she was shocked when Peggy said, "Jack Wilson's a bastard." She sniffed. "Oh, I suppose you think he's a hero 'cos he dragged you out. Eunice would've liked that, people thinking he's a hero." Her tone hardened again. "But Jack Wilson's no hero. He was in there, you know, comatose on the settee, otherwise he might have saved her."

This image of Jack disappointed Lizzie, but she still said that she was glad he had pulled himself together if he was in the house, otherwise she might not be sitting here right now. "I'm really sorry about Eunice."

"She went to a medium, you know."

"Really?" Lizzie didn't understand how this was relevant, but got the sense that she needed to play along to keep Peggy on side.

"Went to try and contact Alfie. She didn't, of course. Instead she got the message 'Jack. Gas'. She thought that meant he was going to be gassed in the trenches, only Eunice got it the wrong way round. No, it was predicting Jack was going to *gas her*."

"That's a bit melodramatic," Lizzie said, noting that you shouldn't put too much store by what a medium told you.

All at once, Peggy's eyes narrowed, and Lizzie shrank under the icy coolness of her stare. "What?"

"Why were you round there anyway?"

Lizzie sighed. She was becoming tired of dissembling – it seemed that keeping a secret was draining, emotionally and physically – and she was rather afraid it was becoming second nature to her. But she didn't think she could risk the whole truth, so she decided to give up only the bare facts and explain about the Red Cross adoption scheme. After all, wasn't it reasonable her charity should extend to paying one final visit to the man she had 'adopted' as a PoW now he was home?

"So it was pure coincidence that you were given Jack to adopt?" Peggy didn't bother to hide her scepticism.

Lizzie raised her eyebrows and opened her hands, palms flat, as if to marvel at the unfathomable nature of chance.

"A right Lady Bountiful." Peggy's tone changed. "They should've left him to rot in that PoW camp, if you ask me."

Lizzie felt affronted on Jack's behalf. "Then William would be an orphan now."

Peggy pursed her lips as she considered the implications of this, but her initial animosity didn't lessen. "Trust him to come back from the war and upset the apple cart."

Lizzie didn't think all the blame could be laid at Jack's door and, despite her original intentions, she blurted out she didn't think Eunice had been coping with motherhood. Peggy shot her a sharp look.

"What would you know about motherhood?" Her casual cruelty cut Lizzie to the quick. "Or about Eunice?"

"What about William?" Lizzie pushed aside her hurt and refused to be deflected.

A brief hesitation. "Jack's mother's looking after him."

"I saw the removal men when I came past." She waited, hopeful Peggy would tell her what she wanted to know.

"A few food parcels and postcards and you think you know him. Well, the war's over now, there's no further need for your charity." Peggy stared at Lizzie. "Did you tell Eunice you'd 'adopted' her husband?"

Lizzie looked down at the table top where she had begun to fiddle with a beer mat.

"You should've told her." Lizzie could feel Peggy's eyes skewering her. "Y'know, if you'd ever met him I'd be thinking you were sweet on him." Peggy paused. "Or do you just like playing God?"

Lizzie's head jerked up and indignation flashed in her eyes, only stayed by Peggy getting up, having noticed a punter at the bar. She said she had to get back to work. Suddenly afraid she would miss her chance, Lizzie asked, as casually as she could muster, if Jack was at his mother's. Peggy swivelled her eyes towards her.

"It's just a question of updating his records at the Relief Fund." The lie fell easily from her lips.

Lizzie wrote down the address Peggy gave her on the back of a beer mat. As she stood up and turned to leave she walked straight into a man who had just entered the bar. Automatically she apologised, then realised it was the drunk who had pestered her weeks ago and whom Jack had ejected. He recognised her too and immediately made a sycophantic bow, like a flunky abasing himself in front of a member of the gentry.

"I do beg your pardon, Milady. My fault entirely."

Lizzie, a little afraid of him, rushed away without responding further.

"Please don't send me to the Tower!" he called after her and laughed.

Peggy stood behind the bar, her lips pressed into a thin line.

"What was all that about?"

He tipped his head in the direction of the door.

"What, with Her Majesty there?"

"Why d'you call her that?" Peggy asked, irritated, as she began to pour him a half of Burton's.

"You jealous? You know she's not a peach like you."

She saw the teasing glint in his eye. She flapped her free hand at him.

"Looked down her nose at me first time…"

"First time?" Peggy stopped what she was doing. "You've seen her in here before?"

224

"A man could die of thirst."

She planted his glass of beer on the bar; a good portion of it slopped over the sides and spilled. "C'mon, Stan. I'm all ears."

He took a slow sip. "Yes, she's been in before. Jack Wilson seemed to take exception to me, er...politely trying to pass the time of day with her."

"Jack Wilson?" She narrowed her eyes.

He took another sip. She knew he was revelling in having her undivided attention. Lord knows he tried hard enough to win her over the rest of the time, despite her giving him her usual curt "Nothing doing!" dismissal which she saved for amorous punters. However, she was prepared to acknowledge that she tolerated his flirting far more than other punters' before she said it.

He wiped away the froth from his top lip. She began to drum her fingers on the counter. "Seemed to me like there was some unfinished business between those two."

"What sort of unfinished business?"

He shrugged. "Dunno. Jack told me to skedaddle. Another time she came in looking for him, but he wasn't here. That was the day, you know, Eunice...the gas..."

Peggy had no idea Lizzie had even met Jack Wilson. In fact, Lizzie had given the exact opposite impression, but now Peggy came to think of it, she had seemed very interested in hearing about him. Peggy considered Jack's reactions to her comments about Lizzie at the hospital after Eunice's death, which at the time she had attributed to his shock and grief. Now she wasn't so sure. Hadn't Lizzie just confessed she'd gone and 'adopted Jack by accident', and now Peggy finds she had been in here – conveniently when Peggy had her day off: Wednesdays.

She saw Stan Bartholomew staring at her, curious. "What's brewing in that delightful little head of yours, eh?"

"Oh, nothing." She began drying up some glasses.

As Lizzie sat on the train, watching the blur of soot encrusted houses and factories belching out black smoke as they whizzed by, thoughts of Jack eddied in her mind. After a while the steady rhythm of the train pounded in her head so that she felt as if her skull might explode. She closed her eyes, but images of Jack remained. She almost missed her stop, and leapt off the train at Ilford just as it began to pull out of the station.

She looked around for someone to ask for directions, but the platform was empty. She walked out of the station and took out the beer mat on which she had written Jack's address yesterday, although she had memorised it and didn't really need to consult it. Further down the road she saw a white-haired woman shuffling along at a painfully slow pace, so she hurried to catch up. Lizzie asked where she could find Barley Lane. The old woman sucked in her breath.

"Barley Lane? It's just a little way down the road. You can't miss it."

Lizzie thanked the woman and turned to move away.

"Mind they let you out again!" the woman called after her.

Lizzie had no idea what the woman was talking about as she followed the perimeter of a high wall and stopped at a tall iron gate, from which a large metal lock dangled. Through the bars of the gate she saw a large, imposing house. Perhaps there was a bell somewhere to announce visitors, To her left she saw a sign on the wall. She walked up to it until she was near enough to read it.

West Ham Borough Asylum, Barley Lane.

Chapter Thirty-seven

A week had passed since Lizzie had taken the train out to Ilford, and she was still consumed by nightmares about madhouses, unable to get well-known images of inmates at the infamous Bedlam – their twisted faces contorted in grotesque torment – out of her head. Her mind roiled with thoughts of Jack in the asylum. As she sat at dinner, she did little other than make patterns in the cooling fast-congealing gravy on her plate, only half-aware of the faint hum of the two male voices around her. Snatches of conversation washed over her: topics such as industrial unrest, strikes and Versailles held little interest. It was only when Elsie asked if she might clear her plate that Lizzie became aware of the conversation.

"I simply thought the man was drunk at first," Edmund said, "and then his behaviour became increasingly extraordinary. I began to think the fellow was quite off his head. Had to let him go, of course, but imagine my surprise when I was told he was suffering from war trauma."

War trauma.

Lizzie's back straightened.

"I understood it was caused by the noise of the mortars and the bombardment – you know, shell-shock. But now they're all back from the war, I can't understand it."

"It's a complicated business," their guest, Dr Ernest Carroll, said. "I haf taken an interest in some of these cases as a matter of fact."

Lizzie had been taken aback, but not entirely displeased, to discover that her previous employer was known to her husband, and had been taken on as the panel doctor at Edmund's factory to augment his public practice. As for her erstwhile employer, he seemed delighted to find her married to this man, and displayed none of the slight social awkwardness she herself felt about their apparent reversal of fortune now that he was reduced to having factory workers for patients instead of the upper classes. Perhaps his foreign origins had played a part in his downfall, but what she really wondered was whether he would discuss her past with her husband – or whether he already had.

"The previous panel doctor at the factory was dismissive," said Edmund as he took a drink of red wine. "He said they can't go around saying, 'Terribly sorry, I can't carry on' now that the war's over. I would have imagined they would be grateful to be out of it."

Lizzie thought that a harsh attitude, but said nothing.

"There was some difficulty about it among a cadre of my fellow medical professionals. Yes, thank you, I will." Dr Carroll accepted Edmund's offer of more wine. "You see, many, like your previous physician, considered these unfortunates were simply trying to wangle a bit of time out of the Front Line during the war. In fact, in certain upper social circles that I moved in back then," he said, without any trace of self-pity, "let me tell you, it was quite acceptable to fake it and laugh about it, which didn't help. But now, they're just seen as malingerers."

"An unfortunate business, Ernest, admittedly." Edmund shook his head. "But I'm afraid, what with that and the unions threatening strikes, I need men who can be relied on to do a productive day's work. After all, there are plenty of others queuing up at the Labour Exchange."

"Just so. But the real issue is we send these chaps off to win the war, and encourage them to behave in all sorts of ways we might consider barbaric and brutal by our normal peacetime standards, and when they come back we expect them to switch again immediately to behaving in a civilised manner, without any emotional or mental repercussions."

"And these poor men haven't had any time to readjust to normal life yet, have they." Lizzie suddenly spoke up.

"Quite correct." Ernest Carroll nodded his head in Lizzie's direction. "Craiglockhart and Netley, among others, were set up during the war to treat officers with neurasthenia – that's the preferred name for shell-shock among officers, by the way, but I use this term for everyone – and now there are places I can refer the other ranks to."

"So you can help these men?" Lizzie leaned forwards in her chair.

"You seem very interested in all this, my dear." Edmund stared at her, his head cocked to one side.

She'd almost forgotten he was there. She flashed him a coy smile.

"Oh, it's just I read an article about how terrible it was that some of these poor war-traumatised men are being put in asylums, as if they're insane." She watched a little crease form between her husband's brows. "Shouldn't we try and help these men all we can after all they've gone through to win this war?"

"No one's saying otherwise, my dear, although I don't think this is as easily solved as simply sending food parcels to PoWs."

Lizzie gave him a pained look at the implied rebuke and turned her gaze away.

"And between them, our medical men are far better placed than we to say how to treat them."

"Just so. But it is important we haf the support of the public."

Lizzie shot a grateful look at the doctor, who then gallantly changed the subject.

Lizzie pushed open the battered old door with difficulty, having to wait until a mass of bodies rearranged themselves to accommodate her entrance. Edmund would be outraged if he knew she was putting herself at risk in this way. She had taken her gargle this morning and she managed to place a handkerchief over her nose and mouth, like many others in here, still fearful any small symptom might be the influenza. Behind her someone's elbow jabbed into her back, so she shifted her position, but it didn't help much as there were just too many bodies for the space. She wondered how her former employer managed in these terribly reduced circumstances. It hadn't been like this when she had first come here, over a year ago, her child safely cocooned inside her womb.

Somewhere amid the din she heard a telephone going unanswered, and occasionally she heard the doctor's voice boom out "Who's next?" until finally the crowd began to thin and she managed to find a seat. She read the notice on the door to Dr Carroll's consulting room, penned in his beautiful copperplate handwriting, *Please take a seat. Patients will be seen on a first come, first served basis. You must wait until you are called.* Next to it was a printed list of instructions to help prevent the spread of the latest influenza epidemic. *There is no order here,* Lizzie thought. *And no receptionist.*

When it was her turn, and the doctor popped his head around the door, she thought how tired he looked, but as soon as he recognised her his face brightened.

"Come. Come," he said as he waved her inside his room. "What a pleasant surprise. But you are not ill, I hope."

She assured him she wasn't as her eyes scanned the room. Immediately she noticed the piles of files, stacked in a haphazard fashion on top of the filing cabinets which lined the walls.

"This Influenza, another wave, there is no stopping it. I will recommend a gargle before you go, just in case. Please. Sit." He indicated an uninviting looking chair. "I must say, I am very pleased for you. Things have turned out well, yes?"

Lizzie smiled and nodded, rather surprised that, in spite of the apparent chaos and his reduced circumstances, the doctor seemed to be thriving.

"So. To what do I owe this pleasure?"

She told the doctor about Jack's history without revealing his name or her relationship to him, referring only to Eunice, her friend from the munitions. She had no idea whether Jack was suffering from war neurosis, but she recalled his reaction to the clattering tray in the Lyon's Corner House back in 1917 as if it was only yesterday. She also knew just enough of the current thinking to suspect that remaining in a war zone without treatment or respite would only have exacerbated his condition, and so she had decided she was willing to try anything to get him out of the asylum. She prayed Ernest Carroll didn't see right through her.

However, she was disappointed to be told that it was much easier to admit someone to an asylum than to get them released. A near relative must give consent first, and then a place needed to be found in a specialist hospital, but only if the inmate was suffering from war trauma. Lizzie listened attentively, but didn't want to hear that these specialist hospitals didn't work miracles, or that some men were irretrievably damaged. She thanked him and said she would go and see the mother.

At his consulting room door, she stopped and asked him if he would like her to put away all of his files while she was there as she had some free time this afternoon. (In fact, she was bored to death and would relish *any* task these days).

Surprised by her offer, he nevertheless accepted.

"Ach, Lizzie, you were always an angel. I have so many new patients with this epidemic, even though I fear I can do little to help them."

Two hours later she had completed her task, pleased she had got an organised system in place. She was rather grateful to be useful, but she did wonder aloud whether the doctor's receptionist was ill.

"No. Not ill." Lizzie saw he looked a little uncomfortable. "Actually, I do not haf anyone."

She said that while she was waiting to see him, she had observed how tempers flared a little when there was uncertainty about whose turn it was to see him. She suggested it might be useful to take the patients' names down when they arrived.

"I could do that for you, if you like."

She saw him raise an eyebrow. At first he was reluctant and he expressed concern that she might get infected, but Lizzie knew also that her marriage had changed her status and he assumed Edmund was unlikely to sanction it. She assured him that she had nursed her husband through the first wave of the epidemic and had not become ill herself, and anyway she was sure he wouldn't mind. Eventually, out of desperation it seemed, Dr Carroll agreed, but said that it would indeed only be temporary, for after the influenza outbreak was over he would likely have very few patients, apart from his factory ones.

"My patients are not over fond of consulting us doctors – they prefer to self-medicate at the chemists on quack remedies or aspirin."

He smiled. She guessed, correctly, that he had no funds to pay her.

Chapter Thirty-eight

Lizzie found the mean-looking two-up-two-down terraced house in Stepney and stood in front of it. She stared down at the doorstep, silently geeing herself up before she finally raised her knuckles and rapped on the door. A small woman with a determined chin and grey hair, which was scraped harshly back off her face and pinned tightly into a bun, pulled open the door just enough to peek out.

"Yes?" There was suspicion in her voice.

"Mrs Wilson?" Lizzie saw that her face was a patchwork of worry lines.

"Who wants her?"

"I'm Mrs Elizabeth Fawcett."

There was no immediate reaction to her name, and she found the woman's unfriendly glare disconcerting.

"I was with Eunice…the day…Jack rescued me. He saved my life…"

"I'm sure you're grateful." The woman's face disappeared and the door began to close.

Lizzie put her hand on the door to prevent it shutting on her. "Mrs Wilson?"

"What do you want?" The door remained slightly ajar.

"Look, I know Jack's in the asylum, and…"

The door slammed in Lizzie's face. The force sent her reeling backwards into the road, and as her head tipped she saw a curtain twitch in the downstairs window, but by the time she had regained her balance there was no further sign of movement. As she stood there, it suddenly came to her that she had been too blunt. She had not considered the shame Jack's mother would feel at her son being in the madhouse. It also dawned on her that people's response to lunacy was not much different from their response to illegitimacy, as she already knew. This hardened her resolve. Lizzie knocked on the door again.

A man, shrugging himself into his coat, came out and walked away down the street. He nodded at her, and indicated with a brisk hand gesture that Lizzie should follow him. He didn't stop until they had turned the corner at the end of the road.

"Prying eyes," he said by way of explanation. "I'm Jack's uncle, Eddie Wilson." He put his hand out, thought better of it and shoved it in his pocket.

"Mrs Fawcett," she said formally in return.

"I recognise you from the hospital, that day...Eunice...You're the one our Jack saved."

She didn't remember him. "Yes. I'm so very sorry about Eunice." Despite her feelings for Jack, she meant it.

"A rum do that, right enough."

"Look, Mr Wilson..."

"Please, call me Eddie."

"Eddie. Jack doesn't belong in an asylum, whatever anybody else thinks..."

"You'd think he'd be the hero, wouldn't you? But now everyone acts like he's some sort of bogey man."

"He's a hero to me," she said quietly. "I want to help him in return."

He stared at her, but not unkindly; more as if he was trying to make her out.

234

"I'm sorry about his mother. She's a very strong woman, but truth is she's not coping well. This business with Jack has really knocked her for six." He looked downcast.

"Jack's not insane." She saw Eddie flinch at her use of the word.

"Yes, well." He stepped out into the road so he could see around the corner, to check Mrs Wilson hadn't followed them, Lizzie supposed, and lowered his voice. "The war's affected him. Up here." He tapped the side of his head with his index finger. "He stayed with us after Eunice died, but I think that must've tipped him over the edge. Ida did what she thought was right."

Lizzie's eyes widened as she realised he was telling her Jack's own mother had had him committed to the asylum.

"I know what you're probably thinking," Eddie said, "but...well, it's a long story." He suddenly looked as if all the life had been sucked out of him.

Lizzie collected herself. "Look, there's a doctor I know. He's interested in returning servicemen who have war trauma. He refers them on to specialist hospitals, not asylums. You should persuade Mrs Wilson to go and see him."

Doubt was in his eyes. "War trauma?"

"Dr Carroll will explain it."

He looked at her as if uncertain whether his skills of persuasion were up to it.

"Do you think you could try? For Jack's sake?"

As Peggy browsed the market stalls where she'd stopped on her way home from Ida Wilson's, she picked up a pair of crisp white linen pillowcases with a crocheted edge which she thought would be a nice addition to her 'bottom drawer' (in effect, an old suitcase) that she had been gradually stocking since she left the children's home, but her mind kept coming back to the puzzle of Lizzie and Jack, and what might be between them. She had stopped by Ida Wilson's ostensibly to see how the family was coping, but also to test the water a little about the pair of them. However, she hadn't even managed to steer the conversation round to it. Jack's mother had seemed taciturn and preoccupied, and even Peggy had been finding it a struggle to keep the conversation going, when Lizzie Fenwick had knocked on the Wilsons' front door.

"Now who's that?" Ida complained. "Some busybody or other, no doubt." She sighed and dragged herself up off the kitchen chair.

Eddie gave Peggy a solemn look as they listened to Ida trudge along the hall to the front door. He'd got up and lingered in the kitchen doorway, his finger to his lips to silence any background chatter. After only a few moments Peggy heard the front door slam.

"Eddie. Just leave it!" Ida called to his back as he pushed past her. She came back into the kitchen and sat down. "Why can't people just leave us alone?"

"Here, finish your cup of tea while it's still warm." Peggy had tried to comfort Ida, but on finding out who had come to the door she'd become impatient for Eddie to return. She'd sat in stunned silence when he came back and told them what Lizzie had proposed. From their reactions, she realised neither Ida nor Eddie knew anything more than she did about Lizzie and Jack, and she omitted to mention to them her own relationship with 'Mrs Fawcett'. Peggy had said her farewells and left, even more convinced that there was something going on with those two.

But what? Why was Lizzie so hell bent on helping Jack Wilson? Surely he was just another PoW to her at the Red Cross. Or was it more than mere charitable feelings on her part? And what about him? In Peggy's experience, a man usually only paid attention to a woman for one reason.

"Do you want those pillowslips, dearie?"

Peggy turned around and saw a pair of very prim old ladies, who looked like they knew a thing or two about starch, eyeing the pillowcases in her hand. She had forgotten all about the linens, which she shoved at the ladies.

"Help yourselves." She turned and walked off.

Lizzie looked up from her work to see Jack's mother entering the surgery. *So Eddie had managed to persuade her after all.* Perhaps the woman wasn't as black as Lizzie's imagination had painted her following their first interaction.

"Ida Wilson," the woman said, yet gave no hint that she and Lizzie had already met, nor made any apology for her behaviour the previous week.

Lizzie was polite to her, but nothing more. Jack's mother took a seat and waited her turn. A tense silence descended on the waiting room. All Lizzie could hear was the ticking of the wall clock. The rhythmic noise began to fill her head. Just as she was thinking that she couldn't bear to sit there one moment longer, Ida Wilson's voice addressed her and asked her how she came to know her son well enough to want to help him so much. Lizzie dropped her pen and scrambled about the desk to retrieve it before it rolled off the top. She stuttered something about Eunice and the munitions factory.

"So you're helping Jack because of Eunice?"

"I suppose so. Yes." She looked across at Jack's mother and then back down at her work. She could feel the other woman's eyes burning into her.

"Well, you must have an awful big heart, Mrs Fawcett."

Lizzie stood by the half-open door of Ernest Carroll's consulting room and chewed her lip as she strained to hear the one-sided conversation. When she heard the click of the telephone receiver being replaced, she dashed back to her desk and pretended to be busy.

"Mr Wilson is being transferred to Moss Side Military Hospital on Monday," the doctor said. "Please make the necessary arrangements."

Lizzie didn't recognise the name since she'd only heard of Netley and Craiglockhart.

"It's in Maghull. In Liverpool. It treats men in the ranks below commissioned officers."

He explained it was run by Dr Richard Rows, a Freudian psychologist (she had no idea what that was) who believed neurasthenia was caused by the repression of some traumatic event, and that by getting the men to talk about this event – 'talking cures' Dr Carroll said they were calling it – it would lose its power over its victim. Lizzie was pleased and disappointed in equal measure. Jack would be free of the asylum, but Liverpool was such a long way away. As if he read her thoughts, Dr Carroll told her no visitors were allowed during the treatment.

Lizzie knew Jack's file was kept in the top drawer of a battered wooden filing cabinet, set aside from the others in the doctor's consulting room, but when she attempted to pull open the drawer she discovered it was locked. Jack's file began to obsess her. Every time she was in the room, her eyes were drawn like a magnet to the cabinet, and she knew Ernest Carroll had noticed her interest.

Often when he was out of the office she went in and gave the top drawer a little pull, but was always disappointed to discover the methodical doctor had remembered to lock it. She would put the flat of her hand onto the drawer as if she could connect with Jack that way; as if the information about him – about his thoughts and feelings, treatment and recovery – would transfer to her. She knew it was foolish, but it became a compulsion. Inside that filing cabinet were his confidential notes; in them, she believed, were clues to the real Jack Wilson.

Chapter Thirty-nine

Lizzie was relieved that the morning surgery was almost over, with only a few stragglers left in the waiting room. Now the latest epidemic was on the wane she found she had little to occupy her. Before she went home she had the dirty cups and saucers from earlier to wash up, but instead she took out a piece of paper from her desk drawer. She stared at the blank page for a couple of minutes before scribbling down a few short sentences. She crossed them out, then rewrote the sentences, the tip of her tongue just visible between her lips, edited them, read through them, scratched through several words and finally let out a little huff of frustration. Maybe she should put her business advertisement away for another day and go and do the washing up, since the charwoman hadn't turned up again.

In the little kitchenette at the back of the surgery, she was halfway through this task when she heard a child's crying, faint at first, then louder. She popped her head back around the door and was surprised to see Eddie Wilson, who carried a fractious and grizzling William in his arms. Lizzie knew at once from the stricken look on the man's face that something was wrong.

"Eddie!" she exclaimed. "What brings you here?"

"It's the boy. He's a bit off-colour."

Lizzie thought it odd that Mrs Wilson had apparently sent Eddie along instead of coming herself, and also because Dr Carroll wasn't their usual doctor. She looked at William's nice, rosy cheeks, but noticed the man looked pale and distracted. She asked him if he was all right.

"Ida was run over by a motor car yesterday," he blurted out.

"Oh, Eddie. I'm so sorry. How is she?"

He made a hand gesture to indicate that it could go either way as he tried to mollify the whingeing child.

"Here, give him to me."

She took William into the kitchenette and found him a bourbon biscuit which silenced him at once. As she held him, she marvelled at the feel of him. His baby blue eyes watched her and her heart lifted. She listened as Eddie relayed the story of how Jack's mother had been crossing the Mile End Road when some sort of fancy motor car had come scorching round the corner, knocked her down and driven off without stopping. Lizzie's gaze kept flitting back to the child.

"Witnesses reckon the car was doing at least thirty miles an hour when it hit her. A woman driver."

His disgust was obvious, but whether it was at the speed of the car or the fact a woman was driving she couldn't be sure. She thought, a little guiltily, of the new motor car Edmund had just bought and how she'd pestered him to let her drive it a little way down the street, but she'd pressed too hard on the accelerator pedal and almost mounted the pavement. In her case, she knew simple lack of driving practice was to blame, but she was shocked that a driver had just carried on and left an old woman in the road.

Lizzie had an idea what Eddie was working up to, and she understood that he was weighing up how best to do it. When he seemed at a loss, she gave him his cue.

"How are you managing?"

"Not very well, to tell the truth," he said, relieved. "I don't know how you women do it."

Lizzie smiled to herself at his poor attempt at flattery just as she noticed a patient come out of the doctor's consulting room. Excusing herself, she moved over to her desk and called out the name of the next patient. By the time she gave her attention back to Eddie, he seemed to have come to a decision.

"Mrs Fawcett, the thing is, I've got to bring home the wages, otherwise we'll be on Carey Street." He gave her a pleading look. "I'm going to have to put the boy in one of those Salvation Army places – just temporary, till Ida comes home, or Jack..." he tailed off.

She asked if any of his neighbours could help.

"This thing with Jack...well, we haven't exactly been getting on with the neighbours. All we get is snide comments about how he's lost his onions."

Lizzie was saddened by such harsh gossip.

"I know Ida wouldn't want Jack's boy going into a children's home, but frankly it don't look like I've got much choice." He paused. "She can't know, of course."

William started to grizzle. Lizzie could see Eddie's sense of embarrassment increasing. "I'm sorry, I shouldn't have come." He made to take the boy from her.

"Wait. I'll help."

Lizzie said the maid could look after the child on the days she worked here. He didn't give her an opportunity to change her mind as he thanked her profusely for her generous offer and agreed to bring William back with some spare clothes when the surgery closed.

That evening in bed, when Edmund reached for her she made no protest. She knew that since she had seen Jack Wilson, and her old feelings had been resurrected, she had been acting in a rather contrary fashion towards her husband. One week she would embrace him with a guilt-fuelled love and affection, and the next she was cold towards him, finding excuses which allowed her to frustrate his desire. But earlier she thought he had taken her fait accompli over William rather well and found no reason to resist him. As she responded to him, however, the child's insistent cry made her husband roll away from her with a muttered curse.

"Elsie will see to him," she cooed as she placed a hand on his chest, but in the darkness she heard his breathing, loud and uneven. She waited, her head snuggled into the gap between his shoulder and his head as she listened to William's wailing.

Come on, Elsie. See to him.

Edmund's voice, icy and polite, cut through the baby's cries.

"While I applaud your charitable instincts, and I am, of course, indebted to Mr Wilson for saving your life, I would nevertheless like to know where you think it will all end."

"Where what will end, my love?" She began to nibble his ear.

William's cries subsided.

"This going about doing just as you please, then expecting me to sanction it."

"I didn't think you'd mind." With her finger she made little light circles on his skin. "Any road, it's only a short term arrangement." She began to stroke his chest.

He put his hand on top of hers to stop her.

"You know very well I am not just referring to you taking the child in, but to your misplaced loyalties. You're my wife first…"

"But…"

Suddenly he lost control of himself and pushed her over onto her back. He rolled on top of her to pin her down, and his mouth came down hard on hers. In the darkness, the shock made her tense her body against him, but she made no other resistance. She sensed his need to feel in control and to be master in his own house. He pushed her legs open with his knee, but, with a groan of despair, he threw himself off her. She heard him mutter a request for forgiveness as he got up and shrugged himself into his dressing gown before leaving the room.

Lizzie lay still on the crumpled bedcovers. She put her arm

across her forehead as she stared into the room's suffocating darkness. *I've tormented him into this,* she told herself. *He deserves to be appreciated for himself: for his many good qualities, and as my adoring husband. He should not be a consolation prize.* She heard the click of the landing light and the sound of Edmund's feet thudding down the stairs. No doubt he would go to his study, pour himself a good slug of whisky and sit ruminating behind his desk, as was his habit when he needed time to think over a problem. She sighed. She might almost have preferred it if he had forced her to accept him to punish her for her waywardness. At least then she could have found fault with him rather than with herself.

Chapter Forty

Eddie Wilson turned up out of the blue with a small gift for William. It was badly wrapped in creased brown paper, which had obviously been used for some other purpose previously. When Lizzie realised that 25 April was the child's birthday, so close to the birth date of her own son, with a forced cheerfulness she went down to the kitchen and got Mrs Ryder to put a lone candle in a cake, not long baked, and insisted she and Elsie come back upstairs to sing 'Happy Birthday' to the boy. Lizzie blew out the candle, but pretended William had done it all by himself. His little eyes blazed with joy as the flame disappeared.

"See, it's magic!" she cried, even as her heart was breaking. "Now, Eddie, how is Mrs Wilson?"

He told her there were signs of improvement. She squeezed his arm and gave him a sympathetic smile. He patted her hand in return, but suddenly snatched it away as if he had forgotten his place. Afterwards she sent Eddie down to the kitchen with Mrs Ryder to make sure he got a hot meal before he went home. She noticed how worn ragged he looked.

Lizzie picked up William and hugged him to her before she carried him upstairs and put him down ready for a nap. When she looked into his bright blue eyes and touched the baby softness of his skin, she felt an emotional charge as strong as if he had been her own flesh and blood. Her child would never have hugs and kisses from his real mother. He would never know who she was, or be told his origins. This terrible thought clutched at her heart and twisted it.

Peggy stood in the Fawcetts' hall, feeling put out but trying not to show it, while the maid went to fetch her mistress.

"Hello, Peg." Peggy noticed the lack of warmth in the greeting. "Come in." Lizzie showed her into the morning room and indicated the armchair by the fireplace, but Peggy remained standing in the middle of the room, facing her.

"Look, I know there's a rabbit off somewhere," she began, and saw the twitch at the corner of Lizzie's mouth. Peggy knew that it had always amused Lizzie when she tried to use one of her northern expressions. "When I heard about Ida I went round to see if I could help and I find out you're doing your Florence Nightingale act again."

"I bet that's not how Eddie put it. He always gave me the impression that he was grateful." Peggy was a little disarmed by this show of confidence, but when Lizzie justified her actions further with "He just needed a bit of help with William until Mrs Wilson gets better," she knew her barb had hit home.

"I mean first the food parcels and now the child. And I hear you got Jack out of the asylum. So, I ask myself, why are you doing all this?"

"It's called kindness."

Peggy ignored the sanctimonious words.

"And there you were again, in her house when Eunice was gassed." Peggy intended her tone to indicate that this was about more than her usual penchant for gossip. "Well?"

Peggy watched Lizzie's gaze flit from side to side and saw how she chewed the inside of her lip, recognising an inner battle was raging within her.

"I'm not leaving until you explain yourself."

Eventually Lizzie sat down and motioned Peggy to do the same.

"If I tell you, promise me you won't go stirring things up."

"Well, that depends." Peggy threw herself onto the sofa and crossed her arms in front of her chest like a petulant child.

Lizzie stared at her, unmoved.

"All right. I promise."

"When I went round to Eunice's that time..."

"That day you had that funny turn?"

Lizzie fiddled with her wedding ring. "Yes. Well, I saw that picture of Jack on the mantelpiece, the one with him in uniform, and...well, I thought it was Harry Slater."

"Who? Oh, right. I suppose they can all look alike in uniform."

"But the thing is...it *was* Harry Slater." Two lines formed between Peggy's brows. "Because that was what he told me his name was."

"You what?"

"Harry Slater and Jack Wilson are one and the same man."

Slowly the truth dawned on Peggy. "Effing hell!" She laid her head back against the antimacassar and closed her eyes, but just for a second before she jerked forwards, eyes ablaze, unable to believe Lizzie was that stupid. "What did you think you were you doing? How could you not know?"

"I had no cause to question his identity. Why would I?"

"Lor', but this is worse than it being some French..." She shook her head, bewildered. "Thank God Eunice can't be hurt by this now." Peggy got up and stood over her. "Trust you, Lizzie Fenwick!"

Lizzie leaned backwards, deeper into the cushions.

"Why in the world did the first ever bloke you let in your drawers have to be Jack Wilson"– Peggy's eyes flashed –"when it suited you to play the virgin with every other man?"

"I told you, I didn't know that's who he was, or..."

"Or what? You wouldn't have opened your legs for him? Pah."

Peggy shook her head and began to pace around the room. "Poor bloody Eunice."

"What about poor bliddy me?" Lizzie cried.

Peggy stopped in front of Lizzie, noticing how her accent came out when she forgot herself. Peggy saw from Lizzie's expression that she hadn't meant to sound so self-pitying, but it had no effect on her.

"What about 'poor bliddy' you?" she mimicked. "Eunice is six feet under an' Jack's still fighting the war with the rest of the nutcases back from France. And here you are." She opened her arms to indicate the room as a representation of Lizzie's life. "Seems to me, *Mrs Elizabeth Fawcett*, you're the only one who's in the gravy." Her face darkened. "Since he came back, are you an' him…"

"Of course not…"

Peggy wasn't sure she believed her. "I can't make head or tail of you. Why don't you hate him? After what he did to you? He pretended to be someone else so he could forget his marriage vows and take advantage of you, and I know you cared about him, and he left you ruined and you thinking him dead. Do you really think he gives a farthing for you?"

Lizzie shrugged. "I can't explain it. Maybe hate and love are two sides of the same coin. He didn't know about our child. I never got the chance to tell him."

"Y'know what I think?" Peggy fixed her with a piercing stare. "I think you need to rid yourself of any romantic notion you might be harbouring about Jack. Thinking of playing happy ever after with him and William as your pretend-replacement son?"

Lizzie looked down at her hands, clasped together in her lap. "I…"

"Happy families? Ha. He loved Eunice, not you! He used you – used you for his own selfish ends when things were bad between them. When he'd just lost his son. To him you were just another silly trollop giving favours to soldiers."

Lizzie's head jerked up and she stuck her chin out in an attempt to stare Peggy down across the room. "Isn't that the pot calling the kettle black?"

Peggy ignored her. "Eunice's death almost destroyed him!" She was shouting now, carried away by her sense of injustice. "And it serves him right. Well, I'll tell you something else for nothing..."

She stopped mid-sentence, regretted her lack of restraint for once and strode towards the door. Lizzie caught hold of her arm.

"Tell me something else for nothing."

Peggy turned on her at the sarcasm and said, "You're wasting your time."

"What do you mean?"

"With your Lizzie, Jack and William fantasy."

"I'm not..."

"William ain't Jack's child."

Chapter Forty-one

Lizzie slumped down on the sofa, took Jack's photograph out of her pocket and looked at it as Peggy's voice swirled in her head.

"You mean Eunice slept…" A small spark of shocked satisfaction coursed through her at Peggy's revelation.

"No! Eunice kept her marriage vows."

"I don't understand."

Peggy stood in silence in front of the fireplace. Her earlier belligerence seemed to have melted away. She stared up at the ceiling, as if collecting herself before she began.

"Eunice lost her and Jack's baby. It was stillborn."

"Oh."

"That was the fifth one she'd lost."

"How terrible."

"I came home and she'd put the baby in Alfie's old basket and dressed him in baby clothes she must've kept hold of, and she was going on as if he was still alive." Her words came out in a torrent, as if the pressure of holding them in had finally given way, then her voice dropped, imbued with tenderness. "He was perfect. He looked as if he was only asleep." She looked across at Lizzie, her eyes imploring. "I could see she was teetering on the edge, but I knew pretending your baby wasn't dead wasn't right." Peggy looked down at her hands, clasped in front of her.

Lizzie gently took hold of her arm, led her to the sofa and sat down opposite her, softened by Peggy's obvious distress, her earlier rancour having dissipated.

"I thought she needed seeing to, so I persuaded her to put the baby in the perambulator – like we were going out for a walk, as that way she wouldn't know what I was up to – and I took her to the free clinic in Old Ford Road instead of her own doctor. I remember even there she wouldn't part with that baby, kept saying he needed a feed. The doctor remembered her – turns out she'd been there before – and he eventually got her to take something to calm her down while he took care of her dead baby. Then we left. Eunice was in a sort of stupor by then. She insisted she push the baby carriage. I don't think she knew there was no baby in it by that stage – she was beyond it and drugged up. It was awful." Peggy clasped and unclasped her hands as she spoke.

"Then?"

Peggy glanced at her then looked away again.

"The doctor, he came to see her next day, and right at the end he said he had a baby that needed a mother. Came out with it. Just like that. He knew about Alfie, and I saw that Eunice trusted him, despite him being foreign. He said it was the fourth baby that'd been left on the doorstep of his East End surgery that month. He had no option but to put most of the mites in the children's home, or worse – I suppose he meant the poorhouse. Eunice wasn't sure at first. He didn't push her, but I said she had a hole in her heart that needed filling, and wasn't she still producing milk?"

Peggy coughed, clearing her throat.

"I pointed to the stain which had seeped through her dress. Bit unkind maybe, but I wanted to make my point. She just stared down at it, not embarrassed like she would be normally, and said, 'Can you bring the child tomorrow?' That was it. She didn't ask if it was a boy or a girl." Peggy swallowed hard. "D'you think I could have a drink?"

Lizzie called for Elsie and asked her to bring up some tea, despite knowing Peggy had meant something stronger. "So you..."

"Kept him? Yes. And Eunice pretended he was hers."

Elsie came in with the tea and there was an awkward silence.

"Would you like me to pour the tea, M'm?"

"We can manage ourselves, thank you, Elsie."

Peggy watched this interaction between mistress and servant, and Lizzie saw the brief look of disdain before she took a large gulp of tea. She rested her teacup on the saucer on her lap and stared down into it. Lizzie watched her for a moment, but she was too impatient to wait.

"So Eunice just took him and went along with it? And Jack has no idea?"

"Look," Peggy leaned forwards abruptly, the movement causing a little splash of tea to slop over the cup and pool in the saucer, "if you had seen the look of contentment on her face when she put that baby to her breast…well, it just seemed so right. Best for both of them in the circumstances."

Lizzie stood up and paced around the room. She was unsure of her own feelings. *Did she believe Peggy? What about the legality of what they had done? Was Eunice in her right mind when she accepted the baby?*

She asked, "And she definitely knew it wasn't her child?"

"She's not – wasn't – stupid, you know. Yes." As if guessing she hadn't won Lizzie over with her argument, she cried, "But she also knew his own mother had abandoned him. If it was your baby, wouldn't you be glad he got a proper mother to look after him instead of the children's home?"

Lizzie had heard the sly note of appeal in her voice before Peggy delivered her perceptive barb.

"Then maybe your own child wouldn't be on your conscience so much."

"Oh, that's a bit stiff!" Lizzie cried, eyes flashing. "You know it was taken out of my hands."

"Tell me, then," Peggy said, defensive once again, "that you wouldn't have done the same thing for that baby's sake, denying Eunice a chance to be a mother into the bargain."

Lizzie didn't know what she would have done.

"Anyway, we couldn't give him back 'cos Dr Carroll didn't know who had left him."

"The road to Hell…" Lizzie stopped, blinked. "Dr Carroll? He was the doctor?"

"Yes."

Lizzie's thoughts were a complete jumble and a dull ache was beginning at her temple. She suggested Peggy should go. Peggy was so unhappy at being dismissed that she flung the morning door wide open, making it hit the wall with a crack.

Lizzie reached out and stroked William's fine downy hair. He was a perfect picture of innocence until Peggy's revelations began to swirl around him. But Lizzie found herself questioning their veracity. *Were they even true, or was she simply being spiteful, trying to get back at Lizzie to have her revenge for Eunice? Or maybe Eunice had been unfaithful, and Peggy was protecting her memory. But why mention it? And what of Dr Carroll?* She knew the absence of doctors who were serving at the Front had meant those left had had to attend surgeries wherever they were needed, and that Dr Carroll had worked at the Mother's Arms clinic occasionally.

She let out a little sigh of frustration and thought how the sting of Peggy's 'happy families' remark had hit home.

Chapter Forty-two

Dr Carroll had gone to Maghull on the invitation of Dr Rows, and until he came back with news of Jack's progress, Lizzie couldn't seem to settle to anything. Her turbulent feelings about Jack melded with wild ideas about her own child's fate and his whereabouts, stirred up by Peggy's revelations. Restless, she went out into the hall and saw the door to Edmund's study was ajar and the light on. She peered around the door and saw her husband sitting behind his desk, sporting a new pair of fashionably round silver-framed eyeglasses, his head lowered over a book. A small wave of guilt washed over her at the sight of him.

He looked up, put his book aside at once and came from behind the desk. "Hello, my darling."

"Edmund," she gave him a look intended to melt the hardest heart, "please tell me what happened to my child."

"Ah." He steered her over towards the small sofa next to the fire. "I knew having that Wilson child here would upset you." The gentleness of his tone could not quite disguise the underlying note of irritation. He took hold of her hand.

"It's not William's fault," she protested in a rather feeble way. She knew his presence had played a part; holding him, knowing his helpless dependence on her, feeling his softness and warmth, not knowing the truth – all of these stirred her repressed maternal instincts.

"I'm afraid I can't tell you anything."

"Can't you?"

"I had nothing to do with it." He gave a little cough. "My sister made enquiries, and through a mutual acquaintance she was introduced to Ernest, who had certain connections in that area."

Dr Carroll. Lizzie turned her head away from Edmund and stared into the fireplace at the leaping flames. "Is that why you gave him the panel job at the factory? As payment for services rendered?"

"Certainly not. He applied without my prior knowledge. He was the best man for the job." She caught the disappointment in his voice that his wife would think such a thing of him. "I'm sorry, my darling. We all thought it would be the least upsetting way for you if he was taken straight away rather than simply prolonging the agony."

Lizzie continued to look into the fireplace. How ironic that her erstwhile employer had now carried through what he had offered at the beginning of her pregnancy. *Has he placed my son with some high born family?* she wondered. But a second thought struck her. *Peggy said it was Dr Carroll who gave Eunice the abandoned baby. The two birth dates – of William and her own child – were only a day apart.* She felt her heartbeat quicken. *Was that baby really left on the steps of his surgery? Or...*

Lizzie became aware of her husband stroking her hand. "It really would be best if we let matters be – for your sake, and the boy's. Put it behind us."

We? Us?

"Perhaps have a child of our own."

She looked at her husband, thought guiltily of the contraceptive device she had been using – ordered from the address on the side of Charlotte Dearden's box before she had reclaimed her belongings to take to Folkestone – and gave him a weary smile.

If only it were that simple, to replace one child with another.

*

Lizzie sat in the Commercial Street surgery, a few desultory files scattered on her desk as she tried very hard not to feel let down by her husband. If only he had proposed before her child had been born. They would be a family unit now, she told herself. However, in moments of more lucid reflection she understood that when Edmund looked at her he wanted to see Elizabeth Fawcett, his wife, not Lizzie Fenwick, the fallen woman with an illegitimate child. She knew her child's presence would be a perpetual reminder of her illicit love with another man – of her former self. She then berated herself for expecting too much of him. He had married her, despite her pariah status – something very few men would even consider. And yet, wrapped up with her feelings for Jack was a sense of something else unfinished, and it unsettled her.

Now she waited until the last patient had gone. "Ernest. Can you spare me a moment?"

The doctor looked up from the notes he was scribbling.

"Edmund tells me he entrusted the placement of my son entirely to you." Lizzie stated this as a fact and tried to keep any note of accusation from her voice.

"This is true. Yes." He appraised the situation immediately. "But you are blaming me for not telling you? And him too, a little, maybe?"

"Yes. Perhaps. No. Not really. Oh, I don't know. I just have this awful sense of being in suspended animation because I don't know what has happened to my child. Was it really necessary to take him from me so cruelly soon?" She spun her thumbs round each other.

"Let me be frank. Edmund's sister seemed to be afraid her brother was going to make a fool of himself. So she wanted to have your child adopted immediately in the hope that he would not feel the need to marry you to save you from ruin. While I cannot say I agree with her reasoning," he gave her a smile of sympathy, "it is my professional opinion that nothing is to be gained by allowing a mother to bond with her child if she cannot keep that child."

"I wasn't given the option."

"I think you knew what you had to do, right from the moment you believed your lover was dead and you were carrying his illegitimate child. And why you had to do it."

She glanced at him, her eyes brimming with tears, and she saw him soften.

"Giving up your child is very hard. For a mother, it is like tearing your heart out. However, to give Mrs Dearden some credit, she came to me on a recommendation because she knew I could place your child with a very good family. Trust me, he will get the very best start in life."

"And Edmund went along with it?"

"Eventually, yes."

This mollified Lizzie, but she was not prepared to countenance Charlotte Dearden had any charity in her heart.

"Could I not see him? Just once, when he is in the park, or..."

"Ach, my dear, I'm afraid that would not be sensible."

Lizzie suddenly lost all reason. "Did you give him to Eunice Wilson? And now he has no mother at all!"

"Who? Ah, Jack Wilson's wife. Of course not." He looked at her with pity. "Why would you think that?"

Lizzie's body sagged; she had almost hoped it was true. "Oh, I was told a doctor – you – gave her an abandoned baby to look after as her own."

He hesitated before he admitted it was so. "But it wasn't your child. Look, I would be breaking a verbal agreement with the adoptive parents of your son if I told you where he is."

"So he is to be dead to me from now on. I'm to pretend, like everyone else, that he doesn't exist." She said it as if to herself.

"It is better if the child does not know he is not the natural child of his parents, *hein*? And with this otherwise childless family, there

256

is the issue of inheritance and so forth. So it is preferable that there should be no contact."

"I can't bear it."

"You cannot expect to get over it just like this." He snapped his fingers lightly. "You must be kind to yourself." He patted her shoulder. "It is a truism, but time, that is the only thing. And sometimes one has to be cruel to be kind."

Those old lies, she thought bitterly.

"Do not forget your good fortune. Try to look to your marriage to find the comfort you seek."

Outside Dr Carroll's surgery, Lizzie bought a newspaper from the news hawker in an effort to divert her mind during the journey home. Having walked half the length of the seemingly never-ending street without seeing any motor taxis – they were still rarer than hen's teeth, despite the men being back from the war, she complained to herself – she decided to jump on a bus which was just moving off. She squeezed herself among the mass of passengers already crammed inside and almost immediately regretted her actions: she could barely breathe.

To prevent the man opposite from exhaling his foul-smelling breath into her face, Lizzie raised her newspaper as a shield. A sensationalist headline about the trial of a middle class couple, whose business was adopting babies for money and then letting them starve to death to save on the cost of looking after them, caught her eye. It sent her mind into turmoil all over again. However, a little fact at the end of the article offered her a glimmer of hope and gave her some focus. She pushed her way off the bus, ignoring the muttered curses of those passengers on whose toes she stepped in her haste to alight. Immediately, she caught another bus going in the opposite direction.

The overcrowded conditions on the second bus matched the first, and she was pleased to get off at the east end of The Strand, unsure where exactly Somerset House was. Here she expected to find the registry of all births, marriages and deaths as outlined at the end of the newspaper article.

Lizzie wove her way through a swarm of oncoming pedestrians until she saw a huge palace-like building. Briefly she noticed its grandeur had been diminished by the urban grime which blackened its once creamy stone exterior, but she was sure this was the place. As she approached the entrance she saw an ex-serviceman, one leg of his trousers fastened up at the knee, leaning on a crutch with a tray of matches in front of him. She saw the card pinned to the tray –*I fought for King and Country. I can't get a job. My family is starving* – and stopped to hand over a few coins. She began to walk off, but he called after her, saying she must take the matches. Lizzie smiled and thanked him.

"God bless you, missus," he said, doffing his cap with difficulty due to a false arm.

In that instant she had a horrible foreboding: what if this was to be Jack's fate as well? Forced to beg on the streets for a few pennies if his rehabilitation didn't work. She couldn't bear to think of it. She hurried away from the man and turned through the imposing entrance arch, emerging into a large courtyard which looked like a series of town houses arranged in a quadrangle. Lizzie had no idea which wing she needed, so she approached an official looking man. With an implacable face, he stiffly directed her to the north wing, where she would find the General Registry. If neither Edmund nor Ernest Carroll were able – or prepared – to give her the information she wanted, then she decided she would try to find it out by other means. Here, she supposed, she might make a start.

The inside of the registry was the opposite of the building's grand exterior facade and did not seem to welcome public access. Nevertheless, she persevered and was pleased when a middle-aged clerk with an open face greeted her with warm civility. Lizzie gave him her sweetest smile as she made her request, then called him back and gave him William Wilson's name as well. He didn't seem in the least perturbed and indicated an austere shabby chair, pushed against the wall, for her to sit on while he made his enquiries.

Lizzie sat down on the hard seat. Almost immediately she began to feel oppressed by the place. What would she do with the information when she got it? Should she be raking up the past like this? She stood up and walked back and forth in front of the chair. The clerk reappeared clutching a heavy leather-bound volume with a marker in it. She swept up to the counter, her eyes bright and eager with anticipation.

"I'm afraid, madam, there's no entry for a male child born to an Elizabeth Fenwick on 24 April."

"Oh." Her shoulders drooped. "But the marker?" She jabbed her finger at it, just in case he had forgotten it.

"Ah, that's for William Wilson," he announced, opening the tome.

Lizzie barely heard him, concerns over identifying and tracing her own child paramount.

"Could you try another name perhaps? Erm," she frowned, "Grimes perhaps?" The dead maid's name was the first one that popped into her head. "Or...or...Oh, I don't know!"

She didn't think it likely either Fawcett, Dearden or Carroll would have been used, but she gave them anyway. Otherwise she was at a loss; if her son's new parents had registered him, they would have used their own surname.

"I can certainly check. If you would wait just a moment." The clerk maintained his helpful expression and excused himself with a small nod of the head.

Lizzie leaned on the highly polished dark wooden counter and began tapping her fingers on it until her eyes strayed to the large tome the clerk had left behind. She opened it at the place marked and ran her finger down the columns. There he was: *William Wilson. Date of birth: 25 April 1918. Mother: Eunice Wilson, Tailoress. Father: Jack Wilson, Printer. Place of birth: Poplar, E14.*

Of course Eunice had registered the birth to make it legitimate. She should have expected that. She looked up as the clerk reappeared, his hands empty.

"Sorry, nothing. Ah, I see you found William Wilson."

"What? Oh, yes." Suddenly an idea came to her. "What about the register for adopted children?" she asked with forlorn hope. She couldn't bear to think her son officially didn't exist.

"Ah, I'm afraid I cannot help you there, madam. Transactions of that nature are not available to the scrutiny of the general public." Lizzie cringed inwardly at his use of the word 'transaction' to describe the adoption of a child. "Besides, there are no formal adoption laws in this country, and therefore no legal registration requirements."

Lizzie felt completely deflated as she stepped outside, her brows clenched in frustrated disappointment, until a thought struck her about Eunice. She went back inside.

"Would you be able to look up a child's death in the register?"

"Of course, madam, if you could give me the name."

"Oh, I don't know the name. It was stillborn, you see, but I have the mother's name."

"Ah." The clerk shook his head. "Stillbirths are not registered. At present you only need a burial certificate at the place of internment."

Lizzie made a little huff of frustration. The clerk suggested she might try the appropriate cemetery. However, she had no idea where Eunice's child might have been buried, and she knew she couldn't face asking Peggy for the details (Peggy would likely not tell her anyway, the mood she was in). Despite her efforts coming to naught, she hid her despair and smiled sweetly at the clerk and thanked him for his help.

Back outside the registry, she squinted as she entered the courtyard again, her eyes unaccustomed to the bright light after the gloom of the claustrophobic interior. She walked back through the arch and out onto The Strand, careful not to look at the wounded soldier selling his matches.

Chapter Forty-three

Peggy lay on the plaid rug, propped up on her elbows as she watched a well-dressed woman playing with two young children: a boy and a girl. Behind them the Serpentine gleamed in the sunlight, and somewhere on the other side of the park she could hear the faint strains of music from a band playing in the open air. She saw the woman gently toss a ball to the smaller child, still wobbly on his feet. He promptly missed it and toppled over from the effort. It was amusing to watch the way the child at first appeared surprised to find himself on the ground, and then he began to wail. At once the woman picked him up and comforted him. The gesture stirred something unfamiliar within Peggy. She wondered what emotions the boy felt when he was picked up and hugged: something her childhood self had never experienced.

The missed ball had rolled near her foot. She reached down and picked it up.

"Cry baby! Cry baby!" the little girl called to the child over her shoulder as she ran up to Peggy, her hand outstretched for the ball. "Please may I have my ball back?"

Peggy heard the accent of a child who didn't want for much. She held the ball out to her. "If you're unkind to your brother, your mother will punish you."

The girl looked only a little chastened before she said, "Miss Dawson is not my mother", took the ball, said a polite "Thank you" and ran off.

Briefly Peggy wondered what relation to the child 'Miss Dawson' was. Governess perhaps, or nanny, judging from the girl's accent. It prompted her to think about her last conversation with Lizzie, which had been unsatisfactory, no doubt.

The more she thought about it, the more she could kick herself for letting her mouth run away with her. She'd allowed herself to get so riled up about Lizzie going with Jack that she'd blabbed about William. Might Lizzie turn her in? She frowned. Lizzie had acted very high and mighty. Just who did she think she was? Forgotten she used to be an ash-cat? That she'd got herself pregnant? And then she'd let her child be taken away, as well. She didn't have the first idea how her son would feel later, when he discovered he'd been given up.

"Well, I know all right," Peggy said aloud before checking herself. She flicked a glance at the figure next to her, stretched out, his arms behind his head, his eyes closed, but he didn't stir.

Rejected and unloved, that's what she'd felt. And what did Lizzie Fenwick know about people telling you your mother is sinful? About being constantly reminded of your illegitimacy and inferiority?

"I could tell her," she muttered, and thought Lizzie would then be wishing she'd gone to Crochet Hook Dora after all. Why didn't Lizzie get it? Between them, Eunice and Peggy had saved William from a mother who didn't want him, from a life in an institution. A place she wouldn't wish on her worst enemy. A place where love is absent.

A vision of a doped-up Eunice, who on very bad days reeled about the house like a drunk and ricocheted off the furniture before collapsing onto the sofa in a Veronal-addled stupor, filled Peggy's imagination, and she squirmed inwardly before she shut the image off. Suddenly the excited cries of the girl who had fetched the ball from her broke into her indignant thoughts.

"Miss Dawson! Miss Dawson! Please!"

Peggy shaded her eyes from the sun and squinted in the direction of the girl's pointing finger. At the same time as she saw the familiar cart with its striped awning, she heard the accented cry of the vendor.

"Hokey pokey, penny a lump!"

She looked over at the long, lean figure of Stan Bartholomew next to her. She'd agreed to walk out with him today just for something to do. Her gaze ran over his features: an aquiline nose with tributaries of scarlet broken veins; a too prominent jutting chin; pale eyebrows and slicked-back straight blond hair. A livid scar was just visible at his hair line – his war wound, he told her – but it didn't draw the eye. What did, though, were his even creamy-coloured dentures that were completely at odds with the rest of him, and had been the first thing she'd noticed about him – other than that he was rather drunk and giving her the glad eye.

Today, however, Peggy saw he was wearing a good suit in her honour. She gave him a sharp prod in the ribs which made him stir. He opened one eye to look at her. She feigned innocence, and then laughed as she pointed at the hokey pokey man. Without demur, he got up, thrust his hand into his trouser pocket to retrieve some change and strode off. Within seconds he was back.

"What flavour?"

Peggy told him, amused at his apparent keenness to please her, but a little warning voice in her head whispered that she mustn't allow herself to get her hopes up. Even though the war had considerably reduced her chances of finding herself a decent husband – or any husband, if it came to it – she still had reservations about the likelihood of him sticking around. Her early experience of abandonment went so deep that she found it difficult to expect anything else.

Finishing his treat, Stan Bartholomew used the reverse of the paper the ice cream cake had come on to wipe his lips, before he crushed it up into a ball and threw it behind him onto the grass. He lay on his side facing her, one hand propping up his head and the other laid flat on his hip as he watched her finish her ice cream.

Aware of his approving gaze, once or twice she flicked him an inviting glance, and when she was almost finished she stuck her finger into what was left and placed the ice cream dollop on the end of his nose. He pretended to be annoyed, and manoeuvred himself so he could push her gently down and lay half over her. He put his nose to hers and made sure the ice cream transferred. She gave a little cry and pulled herself out from under him in mock outrage at his forwardness. He gave a rich throaty laugh as he pulled out a handkerchief from his pocket to offer to her, and when she took it he puckered his lips to indicate she could show her gratitude with a kiss.

"I'm not that easily bought," she said archly.

Once, in his cups, leaning over the bar, he had told her he loved her, wanted to marry her and have a brood of kids. She'd joked that he was already married – to the bottle. No man had ever said those words to her before and meant them. In her experience, during the war men couldn't be trusted. They didn't always come back – and not just because they couldn't.

As Peggy sat on the bus, her hand enclosed by the ex-soldier's long fingers, she suddenly wished Eunice was here so she could ask her advice. It saddened her to think that Eunice was like the mother she had never had; the only person who had shown her some kindness and not expected anything in return, and now she was dead. *God Bless her.* Invariably of late, when Eunice popped into Peggy's head, thoughts of William weren't far behind. She had thought that persuading her friend to accept the child abandoned by his mother was a good idea for both Eunice and the baby, yet a little seed of dissatisfaction had been planted during her conversation with Lizzie, and she couldn't prevent her conflicting thoughts watering it. Her friend's words about 'The road to Hell' came back to her now.

"Stan?"

"Yes, my little buttercup?"

She looked at his daft, love-struck face. "Do you think it's all right if you do a wrong thing as long as it's for the right reasons?"

"What's this, a test?"

"I'm serious."

"Well, I suppose it depends on what the wrong thing is." He looked thoughtful. "And what its consequences might be."

"Hmm." She pursed her lips.

But I did it with the best of intentions, she thought, *getting her to take the child. No one can say I didn't.*

She mulled it over some more. In her mind's eye she saw Eunice, always on edge, constantly looking over her shoulder, and recalled how odd she'd thought it that the child should be both a comfort and a burden to her friend. Then she remembered her own growing anxiety, after Jack came home, that Eunice might give the game away and they'd both do a stretch in Holloway. "If you want a happy ending, just stick to the story," Peggy had told her, and she had, but at a cost. There'd been no happy ending for Eunice.

Suddenly she heard Stan Bartholomew's voice.

"Testing my strength now, are you, by trying to break my hand?" He indicated her tight grip.

"What? Oh." Peggy released her fingers. "Sorry."

"You all right?"

"I'm fine." She wafted his concern away with her other hand, but a vision of Lizzie's good fortune – her nice life and her fancy house – rose up before Peggy. She remembered how Eunice had persuaded her to do the right thing by Lizzie with Fawcett that time. Well, doing the right thing had ended up with her eking out a living as a barmaid – a not quite respectable occupation – while her supposed friend hadn't seen fit to use her charms on the manager she later married to get Peggy reinstated.

"If you knew a secret about someone, would you spill the beans?"

"Not if I wanted to keep their friendship."

"Say, for argument's sake, I don't."

"Well, by keeping their secret – and they know you have the information – you've got a hold over them, haven't you? You get to choose how and when to wield that power."

Peggy nodded.

"But you have to be careful, in case the person you tell the secret to doesn't thank you for it – prefers not to know about it, in fact, and decides to shoot the messenger."

She tilted her head to the side and stared at him with admiration. "Quite the philosopher, ain't we."

For the remainder of the journey, she imagined what it would feel like to tell Fawcett about Lizzie and Jack, then weighed up what she might gain by it.

Chapter Forty-four

Lizzie looked at the note attached to the single folder on her desk. In his usual meticulous handwriting, Dr Carroll explained he would be back by ten o'clock, ready for his surgery at half past ten. She only came in twice a week now, the volume of patients no longer warranting her presence full-time, but she was surprised there was only one patient's folder to be filed. She had plenty of time before the first appointment, so she thought she would get this file out of the way and then she could make herself a nice cup of tea.

Lizzie pulled out the note from beneath the paper clip on the front of the file to expose the patient's name. Her heart missed a beat. She knew this folder belonged in the confidential cabinet in the doctor's office, not out here. *An unusual mistake for him to make.* She glanced at the clock on the wall and across at the outer door, calculating whether she had time to look between the file's covers before the doctor returned. She had only ten minutes.

She picked up the folder, a nervous and anticipatory excitement making her a little light-headed. She began to open it when the shrill ring of the telephone shattered the silence. Startled, she let go of one edge of the file and watched as a single sheet of notepaper detached itself and floated across the desk. Flustered, the insistent ring of the telephone drilling through her head, she reached over and snatched up the stray piece of paper. She clutched it in one hand while she grabbed the receiver with the other.

"Hello? Dr Carroll's surgery," Lizzie snapped. "No, I'm afraid he's not here at the moment. May I take a message?" She held the telephone precariously between her chin and shoulder. "I have made a note of it," she lied. "Goodbye."

She barely noticed how curt she sounded. She slotted the receiver onto its cradle with some difficulty and stared at the quivering piece of paper. The note was addressed to her. Touches of the familiar handwriting made her pulse quicken. She was almost deafened by the roar of her blood rushing around her skull. Lizzie looked at the clock and cast her eyes down to the letter. It was over a month old, with messy handwriting, full of crossed out words and jumbled thoughts.

2 April 1919

Dear Elizabeth,

I believe you know who I am XXX X XXXXX XXX XXXX XX XXXX XXXX XXXX X XXX XX undeserving wretch XXXXX XXXXX. XXXX XXXX XX XXXXXXX XXXX XXXXX XXX XXXX X XXXX XXXXX I owe you an explanation XXX XXX X XXXX XXXX XXXX X XXXX Harry Slater picked your note out of the shell box and sent that first card to you. XXXX X XXXX XX XXXXXX XXXXX XXX. Immediately afterwards he was reported missing in action and when your reply arrived I wrote back in his name. That first time I don't know why I did it because I knew he was already dead, lying somewhere in No Man's Land XX XXX XXXX XXX X XXXXX XX XXX. Then each time you replied I was going to tell you the truth XXXX XXXXX XXXXXX XXX XXXX. As long as no one else knew XXXX X XXX XXXXXX XXX I stupidly thought I could

somehow keep Slater alive. Your letters stopped me
thinking only of death and blood and the hell I was
in. In a trench you only think in the present moment
and nothing else matters XXX X XXXX XXXXXXX
XXXXX XXXXXXX. So I kept on even when
I knew I shouldn't. I looked at your photograph
often XXXXXX wondering about you. XXXX X
XXXXXX XXXXX XXXXX XX I formed a certain
impression of you. XXX XXX X XXXX XXX XXXXX
XX XXXXX XXX XXX XXX X XXX XXX. When
I went to that Corner House it was to tell you Slater
was dead. XXXXXXX X XXXXXX XXX. As soon as I
saw you I knew I would fail, and afterwards when
I held you everything bad went away. X XXXXX
XXXX XXXX XXXXX XX X XXXX XXX XXX XXXXX
XXXXXXXX X XXX XXXXX XX XX.

She stared at the notepaper and listened to the clock ticking her
life away.

Your letters became a refuge. I couldn't live without
them. They stopped me going mad XXXX. X
XXXX XXX XXXX XXXX but I had to be dead to
you when I went back because I was told Slater's
body had been found. His mail would be returned
XXXXXXXXX but I took your scarf as a precious
reminder. I almost bled to death from a shrapnel
wound because I couldn't bear for it to be torn into
pieces to stem the blood XXX XX X XXXXX

Somewhere she heard a little cough. Dr Carroll was standing
next to her. She had not heard him come in. He patted her shoulder

in a paternalistic fashion and she laid her head against the rough wool of his coat.

"The talking therapies are working well, but writing things down was also a part of his treatment," he said. "Catharsis."

Lizzie had no idea what that meant. She remained silent, staring at the note, unable to tear her eyes away.

"I should not discuss patients – I am afraid I am breaking the rules yet again – but I feel I must be frank with you for your sake and tell you that his trauma is mired in the war, in the incident in No Man's Land. He was part of a night raid party of four men, but things went badly wrong. They lost one man to a sniper, and on the way back they were spotted and got caught in a barrage which split them up. When Jack was almost back at the British line he was taken by surprise and thought his attacker was a German soldier. He did what he had been taught to do. When a shell burst above him, the light showed him that he had killed one of his own men. He was unable to speak of what he had done and the neurasthenia probably quickened after that. The body was eventually discovered and identified from the tag."

The doctor fell silent. Lizzie thought about Jack's reaction to the crashing tray, when she barely knew him but was already a little in love with him, and made the connection with the bursting shell above his compatriot's dead body. She looked up at Ernest Carroll, at the expression on his face, and at once she understood.

"It was Harry Slater he killed."

The doctor nodded. "That is where the root of his trauma lies."

She remained motionless, as if in a trance.

"And his feelings for you, because he took on the identity of this Harry Slater, are bound up in his trauma. His guilt over his wife's death simply compounded it." He paused to let this sink in. "Dr Rows tells me he is making satisfactory progress, but Lizzie, you should know that Moss Side Hospital can only go so far in getting him to deal with his demons and helping him to a point where he can try and become a useful member of society."

Eventually she dragged her eyes away from the letter just as an early patient arrived and called the doctor to his other duty.

"Please." He gestured for her to pass the file and note to him.

She clasped it to her chest. "It's addressed to me." She wanted to keep it, afraid that if he took it away everything she had had with Jack would be negated.

"He chose not to send it, so it belongs to him."

With great reluctance she handed him the note and the file.

Other patients came and went for the rest of the morning. Lizzie buzzed around them like a demented bee one minute and sat at her desk in a silent reverie the next, all the while trying to pull her scattered thoughts together.

After Dr Carroll had seen his last patient of the day out, he returned to the subject of Jack Wilson and cautioned her to tread carefully, now more fully aware of her relationship with him.

"I have learned that some men are so damaged they will never truly recover what they have lost in this war. They will never find a way back to this world we live in. It can destroy those who choose to care for them also."

She glanced up at him and saw pity and concern lurking.

"You must not try and love Jack Wilson out of his trauma, Lizzie. For your sake and his. Think of what you have, what you could lose. Think about your future life."

At once she felt as if some sadist had placed a tourniquet round her heart and twisted it tight, and she couldn't help thinking of what she had already lost and what might have been.

Chapter Forty-five

Lizzie observed her husband, his head laid back against the sofa's antimacassar, his eyes closed and a glass of whisky in his hand, a look of contentment on his face as he listened to the sweep of a Vaughan Williams piece playing on the gramophone. He often liked to relax in this manner before retiring to bed. They had been out for an evening of gaiety at the theatre, where they had been invited to share a box with the owner of the chemical plant Edmund now managed and was a minor shareholder in. The owner's wife had spent the entire evening discussing her eldest daughter's coming out, because the Court presentations were restarting now that the war was over. Talk of such debutante glamour would have appealed to Lizzie's romantic imaginings before the war, but now, as she watched Edmund, his lips moving wordlessly in time with the melody – a habit of his – the thought that there was something deeper missing from her real-world life returned to unsettle her, as it had quite often of late.

She leaned against Edmund and placed her head just under his chin while her left hand rested on his chest. She could feel the calm rhythm of his heartbeat as the mellifluous music lulled them into a gentle somnolence.

"I'd like to be able to earn my own money again." She began to pick a piece of lint from his waistcoat.

"I can look after you perfectly well, my darling." His hand came up and stroked her hair.

She sighed. "Yes, but I'm bored."

She felt his chest rise and fall against her hand. "It's a pity you find the domestic sphere so dull. I thought helping out Ernest would stave off the boredom."

"I could put my typing skills to better use." She felt a slight stiffening of his torso. She tilted her head, looked up at him and saw his eyes were now open and his expression more attentive, as if he realised he needed his wits about him.

"This house will not run itself, you know," he said. "The servants need direction and sound management. Mrs Ryder has been here a long time and is very set in her ways, and Elsie is rather inexperienced. The running of the household needs your firm hand. Besides, do you think it fair that women such as yourself take up any form of paid work in the face of mass unemployment among returning soldiers?"

Secretly she thought she, along with her fellow working women, deserved more consideration for their contribution to the war effort, but she didn't say so – it wouldn't further her argument. Instead, she explained that she didn't mean going out to work or taking a job away from a man who needed it.

"I want to advertise a typing service in the newspaper. Use my Corona."

Behind his gaze she saw him making an evaluation. She was fully aware that holding the purse strings enabled him to maintain his authority more than if she had her own resources.

"It would allow me to remain at home and give me something worthwhile to do. But because I'll be here, I can still manage the domestic affairs."

Lizzie saw the two lines deepen between his brows.

"I like to relax and forget about work when I come home. I don't want it turned into some sort of commercial domain."

In her head, Lizzie had gone through all these arguments already and had prepared her answers.

273

"Oh, I know an Englishman's home is his castle, so I could use the spare attic room as an office, and that way I wouldn't disturb the household at all. You won't know I'm there! And I promise not to mention it over dinner."

She saw that he was torn between his love for her, his need to make her happy, and his own authority as the man of the house. Lizzie pressed home her claim.

"It would be so much better to have something of real interest to occupy myself with, something fulfilling to give me purpose during daylight hours."

She watched her husband consider this. Perhaps he was prepared to risk a little of his power in order to keep her fully occupied within the confines of the house, because this was more likely to ensure she didn't find herself in any low grade circumstances which might compromise her – and him.

"Very well," he said eventually. She leaned towards him and kissed him on the cheek. "But it mustn't interfere with your domestic duties." She heard the note of resignation. "And you put a box number on the advertisement."

She got up, increased the volume on the Vaughan Williams and pretended to enjoy it.

Chapter Forty-six

Lizzie heard the front door bell followed by voices in the hall. She tensed, listening. She picked up William and hugged him to her.

"We've had a fine time, haven't we?"

In response the boy banged together two alphabet blocks held in his pudgy little hands. Here was Eddie now, come to collect him and take him home. Energised by Edmund agreeing to her typing service plan, Lizzie was determined to appreciate her life, fulfil her domestic obligations and duties. She had told herself she must not allow her regret at William's departure to get the better of her.

When Elsie announced it was "Mr Wilson", Lizzie was forced to try to compose herself in an attempt to be ready to say her farewells. She held William aloft, asked the girl to show her visitor in, and was so busy making a fuss of the boy in her final few minutes with him that she didn't hear what else the maid said.

"Here's your Uncle Eddie, come to fetch you."

Lizzie spun the child around in the air like a propeller before she came to a halt and planted a noisy kiss on the top of his head. Feeling slightly giddy from her playful exertion and aware of a presence in the room, she turned to face her visitor. A man stood in the doorway, nervously fiddling with the cap held in his hands.

"Hello, Mrs Fawcett," Jack Wilson said and stepped into the room. He shoved his cap into the pocket of his plain suit.

Lizzie tried to hide her shock by focusing on the top of William's head, but her gaze could not remain there long. She looked up.

"Mr Wilson." She said it in such a way as to confirm that she already knew his identity; that he wasn't Harry Slater.

"I'm sorry to come here uninvited," he said, an expression of contrition on his face, "but my uncle had a chance to do extra work at the docks and my mother's not quite well enough to make a trip yet."

She wasn't sure that was true, but she gained the impression from his tone that he knew he was taking a risk by seeking her. A fizzing sensation ran through to her nerve ends as she struggled to keep her voice calm.

"No, no, it's good of you to come. Ah, here." She held the boy out to him. "I'll just ask the maid to get his things. Please excuse me." She hurried out of the room in case her knees gave way.

In the hallway, Lizzie paced a repetitive circuit.

What shall I say? What will he say? What shall I do? What will he do? What if?

Her gaze travelled around the elegant hallway and settled on Edmund's closed study door. Lizzie knew he was in there. On impulse, she moved towards the door and her fingers slid round the cold metal of the ornate door handle. Her husband was keen for her to end her acquaintance with the Wilsons. He hadn't been very enthusiastic about her helping them, especially latterly, so perhaps she ought not to involve him in this. She could deal with Jack on her own and get it over with. No need to disturb Edmund. She let go of the door handle.

Holding her tension inside herself, Lizzie went back into the morning room. With his back to her, unaware of her presence, Jack held the boy and pointed through the window at something outside which had caught his attention. She looked at his shoulders, slightly hunched now, and let her eyes linger on the way his wavy hair caressed the back of his collar. She observed the affectionate way he held the child and felt an overwhelming desire to tell him she had borne him a son. But Dr Carroll's warning voice floated at the edge of her consciousness and she fought off the urge.

"Look, a magpie. Mag-pie."

She watched the boy respond by giving Jack a gummy smile, exposing four tiny milk teeth while he patted Jack's cheek and made a gurgle in his throat.

"'Da-da'. Say 'Da-da'"

She felt her heart ready to break once again.

Jack looked over his shoulder into the interior of the room, and seeing her there he made a sudden turn. She saw pain flash across his blue-grey eyes and noticed the weakness in his right knee – the result, she assumed, of the shrapnel wound he had written of in his letter. Her gaze strayed to his jacket sleeve searching for a flash of green, but saw nothing. Then her eyes appraised him and greedily took him all in.

He had gained weight, lost the grey pallor and sunken eyes she had seen several months ago in the King's Arms, and the scatter of small red scars that had pitted his face had faded a little. She thought, with hidden pleasure, how much he again looked like the soldier she had given herself to almost two years ago. This recaptured romantic image of him made her feel as if all her good intentions might fall by the wayside and her repressed emotions come flooding out. At the same time she heard words begin to tumble out of his mouth, falling over each other: gratitude mixed with explanations mixed with regret, but not making complete sense. She felt they were dancing on the edge of a volcano.

"How is your mother?" she said abruptly.

For a second he looked confused, but then he recovered himself.

"Almost back to health. Thank you."

Lizzie pretended to be pleased to hear of it, and because she felt it would look odd, heartless even, if she didn't also offer him her condolences for Eunice, she voiced them. She saw a slight contraction around his mouth, but he thanked her. She enquired after his own health, again unsure whether she should broach it, but he told her he felt quite well.

An unnatural stillness descended on the room.

"My, this here lad's going to be a heavyweight, I reckon." Jack broke the silence and bent down to put William back on the floor, removing a barrier between himself and Lizzie. He stood up and faced her. "I'm starting over. In America."

Lizzie's face went slack and she couldn't stop a little "Oh" from escaping her lips as the tears pricked her eyelids. All at once she heard herself saying, a catch in her voice, "I'll always be glad it was you and not the real Harry Slater."

At the mention of Slater, she saw a vein throb in Jack's neck and his gaze shoot towards the door. At once fearful and regretful that the mention of the man he had impersonated and whom he had accidentally killed would cause some horrific reaction, she reached out a tentative hand to him. He stepped towards her, and before she knew it, he had gathered her up in his arms. Her unresisting lips yielded to his and the world stopped turning on its axis.

Somewhere a child began to cry. Reluctantly they broke their embrace, just ahead of a rich, commanding voice exploding into the room.

"Lizzie."

She jerked her head around, registering the unfamiliar harsh tone.

"Oh, Edmund," she said, flustered, stepping further away from Jack as her husband strode like a colossus into the room. "This is William's father. Mr Wilson. He…"

"I know who he is. We have met before. In the hospital." Speaking over the noise of William crying, Edmund was coldly polite and dispensed with the usual courtesy of shaking their visitor's hand. "I trust your mother has now recovered fully?"

"Yes, thank you. I am indebted to you and your wife for caring for my boy meantime." Jack's reply was equally without deference as he picked up William, who instantly stopped crying.

"No need to thank me. My wife is the one who deserves your... gratitude, but I think you more than repaid her with your previous heroic deed."

She watched Jack press his lips together.

"However, seeing to your son has been good practice for our first child, has it not, my dear?" He moved and stood next to Lizzie as he put a proprietorial arm around her waist.

Jack let his eyes wander down Lizzie's body to her stomach and then back up again to her face.

"I trust you can now get on with your own life." Edmund's meaning was clear: *let my wife be.* "Elsie has the boy's things." He swung his arm in the direction of the open door, where the maid waited for Jack to take his leave. "Good day to you, Mr Wilson."

Jack gave him a curt nod in acknowledgement of the dismissal and let his gaze rest on Lizzie for a moment before he walked out of the door.

She stood beside her husband until the front door banged shut, then she disengaged herself from Edmund's arm. She walked over to the window and faced out into the garden, clutching her arms to her chest, her back to the room. After a moment or two, as she gathered her shredded emotions together she turned around, prepared to face her husband, a stiff half-ashamed, half-apologetic smile fixed on her face, but the room was empty.

She was entirely alone.

Chapter Forty-seven

Lizzie awoke from a fitful doze, aware of a sick excitement which lurked in the base of her stomach. Swinging her legs over the side of the thick mattress, she padded across the bedroom floor to check the time by the clock on top of the chest of drawers. She peered at it in the gloom, but could barely make out the position of the hands, so she pulled open the curtains just enough to let in a thin shaft of early morning light. She watched the dust motes dance and fall towards her until she heard Elsie tap lightly on the door before coming in to bring Lizzie the usual cup of early morning tea.

"Good morning, Elsie."

The housemaid seemed surprised to find Lizzie up and out of bed. "How are you feeling, M'm? I hope your headache has gone."

"Yes. I feel better now, thank you."

Elsie left, knowing Lizzie required nothing further from her while she got dressed.

Lizzie sat at her dressing table in her silk chemise. Occasionally she took a sip of tea, glancing at her reflection in the dresser mirror before she carried on with her toilette. She applied her Helena Rubenstein Valaze vanishing cream, putting tiny blobs of emollient onto her alabaster skin before rubbing them in, using only a light pressure, in small circular motions. With her index fingers she smoothed her eyebrows into neat arches, satisfying herself of their symmetry before she smeared a faint bloom of rouge to her cheeks.

Finally, she dabbed a few drops of *Tilleul d'Orsay* scent on the inside of her wrists, behind her ears and at the base of her throat.

She got up and opened her wardrobe. Flicking through her small but carefully chosen items of fine clothing, she gently rubbed the materials between her thumb and forefinger, delighting in the sensuous feel of the various velvet, silk, crepe de chine, georgette, wool, satin, tulle and linen garments. She selected an outfit, scrutinised it, held it up against her and looked at her reflection in the mirror before relegating it back to its space in the wardrobe. She repeated this process several times, each time dissatisfied with the look.

On a sudden whim, Lizzie searched towards the edge of the rail and took out an old favourite she had not worn in almost two years. It was of a much lesser quality than many of the other items she had been able to buy after her marriage, but she had kept it for sentimental reasons. She put the green and cream check dress against her and looked at her image for several minutes. This outfit had suited her once. She returned it to the rail, and eventually settled on a mid-calf length bottle green self-patterned dress, selecting a pair of pale button-strapped leather shoes, lightweight kid gloves and a fashionable cloche to complement it.

As she came down the stairs, Lizzie's eyes lit on the pile of envelopes on the hall table. She hurried towards them. Her gloves, hat and handbag put to one side, she counted each letter, her smile widening as she got to ten, eleven, twelve…*fifteen*! All were replies to her advertisement for her typing services, forwarded on to her by the newspaper. She held them against her chest for a moment before she opened her bag and stuffed the whole lot of them into it. About to close the bag, Lizzie checked the small inside pocket, but her fingers only closed around a key. She made a little clicking noise with her tongue.

In the morning room, a quick look in the escritoire produced the missing item. She must have left it there yesterday evening. It was next to a silver medal suspended from a dark blue coloured ribbon edged with yellow. With a smile, she rubbed her thumb over the cold metal: 'For Courage' it said. It had been awarded to Edmund for his act of civilian bravery when the munitions had exploded. She knew it went some way to alleviating the disappointment he felt at not being allowed to enlist when war broke out because of his eyesight, but she was glad now that he hadn't gone to fight. She laid the medal down and took the newspaper cutting – a notice announcing the date of the unveiling of a statue in memory of the eighteen schoolchildren killed by an enemy bomb on 13 June 1917 – wondering if Edmund had seen it and whether he would understand its significance. He had made no mention of it before he went off to work, but his farewell kiss had had an unusual degree of affection in it. Or had she just imagined it?

Lizzie glanced up and looked through the tall windows in front of her which afforded such a lovely view into the walled garden beyond. She was pleased to see flowers had now gradually begun to replace the vegetables necessitated by the food shortages during the war – the tall spires of the dark pink foxgloves, spectacular at the back of the far border, contrasting with the showy blue bowl shaped spikes of the delphiniums and the orange, yellow and mahogany of the marigolds which blossomed profusely in front of them, nestled close to a large cluster of pinks with their silver-grey foliage. Suddenly a vision of Jack and William standing there a month ago flashed in front of her; she put it out of her mind.

She turned and walked into the hall where she stood in front of the wall mirror. She pulled on her dark green cloche, which allowed her neatly bobbed Titian hair to frame her features perfectly, and addressed her image.

"You'll do, Mrs Elizabeth Fawcett."

*

In the back of a motor cab, Lizzie watched scenes from the East India Dock Road flash past, and her mind swung to and fro like a clock pendulum. One minute the replies in her handbag encouraged her to imagine renting an office in a prominent street and employing staff, and the next, glancing at the cutting she held in her hand, she contemplated a different fate.

"Here we are, missus," the cabbie's voice broke into her reverie. "Poplar Recreation Ground."

Jolted out of her daydreaming, she grabbed hold of her bag and almost jumped out of the cab onto the roadway. She paid her fare, turned and saw ahead of her in the distance a mass of sombre-clad adults and children in school uniforms standing around a tall covered structure which towered over them. As she got nearer she felt the emotional charge in the air of heartbreak and grief and remembrance at this memorial for the school children killed in the Upper North Street bombing raid.

Edmund and she had been just two of thousands of members of the public who had contributed to the memorial fund, so she reasoned he could have no objection to her presence here. She stopped on the edge of the gathering and listened to the Mayor of Poplar's in-memoriam speech, but found her gaze drawn by the faces in the crowd, occasionally alighting on an individual who, on first glance, seemed to be familiar, but turned out to be a stranger. Only the eventual unveiling of the handsome Victorian Gothic memorial finally pulled her attention away.

She appraised its marble and granite pedestal, and its childlike angel carved from white stone which towered like a winged guardian over all those lost infant souls beneath it. Schoolchildren in their Sunday best for this special commemoration came forward in a solemn line and laid wreaths, which eventually covered the entire base of the pedestal in a riot of bright summer colours. A final prayer to mark the end of the ceremony saw Lizzie dip her head and look down at her gloved hands, clasped in front of her. A little voice in her head reminded her that Edmund, the man she had promised to 'love, honour and obey' on their wedding day, had given these to her.

"He's not coming."

Lizzie's shoulders stiffened at the familiar voice, but she didn't turn around.

"I said, Jack's not coming."

A painful tightness gripped Lizzie's throat. She forced herself to turn around to face Peggy, who stood there, all twitching lips and narrowed eyes.

"I've come to pay my respects. A fitting memorial, don't you think?" Lizzie bestowed on Peggy a quick false smile before she started to walk away down the path in the wake of the dispersing crowd's ghostly trail. Immediately she heard the annoying clack, clack of a woman's shoe heels following her.

"He sailed from Liverpool for New York a week ago."

A whole ocean now lies between us.

Lizzie attempted to increase her pace, but the energy seemed to be draining out of her.

"You're well out of it," Peggy called after her. "At the risk of sounding cruel, the truth is it's a nursemaid Jack Wilson needs, not a wife. You'd have had to chuck in your nice life and it'd put the kybosh on all your future plans for that business you were all excited about."

Suddenly, Lizzie's legs would not move and she rounded on her pursuer.

"Tell me, Peg, is it being left on the shelf that's made you so bitter?"

Lizzie saw the spiteful barb had hit home.

"At least I'm being true to myself. Can you say the same?"

"I never lied to Edmund," Lizzie found herself saying in self-justification.

Peggy regarded her for a moment as her mouth curved slyly. "Lying can be done without words."

"And you know nothing of my feelings for my husband."

Peggy shrugged her shoulders.

"Look…"

"Here. I almost forgot." Peggy shoved something soft into Lizzie's hand and walked out through the park gate, where she turned right onto the East India Dock Road without a backwards glance.

It took Lizzie a few seconds to register that she was holding a pale remnant of her green silk scarf.

In the flat above Ernest Carroll's surgery, from which Lizzie now ran her embryonic typing business, she put the kettle on to boil on her little gas stove and returned to her work. Her new assistant had gone out to deliver some urgently needed typed documents to a client in the City of London, and Lizzie expected the arrival of the doctor in about five minutes' time. They had fallen into the habit of taking tea together after his morning patients had been seen on the two days a week he wasn't the panel doctor at Edmund's factory.

Lizzie tapped away at her work, only stopping when she heard her visitor's footsteps on the stairs.

"As busy as ever, I see." Ernest Carroll looked around the room.

Lizzie rolled her eyes in mock horror. "We're snowed under. I'm seeing typewriters in my sleep, and" – she held up her hands – "I think my finger ends are turning into little flat spades."

"Perhaps you can take up gardening as well," he suggested, flicking a glance at the barren window box outside the small casement window.

She gave out a low laugh. "As if I have the time!" She balled her hands into fists and flexed her fingers.

"Stiffness in the fingers? Be careful you don't get arthritis."

"I thought your surgery was finished," she teased him.

He looked around and raised his eyebrows at the piles of foolscap paper leaning at precarious angles against the skirting board at the edges of the room. "You will soon be needing more staff, and then, I suppose, somewhere bigger will be necessary."

"As a matter of fact, I've already looked at a little place just off Fenchurch Street." A tick of satisfaction twitched at the corner of her mouth. "It's busier there, more commercial."

"Indeed it is."

"You see, I've just negotiated a contract that will require two typists working full-time on it. And if I'm to grow the business I need to spend more time promoting it rather than doing the typing myself."

He looked at her with admiration, but his eyes twinkled when he asked, "And what does Edmund think about all this...ambition?"

Lizzie tilted her head and looked at him from under her eyelashes. "Well, he'll have to get someone other than you to spy on me for a start, even though he did finally agree to me branching out."

She laughed and handed him a cup of tea.

"Thank you. You are lucky, Lizzie, that marriage to such a man as Edmund has not limited your opportunities. Rather the contrary, in fact."

A faint fleeting echo called out to her from the past of a man in a soldier's uniform with black wavy hair, blue-grey eyes and a dark moustache above a lop-sided grin. She reached out and ran her fingers over a line of keys on her Corona machine and smiled a bittersweet smile.

THE END

Author's Note

I have altered one historical fact. On 19 January 1917 a fire broke out in the Brunner Mond TNT factory in Silvertown, East London, causing fifty tons of TNT to explode, killing seventy-three people, injuring 400 and causing substantial damage to the local area. This was my inspiration for Silvertown Munitions, but in my novel the explosion occurs eleven months later, on 19 December 1917.

Acknowledgements

There is a plethora of work written about the Home Front during World War I. Those that I have found most useful are: *On Her Their Lives Depend: Munitions Workers in the Great War* by Angela Woollacott; *Zeppelin Nights* by Jerry White; *The Home Front. Civilian Life in World War One* by Peter G. Cooksley; *Great War Fashion – Tales from the History Wardrobe* by Lucy Adlington. Attitudes towards illegitimate children and the history of The Foundling Hospital are described in *London's Forgotten Children: Thomas Coram and The Foundling Hospital* by Gillian Pugh. I am also indebted to *The Times Newspaper Archive*.

Thanks so much for reading *A Kiss from France*. I'd love to hear how you enjoyed it so if you're inclined, please comment via a review.

Lightning Source UK Ltd.
Milton Keynes UK
UKOW04f1835141115

262699UK00002B/32/P